THE
HEAVENLY GRILLE
CAFÉ

Published by Piscataqua Press
An imprint of RiverRun Bookstore, Inc.
142 Fleet Street | Portsmouth, NH | 03801
www.riverrunbookstore.com
www.piscataquapress.com

Printed in the United States of America

ISBN: 978-1-979379-73-5

THE HEAVENLY GRILLE CAFÉ

By

J. T. Livingston

*W*e've all heard stories about it, just as we've all wondered whether or not it really exists. We've wondered what it's really like – will we all live in mansions built on streets of gold; will our pets be there; will homosexuals, perverts, rapists, or murderers live among us; will Aunt Jane have to pick among the five husbands she outlived; will there be toilets and fast foods; will we be expected to work, or will we just lay around eating bonbons and brownies all day? Oh, yes, we have all heard the stories associated with that wonderful place that really does exist. Far above the earth's atmosphere lies a beautiful, tranquil encampment known to mere mortals as HEAVEN. Words have yet to be created that would fully and accurately describe the beauty, as well as the encompassing peace and serenity, associated with this truly miraculous, spiritual domain.

Since Heaven really does exist, then we also have to wonder about the stories that have been told for centuries about its inhabitants – those inhabitants known to us as ANGELS. You see, just as there really is a Heaven, there are also angels who inhabit it; and, you have to realize what a fabulously collective group of souls these inhabitants of Heaven present. Our human visualization of them probably finds them floating around on their designated clouds, adjusting their brilliant halos throughout the day, and flapping their earned wings in pride – but the truth of the matter is that some of those angels are actually allowed to return to earth, in hopes of persuading more of us mere mortals to turn our lives over to the Lord – you know...before it is too late. For those of us who have read the entire sixteen-volume set of the "Left Behind" series, we know what life will be like for all the non-believers, don't we? That brings us to the focal point of this particular story. It is a story about a group of angels, once again... quite a special, collective group of angels...who have been assigned their earthly duties working at a dining establishment known as the Heavenly Grille Café.

Max is the angel-in-charge of the Heavenly Grille Café. Somewhere in his distant past, Max had a last name, but in his role as an angel, he does not require one. There is no need for angels to use their given last names because there simply is no need for them in Heaven. So what happens if there are two million angels named Max in Heaven, you might wonder? Fear not, because the explanation is not a complicated one. Quite simply, the angels just know. All they have to do is close their eyes and visualize the Max they need to talk to, and – POOF! – just like that, they are immediately transported into the presence of that person. Just imagine the savings in fuel costs alone once we get to Heaven!

Not every angel is allowed the privilege of returning to earth, and even fewer angels ever acquire the privilege, and responsibility, of working with Max at the Heavenly Grille. Quite the contrary, working with Max at the Heavenly Grille is an honor bestowed only upon those angels who have truly earned their figurative wings - not necessarily through longevity, but through proven obedience, dedication, and love to their Heavenly Father. It is one of the most prestigious positions any angel may hope to achieve, and since Max is the angel-in-charge, he is given free authority to select his "employees" for the Heavenly Grille. Naturally, Max has to answer to someone, too, so he is always extremely careful to select just the right group of angels to accompany him on his assignments. Most of the angels working with Max at the café stay for a five-year assignment because that is usually the longest time that the Heavenly Grille remains in any one location. There has been one exception to the five-year assignment; it involves an angel who has been with Max at the café, every day, for the last fifty years. That angel's name is Bertie - just Bertie - no last name.

Now that you have a better, general idea of Heaven and how some of its angels operate, what do you say about kicking back and making yourself comfortable for a bit? Go ahead, grab a snack, turn off the television, give your computer a much-needed rest, prop up your tired feet, and allow yourself to be entertained by this wonderful group of angelic characters. Who knows, maybe they'll *even recruit YOU before the book ends. There is no doubt that you will be forever glad that you welcomed them into your life!*

"For He shall give His angels charge over you, to keep you in all your ways."

-Psalm 91:11(NKJV)

CHAPTER 1

Summer 2011

Bertie checked herself in the wall mirror that hung outside the ladies' restroom door. She dabbed on some pink lipstick, her favorite color, pinched her cheeks for some extra, natural color, and ran her fingers through her thick curls; she was careful not to disturb the halo headband perched upon her head. "You are one fine looking woman!" she laughed as she gave her reflection a final nod of approval and straightened her crisp, white apron. She was still laughing when she reached the front door and flipped the CLOSED sign to OPEN. It was seven o'clock on a beautiful Monday morning and she couldn't wait for the day to begin. She took a long, deep breath, closed her eyes, and whispered the prayer with which she began every day. "Okay, good morning, God! Here we go! I hope this will be a blessed day for you, filled with few disappointments; and, to start your day off on a positive note, I sincerely promise that I will do my best to hold my tongue today and to make you proud. As always, Lord, use me to do your will. Amen!"

Bertie opened her eyes and glanced quickly over her

shoulder at the enormous black man, who was whistling loudly and extremely out of tune, and smiling back at her from the café's kitchen. She shook her head and grinned back at the man. Who knew anyone could actually whistle out of tune! "Looks like the first car is here. Get the fire started, Max!"

Max chuckled and nodded. "Oh, don't you worry none, Bertie; this fire stays lit!" He gave her a thumbs up. "It's going to be a good day, Bertie, oh, yes it is!"

Max was the owner/operator of the Heavenly Grille Café, a pristine diner with flashing neon lights that welcomed his customers continuously. The café's current location was situated along an isolated stretch of Highway 19, close to the Florida and Georgia state lines. Instead of golden arches that monopolized the interstate, the Heavenly Grille hosted a huge, golden halo that seemed to actually float above its roof. Visitors to the café never failed to wonder, and ask, how the halo managed to stay afloat, because there were no obvious means of support beams or wires to hold it in place. Max always laughed and winked, telling everyone that God kept it afloat. Some people would smile and wink back, others would nod in agreement, and, some would look at him like he had grown two heads before they quickly exited the café. As much as people wondered about the physics involved with the floating halo, no one seemed to really question or challenge Max's explanations; nevertheless, that didn't stop them from continuing to wonder about it and to tell their friends and neighbors about it. If their curiosity about the halo ever reached a point of overt concern, and that had happened once or twice in the past, then Max would simply pack up and move the café to another small town. He had tried relocating the café to the larger cities, because residents there tended to be more concerned with catching cabs and making a buck than in wondering how the café's halo stayed afloat, but he preferred the spiritual intimacy that he found so exhilarating in the smaller cities and towns across America.

Max would routinely relocate the Heavenly Grille every five years, regardless of people's curiosity, because of one important factor – he didn't want people to begin to wonder why he and the other café employees never seemed to age. Of course there was a very logical explanation as to why they didn't age, but Max wasn't at liberty to divulge that information. The fact of the matter was that all of the employees of the café never aged because they were angels. That's right – angels! It was important to Max, not to mention to God, that he reach as many people as possible while operating the Heavenly Grille; and, over the past one hundred years, Max and his employees had managed to reach thousands upon thousands of people – some, just in the nick of time, too.

Bertie was the only café employee who had been with Max for more than the normal five-year assignment, and she was very, very good at her job. She usually served a dual role as both hostess and waitress, and was the first person people met upon entering the establishment. She stood 5'2" tall and weighed a healthy 140 pounds. She currently wore her curly, dark brown hair at chin-length, always tucked behind her ears; but, over the past century, she had sported every hairstyle imaginable, from braids to buns. Although her hairstyle may have changed many times over the years, it was the light in Bertie's intense blue eyes that never changed. Her eyes were both captivating and illuminating on their own, but it was her exuberant smile and boisterous personality that seemed to most capture and engulf the attention of her audience.

Bertie took a last look around before opening the doors to the café's first customers that Monday morning. Yes, everything was in place. The blue- and white-checkered tablecloths were clean and crisp; they looked so pretty against the pale blue walls accentuated with large, cumulous clouds. The cherub salt and pepper shakers, like Bertie, also served a dual purpose; they also held a slot for the café's customized napkins, which were engraved with the Heavenly Grille Café logo – a golden halo with the words, "God loves YOU!" embossed on them.

Bertie took personal pride and satisfaction in knowing that the café was ready for the day's real job. It was true that while the customers might leave with positive thoughts about the friendly service and the scrumptious meal they had received, and simply go on about their day, they would also leave with a little something extra. They would leave the café knowing that they had to return for more – for something more than just the good food and pleasant employees. They might not realize initially what that "something more" was, so it was Bertie's job to ensure that they would eventually find answers to the many questions for which they inwardly searched.

Bertie adjusted the halo hairband on her head, removed the key from her apron pocket, and unlocked the front door. A little girl around the age of four walked in, her mother trailing behind her, and smiled up at Bertie.

"Well, good morning, beautiful!" Bertie smiled as she bent down to look into the child's innocent and bewildered eyes.

The little girl's smile widened as she continued to beam at Bertie. She tugged at her mother's shirt, pointed at Bertie's halo, and whispered, "Look, Mommy! She's an angel!"

"Out of the mouths of babes!" Bertie laughed as she patted the child on the shoulder.

CHAPTER 2

-Heaven-
Martin Assigns A New Angel

*M*ax's primary assistant in Heaven was an angel by the name of Martin, who, like Max, was a tall, black man. However, the color of their skin and their height were their only similar physical features. Where Max was muscular and robust, Martin was thin and weakly in appearance. Where Max was personable and outgoing, Martin was perspicuous and rather introverted. Regardless of their physical and emotional differences, the two men had been best friends in their former, earthly lives, and their relationship only intensified and strengthened when they obtained their wings from their Heavenly Father. The other angels often joked among themselves that the most prestigious assignments must go only to those angels whose names began with an "M". Naturally, that wasn't true – just merely coincidental.

Martin was not only Max's best friend in life and in death, but he also served as mentor to some of the senior angels – one of which, and to his often regret, was Bertie. Even though Bertie had been an angel for one hundred years, there was still much for her to learn, and Martin was more often than not challenged, yet also *determined, to perform his job to perfection. Bertie had proven, on more than one occasion, to be one of his biggest challenges. He took immense satisfaction, not pride – because he was convinced that pride was indeed a sin - in knowing that his mentoring and persistence had helped produce an angel of Bertie's qualifications and caliber, even though it had taken her fifty years to attain her figurative wings. His patience was tested every time she argued with him about those wings; she refused to acknowledge the fact that there was a difference between the wings representing a figurative symbol, and not a literal symbol, of angelic achievements.*

Martin was tedious and particular about angels fully meeting all qualifications and readiness for their respective assignments, so he was surprised at the uneasy feeling and second thoughts he was now having about the latest assignment for Doug, his newest protégé. He was recommending Doug for one of the prestigious assignments at the Heavenly Grille Café. He and Max had discussed the situation at length, but Martin still had some doubts as to Doug's readiness to return to earth. One of the reasons triggering Martin's doubts was the fact that Doug had only been dead for fifty-eight years; so, there was always the slight possibility that someone might still be alive who could recognize him. However, at the end of the day, Martin agreed to take the risk because he knew that Doug needed this assignment in order to truly move on – to finally let go of his past life and accept the one that awaited him.

Martin rubbed his chin between his bony thumb and index finger, and began pacing back and forth, eventually forming a complete circle with his thoughts and concerns about Doug. There was nothing in Martin's heavenly space to distract him from his prayers and thoughts. There were no phones, no buzzers, no sirens – nothing to distract him from the final decision he had made regarding Doug. He was surrounded by an endless, subtle aura of whiteness – a whiteness whose eternal partner was a peaceful, serene bright light made up of shards of gold and white beams. The only tangible object in the area at the moment was a HUGE white screen with scrolling black lettering moving slowly from left to right. The screen served as Martin's data base containing information on events pertaining to every angel's life, death, and hereafter experiences. Neither a touch pad nor voice activation were required to operate the screen; it operated simply and efficiently, never crashing or requiring rebooting, via Martin's thoughts and prayers – and only his. Even Heaven requires some form of security – for the time being at least.

Martin opened his eyes from prayer and focused, once again, on the information emanating from the huge screen. A brief outline of Doug's life, and angelic qualifications, quickly appeared on the screen.

Angel was born on January 1, 1933 to parents, Joseph and Camille.

Angel was younger brother to sisters, Emily and Rachel.

Angel was baptized at the age of 10.

Angel joined the United States Army in 1951 at the age of 18.

Angel became one of the estimated 33,686 battle deaths during the Korean War; angel died at the age of 20 on July 16, 1953, the last day for the Battle of Pork Chop Hill.

Angel lived a Christian-filled life until his untimely death.

Angel has achieved exemplary angelic ratings and performances since his arrival in July 1953.

Angel has met all angelic requirements for return-to-earth-assignments (first of which is to have been dead a minimum of 50 years).

Martin could have requested additional, more detailed information about Doug, but he already knew all the minute, in-between details. He felt, in his heart and after all his discussions with Max, that Doug was ready for the Heavenly Grille assignment. He also knew that Max and Bertie would continue to guide him in his heavenly duties and requirements.

Martin's only outstanding concern regarding Doug's readiness for the assignment was his ability to control his temper. Naturally, Doug's propensity toward a quick temper had not been an issue in Heaven, but it had caused him some problems during his life as a mortal. "Oh, well," Martin sighed, "It's in God's hands now. Only time will tell, I suppose…and that's certainly one thing there is no shortage of here in Heaven!"

"For we are His workmanship, created in Christ Jesus for good works..."

Ephesians 2:10 (NKJV)

CHAPTER 3

-Tampa-
Amanda's Journey Begins

It was only nine o'clock on Monday morning when Amanda Turner had dutifully cleaned out her desk, waved and mumbled her final good-byes to her now former co-workers, and carried the small cardboard box containing her personal belongings to Old Faithful – her 2002 Isuzu Trooper - which was still running strong at 135,000 miles. The used car had been a high school graduation present from her father, Stephen, just three short years ago. Her father had been her only living relative, as well as her best friend. They had spent every possible moment together and he had raised her single-handed since the day her mother, Regina, had been killed in a freak car accident when Amanda was only seven.

Stephen Turner had been diagnosed with advanced colon cancer one month before Amanda graduated high school. Prior to his diagnosis, he had suffered and worried in silence for two years with mild-to-moderate rectal bleeding. He performed a self-diagnosis and determined the culprit to be painful and persistent hemorrhoids, and since he had always distrusted doctors, he did not have his symptoms checked out until his condition was too advanced…and too late. The day he had to tell Amanda the truth about his condition was one of the hardest days of his life. Stephen had fought the disease with his normal quiet integrity and strength for the next thirteen months, always convinced that he would win the battle against the ferocious and unforgiving cancer. He put up a tremendous fight, but he did not win that battle.

The agony of watching her father's valiant, yet futile, attempt to survive ripped through Amanda's heart; she was an emotional wreck as she watched her father grow weaker and thinner, but she made every attempt to make him laugh and to make as many memories as she could for them. She took pictures and made scrapbooks of all their activities, listened to his Patsy Cline collection with him practically every night, baked his favorite desserts, drove him to all his appointments, and cried with him when his pain was too much for him to hide. She became the same dutiful caretaker to him that he had been for her for her first eighteen years. Even when Hospice stepped in to help during his final months, she never left his side. She was alone with him, holding his hand, and singing along with Patsy Cline when he died at home thirteen months after his initial diagnosis.

Her father had prepared her for his death the best he could, showing her how to manage the household expenses, and where important legal documents were stored. He had purchased a small insurance policy that was enough to pay for his burial and allowed Amanda to remain in the family home for another year after his death. Looking back in hindsight, Amanda knew she probably should have sold the home before she ran out of insurance money, but she had not been able to allow herself to leave the only home she had ever known - the home where she still felt her father's strength and presence in every room.

Amanda kicked a loose rock and looked back at the office building. She sighed and tried to ignore the heaviness that settled upon her chest. She was determined not to cry, not again, not now. She opened the back door to Old Faithful and moved a mountain of other boxes and clothing aside to make room for the cardboard box she carried in her arms. She closed her eyes, bowed her head, and whispered, "Okay, God, what now? What do I do now? Where do I go? I have no family, I've been evicted from my home, I've lost my job, and... I have a whopping seven hundred dollars between me and total desperation. So, how about it, God? I'm here, your child, out of answers. I'm waiting, God. I'm waiting...where exactly do you suggest I go?"

Amanda Turner had never felt so alone in her life.

She closed the Trooper's back door, lifted her head, and looked toward the captivating Tampa Bay skyline. She hated to leave her home town, but the economy was crushed and the job market more dire than it had been in decades, so she felt she had no other choice but to leave. She just didn't know where to go. She raised her eyebrows, tilted her head, and quirked, "Hmmm? What was that, God? I'm still not hearing you!"

A pedestrian, walking by the parking lot, gave her a strange look and hurried past.

Amanda shouted after him, "Oh, yeah, you'd better run! Crazy woman here! No telling what she might do!" She watched the stranger until he was out of sight. "Well, Lord, I can't stand here all day waiting for you to make up your mind, that's for sure. My luck, they'll arrest me for loitering..." Amanda got behind the wheel and started up the car, guiding the air conditioning vent until the cool air was blowing directly in her face. She backed out of the parking space and looked in her rear view mirror for oncoming traffic before easing her way onto the exit ramp that would take her north across the Howard-Frankland Bridge. "I bet I've crossed this bridge hundreds of times," she sighed, "Usually with a destination in mind, but...I have absolutely no idea where I'm going now." She turned on the radio, lit a cigarette – nasty habit that it was – blew out the cancer-inducing smoke, and smiled. "Faith...gotta have it; gotta love it! Okay, Lord, here we go..."

Amanda had been on the road for almost six hours and God still hadn't responded to her incessant questioning about her destination. Her growling stomach reminded her that she had not eaten anything since a peanut butter and jelly sandwich the night before. She pulled off the interstate at the next exit and looked around for a fast-food joint. She obviously had chosen the wrong exit because there was only one gas station and a few vintage Floridian homes. She continued down the road for about a mile and was about to make a U-turn when she noticed a golden hue up ahead, around the bend. The golden hue was coming from a blue and white restaurant on the left. A small parking lot graced the front of the restaurant. Amanda pulled into the parking lot and stared in awe at the source of the golden hue - a huge, golden halo that appeared to be *floating* above the restaurant's roof.

She got out of her car, stretched her arms high above her head, and twisted from side to side. She tossed her cigarette stub on the ground and grinded it with her foot to make sure it was out. She grinned at the handmade sign that hung over the front door and identified the establishment as the Heavenly Grille Café. "Heavenly Grille Café, huh? So this is where you want me stop, God?" She shook her head, reached inside the car for her purse, slammed the door, and turned toward the café. "Well, okay then. A girl's gotta eat, right?" Looking upward, she shook her head and wondered aloud, "How the heck does that halo stay afloat?"

She never saw the man, directly in her path, bent over to tie his shoe laces. "Oh, my God!" she shrieked as she tripped unceremoniously over him.

The man grunted, turned quickly, and caught her in his arms before she hit the pavement.

Amanda landed squarely atop the man and stared into the

most absolute greenest eyes she had ever seen. His eyes mesmerized her into temporary paralysis; she could not, nor did she want to, move. It was several moments before she took a breath and quickly pushed herself up, inadvertently poking the poor man in the ribs with her elbows. "Oh! I am so sorry! Please forgive me. Are you hurt? Here, let me help you up. I'm so sorry."

The man's laugh was soft and gentle, and strangely comforting, as they both struggled to reclaim their former vertical positions. The man stood and brushed sand off his well-worn jeans. "It's okay, really. I'm fine, no problem. What about you?" He touched Amanda's shoulder to help steady her.

His touch was absolutely electrifying, causing Amanda to shiver and jump back. She rubbed absently at the shoulder he had barely touched. "Me? No...yes...no, I'm good. Yeah, I'm... okay. You're sure you're okay?" She asked again, staring into his eyes. Oh, yes, they were indeed the greenest eyes she had ever seen. The greenest eyes on the most handsome face she had ever seen. The most handsome face on the most perfect body she had ever seen. She stared at him for a moment longer before finally accepting the hand he held out.

"Why don't we try this again, shall we?" he smiled down at her. "Hello, my name is Doug." He looked toward the café and grinned. "And... I think I work here. Any chance I can I buy you a cup of coffee? Or, maybe...a peanut butter and jelly sandwich

CHAPTER 4

Bertie Greets Amanda and Doug

The café was only half-full with customers, all of whom were enjoying Max's home-made meals that consisted mostly of good, old comfort food. Word had spread quickly throughout the small community that the Heavenly Grille was the place to go for cooking that was even better than Mom's. Max was working in the kitchen, looking out at the crowd, and whistling one of his usual out-of-tune melodies. He stopped every once in a while to say hello to one of the regular customers.

Bertie was standing at the counter, outside the kitchen, waiting patiently for Max to finish an order. She turned when the front door opened, sounding the angelic chimes that jingled whenever someone entered or exited the café. A wide grin spread across her face when she recognized the tall, handsome man who entered. She looked back toward Max and said in a low enough voice that only he could hear, "Well, I'll be damned, will you look who old Martin decided to send down for this latest assignment!"

Max pursed his full, generous lips and drew his eyebrows

together in what he hoped Bertie would recognize as a frown. "Bertie! Watch the language, girl; do you want to be put on probation... AGAIN?"

Bertie grinned at him and shrugged, "Oh, don't go getting your big girl panties in a wad, Max. I've become a pro at being on probation, and besides, He knows it's just a figure of speech. Besides...we all know that I'll never be damned! Besides, you gotta admit, my colorful language keeps Heaven a little more interesting..." She laughed out loud, reached across the counter and pinched his puffed-up cheek. "You're just so damn cute when you get all worked up over something, you know that, big fella?" She picked up the order that Max had placed on the counter and smiled again. "You probably knew all along who was coming down, but I had a feeling it might be Doug checking in here next. We can definitely use the extra manpower, for sure, especially on the night shift. So...close your mouth, Max, and take a deep breath. If you think you have your hands full with me, let's just wait and see what little Dougie here brings to the table! From the stories I've heard about him, he had quite a temper in his day!"

Max's attempt to look stern failed miserably. He knew Bertie never took things too seriously so it wouldn't do any good to scorn her for her inappropriate language. He sighed and shook his head in defeat. "Compared to you," Max grinned, "Doug should be a pussy cat..."

Bertie grabbed the plates of food and smiled at the young couple as she whizzed past them. She winked at Doug and said, "Be right with you two; just let me take this to those hungry truckers over there. Max's cooking has been known to tame the savage beast."

Amanda inhaled the enticing aroma of what she assumed must be the daily special posted on the chalkboard inside the front door: barbecue meatloaf and REAL mashed potatoes, smothered with brown, onion gravy. She hadn't realized just how hungry she was until she got a whiff of the food carried by the passing waitress. "Oh, my God, that smells soooo good," she sighed, trying to inhale another quick wisp of the food's aroma. She looked up at Doug and asked, "By the way, did I hear you right outside...you said you worked here? Because that waitress didn't seem to know you at all."

Doug smiled back at her and rubbed the back of his head, which was covered with thick, coal-black hair. "Close...what I said was that I *think* I work here."

Amanda took her eyes off the food the truckers were devouring long enough to say, "You mean you don't know...?" However, before she could finish her question, she noticed the waitress approaching them - this time with her arms outstretched widely in greeting. At least, Amanda hoped it was in greeting.

Bertie zeroed in on Doug and pulled him to her in a tight, strong hug. When she finally released him, she stood back, placed her hands on her hips, and looked up into his smiling face. "You've gotta be Doug, right? I heard you were a looker, but, damn, you really are one of the best looking men I've ever had the pleasure to lay these old eyes on!" She punched him on the shoulder and laughed out loud. "We've been expecting you for a couple of days now, boy. Where have you been?"

Doug had returned her bear hug and was now grinning back at her as if he'd known her all his life. He felt like he knew her already because he had certainly heard enough stories in Heaven about Bertie. The other angels had nicknamed her the *naughty angel* because of her uncontrolled compulsion for cursing. "Yes, I am Doug...and you must be Bertie? I've... heard a lot about you. It's very nice to meet you, Bertie." He looked toward the kitchen at the huge black man who was waving back at him. Doug returned the wave. "And that must be Max. I'm really sorry I'm so late, but I got a little side-tracked and my trip was delayed a couple of days. I hope you still have an opening for me."

Bertie stood looking up at the handsome man, who to mortals might appear to be in his late twenties to early thirties, and said, "Are you kidding, handsome? I've saved an apron just for you; had a hard time finding one in your size, but I finally did."

Doug stepped back, obviously checking out the frilly, white apron that Bertie sported, and threw his hands up in mock defense. "Come on now…is that really necessary? Somehow, I just cannot see myself wearing an apron…"

Bertie laughed and punched his shoulder. "Aww…too macho for a pretty apron, are you? Hey…just picking at you, kid. No, you won't have to wear an apron if you don't want to." She looked over at the pretty young girl standing next to Doug and punched him on the shoulder yet again. "Hey, where are your manners? Who's this pretty, little thing with you? We were only expecting one for the job, even though…there's plenty of work around here for more."

Doug smiled, looking back and forth between Amanda and Bertie. He scratched his head and said, "Well, this is actually a little embarrassing because…well, I didn't get her name. We just…sort of…bumped into each other in the parking lot."

Amanda offered her hand to Bertie. "Hi there, name's Amanda. He's being too much of gentleman. The truth is…we more than just bumped into each other. It was more like a collision. I actually tripped over *Doug* in the parking lot."

Bertie ignored Amanda's outstretched hand and, instead, pulled her into a motherly embrace, not quite as aggressive as the one she had offered Doug. "And you lived to tell about it? I won't even ask how you managed to trip over something the size of this handsome devil. Well, never mind about all that. The two of you look mighty hungry to me. What do you say we find you a table and get you fed before we put Doug to work? By the way, handsome, you're scheduled to work the night shift, so you still have a few hours. You'll have plenty of time to get settled into your apartment before you have to tackle the evening crowd."

Bertie grinned at Doug's obvious discomfort. They both knew that angels did not require food or water to sustain their Heavenly bodies and that they never experienced hunger pains. It didn't mean that they couldn't eat...it just meant they didn't have to. She winked at Doug as she led the way to a corner table.

Doug just shook his head and grinned, while Amanda was quick to follow Bertie to the offered table. "Oh, thank you!" she laughed. "I want some of whatever that was you took to those truckers. And, I would absolutely die for a cup of coffee, please."

"Oh, we won't require that you die first... will we, Doug? Bertie grinned and slapped Doug on the butt just before he slid into his chair. "Take a load off, handsome. I'll be right back with some food and coffee. After that, I'll show you around the café. The night shift can be pretty hectic at times, but something tells me you won't have any trouble with those customers."

Amanda grinned as Bertie left them alone at the table. "I really like her. She has a way of making you feel right at home, doesn't she?"

Doug rubbed his shoulder and smiled back. "Yes, she does; and, that's probably a good thing, because I have a feeling I'll be here for a while"; and, thinking to himself," *Oh, it's going to be an interesting five years, I can tell..."*

CHAPTER 5

Amanda Taken Under the Angels' Wings

Dusk was settling in when Amanda looked up from her second helping of Max's famous banana pudding. She closed her eyes and placed her hands comfortably over her belly. "I have NO idea where I managed to put all that food. It's been a long time since I've tasted anything so good. My Grandma used to make banana pudding like this – it's made with REAL pudding, not that instant, boxed stuff. There's a big difference in the taste, you know, using the real stuff, I mean."

Doug grinned at the beautiful young woman sitting across the table from him. A sudden sadness crept into his soul, one he couldn't quite explain to himself or get a grasp on, but he quickly shook it off and took another sip of black coffee. "Yes, it was pretty obvious that you enjoyed your meal," he said.

Amanda tossed a napkin at him, which he reflexively caught in mid-air. She added cream and sugar to her cup of coffee and grinned back at him. "Well I had to eat enough for both of us. Weren't you hungry? You hardly touched any of that yummy food."

Doug shook his head. "Not really. I... actually had a late lunch a couple of hours before I got here. I'll probably have something a little later on tonight, though."

"That's right. You start working the night shift tonight, right?"

Doug nodded. "How about you, Amanda? Where are you headed now that your belly is obviously full? It is full, isn't it?"

Amanda pushed back from the table a little and exhaled slowly. "Yes, my belly is quite full, thank you very much. As to where I'm headed? Well...I wish I knew..."

"What is that supposed to mean? You don't know where you're going?"

Amanda wrinkled her nose and offered a half-smile. "Not really, no. You know, I don't usually tell total strangers the story of my life, but... you don't really feel like a stranger anymore, so here goes. I'll give you the short version. Within the past year and a half, my Dad, who was my only living relative by the way, died from cancer; I managed to lose the house he raised me in; and, this morning, I lost my job due to new management and company downsizing, and all. So... here I am, I don't even know where this is by the way, but everything I own is packed inside my car." She looked at her watch and continued, "I left a Tampa parking lot about eight hours ago with no real destination in mind. I drove for six hours, only stopped once for gas, and then that awesome glowing halo outside caught my eye and lured me here to get something to eat. Actually, now that I think about it, if it hadn't been for the glow from that halo, I don't think I would have ever found this place. It's a little off the beaten path."

Doug sat listening to her story with his hands clasped together and positioned beneath his chin.

Amanda felt those piercing green eyes staring at her and looked up. "Oh, God, don't look at me like that. Pity is the last thing I need."

Doug continued to stare at her and, without any warning, reached across the table to take her hand in his. "I'm very sorry for the loss of your father, Amanda. That must have been hard for you. You said he was your only living relative?"

Amanda exhaled and nodded. "Yep, it was just the two of us. My mom died when I was seven, freak accident...but that's another story. He really was a great father. I miss him... so much."

Doug released her hand and sipped at his coffee before responding. "So, you really don't know where you're going? No destination in mind?"

Amanda held her coffee cup in both hands and stared into it. "Nope, not a clue. If this was hot tea instead of coffee, maybe the tea leaves would provide me a hint of where I should go. But...I've got a little money saved, not a lot, but hopefully enough to hold me over until I can find a job and a place to live."

Bertie and Max were more than half-way across the room, but since angels have exceptional hearing ability, they couldn't help but eavesdrop on Amanda and Doug's conversation.

"Oh, Max," Bertie sighed. "We've got to do something to help that poor girl. She's so young, and she's all alone in this world."

"Well, Bertie," Max nodded. "Maybe that's why she's here. Do you really believe it was only a coincidence that she tripped over our Doug in the parking lot?"

Bertie looked deep in thought, and after a few moments, her sassy-blue eyes came to life, sparkling with obvious inspiration. She stared at Max, raised her eyebrows, and began nodding her head.

Max watched her and shook his own head slowly from side to side while pressing his huge lips together in an obvious pout. He and Bertie had worked side by side for fifty years and he knew only too well what that sparkle in her eye probably meant. "Quit nodding your head, Bertie. You look like one of the bobbling head things in people's cars." He shook his finger at her grinning face. "No, Bertie, don't even

21

go there. I know exactly what you're thinking, and NO! It is NOT going to happen."

Bertie continued the exaggerated nodding her head. "Oh, come on, Max, lighten up! Think outside the box for a change! Isn't that what people are saying these days?" Bertie pinched his cheek and laughed heartily. "Come on, Maximus…pretty please?"

Max crossed his arms and shook his head again, "No, absolutely not! It is against the rules."

Bertie punched his shoulder. She had an unwelcomed habit of punching people's shoulders when she was trying to get a point across. "Give me a break, Max…against whose rules?"

"My rules!" Max whispered loudly.

"Oh, shush!" she grinned, punching his shoulder yet again. "Your rules don't count!"

Max continued shaking his head, but Bertie could tell he was weakening.

"Come on, Max…"

"It's too dangerous, Bertie."

"Oh, hogwash! Dangerous for who?"

"Dangerous for *whom*," Max corrected her. "We've never had a mortal work at the Heavenly Grille, and you know it. Just think of the consequences if she happened to guess upon the truth?"

Bertie shrugged. "So what if she did? So what if she finds out we're angels. Would that be so terrible?"

"Bertie…you know as well as I do that we are supposed to keep our real identities a secret. Only the children guess the truth."

"Yep," Bertie nodded, "That's true, and nobody listens to the little children, do they?"

They were both quiet for a moment as they continued to watch, and listen to, the young couple sitting at the corner table. Most of the diners had left and gone home to their busy lives. There were only two other customers currently in the café and Max and Bertie both knew they only had about an hour before the night crowd began arriving.

"Oh, what the Hell," Bertie sighed in exasperation. "Come on, Max! We don't have much time before this place is packed again with customers. Look at that poor child. She has no one. She is truly all alone in this world. You know it's the right thing to do."

He had once been known as Maximus, an undefeated gladiator whose final battle had been lost to three man-hungry tigers. He had fought and died galantly, but the gentle giant who had operated the Heavenly Grille Café for the past one hundred years now smiled back at the naughty angel who had worked by his side for so long. "Okay, Bertie, I still feel like this might be a mistake, but, you win... this time."

Bertie reached up and gave his cheek a playful slap. "That-a-boy, Maximus! You see... thinking outside the box isn't so hard, is it? You won't be sorry, big fella."

Max watched as Bertie made her way to the corner table, coffee pot in hand, and looked upward. "I can only hope and pray not... I surely do."

CHAPTER 6

-Heaven-
Bertie's Arrival in Heaven

*M*artin paced back and forth, hands behind his back, glancing periodically at the huge screen before him. He grabbed the back of his neck with both hands and closed his eyes, praying that Max would be quick to remind Bertie of the possible consequences should Amanda ever discover their true identities. Why, it could jeopardize their entire operation at their current location; and, surely they recognized the cause of the sadness that had crept inside Doug when he was talking to Amanda. The newly assigned angel was subconsciously mourning a life he never had the chance to experience – a chance at love, marriage, children, and grandchildren.

Martin ceased pacing, closed his eyes, and sighed heavily as his thoughts focused on Heaven's naughty angel.

Bertie had been a true test of his patience since her arrival in Heaven one hundred years ago. He knew from the moment they met that he would have his hands full mentoring her. Thinking back to her arrival date in December 1911, Martin couldn't suppress a small smile...

It had been business as usual that day. The reception area had been full with almost one hundred new arrivals, all of whom, exhibited a sense of serenity and peace, accepting the fact that their earthly lives had ended and they would now be spending eternity with their Heavenly Father. All, that is, except for one.

"Hey, what the Hell happened? Where am I? Who are all you people? Hey! Somebody answer me!"

Martin exhaled, prayed for patience, and made his way to the very back of the waiting area. It was there that he found Bertie twirling around, alternating between lifting her robe and punching people near her on their shoulders.

"Hey, you!" she shouted to an elderly man in front of her, punching him on his right shoulder. "Do you know where we are and what the Hell is going on here? One minute I'm walking down the road, headed to Fern's Market, and the next thing I know, I'm here in marshmallow world. Damn! Have you ever seen so much whiteness? There's no color at all in this place."

Suddenly, seemingly out of nowhere, the skinniest, tallest black man she'd ever seen in her life appeared at her side. "Well, I'll be damned!" laughed Bertie, "I take it back; there is some color in this place after all." She gave the black man a welcoming punch on his shoulder. "Well, hey there. Man, you are one skinny, black man. You look like you could use a good meal! Speaking of which, I'm hungry. Do you know where a gal can get something to eat around here? And, again.... where the Hell am I? I mean, there's like, nothing here, just a bunch of WHITENESS." She looked over at the skinny, black man, who did not appear to be in a very hospitable mood.

Martin sighed inwardly. It had been a few hundred years since he'd had a truly difficult recruit on his hands. "Trust me, you're not really hungry. We don't get hungry here, but there is food to eat, nonetheless. Please, Miss...Bertie, come with me." He tried to take her elbow and lead her away.

Bertie pushed him away, almost knocking him on his Heavenly caboose. "Whoa there! Easy, fella. These other folks may be willing to follow you anywhere, but, I don't know you from Adam and, trust me, it will be a cold day in Hell before I follow you anywhere. Just who the Hell do you think you are, anyway?"

The people around them began slowly moving forward and Bertie began to follow them.

Once again, Martin attempted to grab her elbow, this time with a firmer grip. "You're not ready, Bertie; you won't be going with them just yet."

"Hey! How do you know my name?" Bertie quipped as she watched the throng of people quickly dissipating into the all-encompassing whiteness. "Where are they all going? What's going on here? Where am I? What are you going to do to me? I know Judo so don't you go trying any funny stuff with me!" She looked around her at the empty space surrounding her. It was just her and the skinny, black man now. "And where in Hell are my clothes?" She pulled at her robe. "I look awful in white; it washes me out."

Martin waited patiently while Bertie continued to mumble to herself, allowing her all the time she needed to remember. When she had quieted down, Martin looked at her and smiled. "Let's try this again, shall we?" He held out both arms in welcome and embraced her. "Hello, Bertie. My name is Martin. I will be your mentor for however long it takes."

Bertie looked more confused than ever but allowed herself to be embraced by the stranger who stood before her. "However long it takes for what?"

"For your transition phase to be completed."

Bertie bit down hard on the inside of her cheek and nodded. "And just what am I gonna transition into? Oh, wait, now I get it. I know what's going on here. You're one of those alien, Martian creatures and I've been abducted, haven't I? Well, you sure as Hell ain't gonna be doing no experiments on me, that's for damn sure!"

Martin frowned and shook his head. "Try again, Bertie."

A blinding white light, streaked with brilliant gold shards, pierced the area surrounding Bertie and she suddenly remembered what had happened. She would have loved to have sat down at the moment she realized she was dead, but there was no place to sit. "Whew...oh, wow...let's see...I remember I was walking to Fern's Corner Market. My best friend, Fernie, lives and works there. She had loaned me a new book to read. You see, I was baptized a few weeks ago, and I have so much to learn about God 'cause my parents weren't very religious folks, so they didn't bother teaching us anything. But my friend, Fernie, had this new book called "My Life in Christ" written by some saint."

Martin nodded. "Yes, St. John of Kronstadt..."

Bertie began pacing. "Yep, that's the fella. Anyway, I tried to read it but it just wasn't making much sense to me, so Fernie had suggested I bring it back and we would sit down together and read it once or twice a week. Fernie knows EVERYTHING there is to know about God; she's the preacher's daughter and we've been best friends since we started walking and talking." Bertie looked around her and swallowed hard. "Damn...I'm really dead, huh?"

Martin held open his arms and welcomed Bertie, once again, into his embrace. "Yes, Bertie... you are. You were hit from behind by one of those new automobiles. There was a malfunction and the driver lost control of the vehicle, I'm afraid. The young man who was driving was very distraught about what happened."

"He was distraught! How the Hell do you think I feel?" Bertie pulled back and rubbed up and down on her arms. "Hmmm... I feel fine. No broken bones. No pain. Are you sure I'm dead?"

"It was an instant death, Bertie. You felt nothing, no pain."

"But it's so unfair, I can't be dead..." Bertie replied softly, something totally opposite her naturally boisterous personality. "I'm only twenty-six years old. I have a husband and... OH, MY GOD, my kids! I have two small kids! Who's going to take care of my kids?"

Martin placed his hand upon her shoulder and immediately calmed her down. "Your children will be fine, Bertie. Trust me. It's you I'm worried about now."

"Why the Hell are you worried about me? I'm dead, remember? What else can go wrong?"

When Martin turned and began walking away, Bertie was quick to follow. "Hey, Bones...I mean...oh, Hell, I've forgotten your damn name... Hey! Wait for me! Why did you say you were worried about me? Damn! Slow down, will you! This isn't a race, is it?"

Martin placed his palms together in silent prayer and thought, "This one is going to take some time, Lord. Please.... grant me the patience that will most definitely be required. . ."

"Hey, you! Martin, right? You're absolutely positive that I'm

dead? I mean, you could be wrong, you know!" Bertie raced to catch up with the skinny, black man.

Martin sighed as she caught up to him and punched him on the shoulder. He shook his head and prayed silently once again. "Patience, Lord...please grant me patience..."

"...knowing that the testing of your faith produces patience."

-James 1:3 (NKJV)

CHAPTER 7

Amanda's Dream

The radio alarm sounded promptly at 5:15 AM. Amanda turned over in the comfortable twin-sized bed and searched in the early morning darkness until she found the snooze control button. She pushed it down and turned back over, pulling the white, down comforter over her head. She immediately returned to the strange dream she had been having before the alarm sounded.

"Amanda?"

The voice was soft and gentle, almost ethereal, and seemed to be coming from somewhere above Amanda's head. She spun around in all directions before finally looking upward. The darkness that had previously enveloped Amanda's dream suddenly dissipated in short bursts of brilliant light. Amanda was surprised, not scared, to see a woman's smiling face smile looking down upon her. It actually took her a few moments before she recognized the face. It was her mother's face.

"Mama?" Amanda whispered hoarsely, clasping her hands over her mouth in disbelief.

The woman continued to smile at Amanda and simply nodded. Almost as an afterthought, the woman slowly turned her face to the right as yet another image began to materialize in the clouds above Amanda's head. This was a face she recognized immediately. It was her father's face.

Amanda fell to her knees, lifted her hands heavenward, and began crying tears of joy and longing. She gulped in huge gasps of air as she tried to regain some control of her emotions, so afraid that if she closed her eyes for one second, the images would disappear. "Oh, Daddy... oh, my God... Daddy...it's really you..."

The two images smiled in unison as the woman laid her head upon the man's shoulder.

"Hey there, baby girl," the woman said. "My, what a beautiful young woman you've become, but then...I knew you would."

Tears continued to stream down Amanda's cheeks. She had her parents with her, both of them, and there was so much she wanted to say to them; but, she couldn't seem to find her voice.

Stephen Turner finally broke the blissful silence among them. "You look wonderful, Princess, and I hope you know how very much I miss you, but, this place... Heaven...oh, Amanda, it's amazing, so amazing. Everything is just as you and I use to talk about...the beauty and the peace...but, most importantly, Princess, I found your mother." He looked over at the woman beside him, the only woman he had ever truly loved, and kissed the top of her head. "I wish we could take the time to tell you about everything we have seen here, but, that's not why we've come to you today. We really don't have much time, Amanda."

Amanda nodded her understanding and wiped the tears with the back of her hand. She wanted to speak to her parents but she still had trouble getting her voice to work for her.

"Amanda, you must pull yourself together now and listen to what we have to say; it's very important," her mother began explaining. "You must understand that you did not end up at the café by chance. There's a reason why you are working there and today is a very important day because you will meet someone today who needs your help. You may not think there is anything you can do to help this person, but you must trust and believe that God has put you there for a very specific reason. It's very important that

you keep your eyes, and your heart, open so that you'll recognize this person. Do you understand, dear?"

Amanda cleared her throat and finally found her voice. She managed to choke out a response to her mother's question. "What? Who? What are you talking about?"

Her mother's mouth opened as if to speak; however, before the words came, her image began to slowly vaporize.

"Oh, no!" Amanda screamed, "Don't leave, Mama! Please, don't leave me..." It was too late. Her mother's image was gone and Amanda began to panic when her father's image began to shiver and blur. She reached upward in a vain attempt to keep him with her. "Daddy, no...please...not you, too! Please stay with me. I miss you so much..." Tears once again flowed freely down Amanda's cheeks.

Her father's eyes misted over and he whispered back to her as his voice and image grew dimmer. "I miss you, too, Amanda, but you're going to be fine, Princess, trust me; but, you need to remember what your mother said and be watching closely today so that you'll be ready to help this person. I'm sorry, Princess...I have to go now. Remember what your mother said; it's very important...keep your eyes, and your heart, open."

Amanda was crying openly now, tiny wails and gasps seeking escape from deep within her heart. "Please don't go, Daddy..."

Her father's image was almost gone when she glimpsed one final smile and heard him whisper something to her. "I love you, Princess..."

Amanda bolted straight up in bed just as the radio alarm blared for the second time. She had the station set to one that played non-stop country oldies. Patsy Cline, her father's all-time favorite country singer, was wailing that she was "falling to pieces" and Amanda couldn't help but think that she knew exactly how she felt.

The dream had shaken her to the core and she didn't know quite what to make of it. It had all seemed so real, but it had been a dream, and dreams weren't real. She threw her legs over the side of the bed slowly and twisted up her shoulder-length blond hair, clamping it with a hair clasp she kept on the bedside table. She reached for the pack of cigarettes that she also kept on the table before remembering Bertie's strict rule that no smoking was allowed in the apartment. Amanda stared at the cigarettes with a bit of longing, but it seemed too much of an effort to go outside this early in the morning to smoke. Suddenly, with no real understanding of why she was doing it, she picked up the pack of cigarettes and took them into the bathroom with her. She looked into the small mirror situated above the sink and saw her wet cheeks. She wiped one cheek to verify the tears were real.

The dream suddenly came back to her. She closed her eyes, remembering everything about the dream, trying to recapture the image of her parents. They were together…at last.

She looked at herself in the mirror, looked at the pack of cigarettes in her hand, and smiled back at the young woman staring at her in the mirror. "You didn't mention the cigarettes, Daddy, but I know how you felt about them. If it's any consolation, I don't think I ever actually inhaled any of them…"

She lifted the toilet lid and, one by one, broke the remaining cigarettes in half and flushed them. She closed her eyes, trying to recapture the blissful image of her parents, together once again…in HEAVEN! There was no doubt in her mind that it had been more than a dream. Her parents were definitely trying to tell her, or to warn her, about something or someone. Her father had always been there for her when he was alive, and he was still with her today. She smiled as she thought of the two of them together again. Her mother was even more beautiful than the pictures Amanda had constantly looked at while growing up.

She pulled off the baggy tee-shirt she always slept in, one of father's old shirts, and stepped into the shower. She hummed along as Patsy Cline crooned the last verse of her father's favorite song. "Okay…I promise to keep my eyes, and my heart, open," she whispered as the song came to an end. *"You tell me to find someone else to love, someone who'll love me, too; the way you used to do; but each time I go out with someone new, you walk by and I fall to pieces..."*

Fifteen minutes later, Amanda was dressed in her blue and white uniform, complete with the halo hair band. She laughed at herself as she adjusted the hair band, remembering how she had pleaded with Bertie not to make her wear it on her first day at work at the café, almost three weeks ago. She wobbled her head from side to side, causing the halo to bounce around. "I still don't like having to wear this silly thing, but, hey, what the heck. The kids always get a kick out of it."

She took a last look around the tidy studio apartment that was situated above the left side of the café. Her twin bed was actually a day bed that doubled as a sofa in the day time. The kitchen was extremely compact but had all the basic essentials for sustaining life, especially for someone who did not cook for a living. The apartment was always well lit with natural light even though it only had two, tiny windows. One was above the kitchen sink, overlooking a serene, wooded forest behind the café. The other was a tall, narrow window, to the left of the front door, which faced the front parking area. There was also one other door located at the far back right of the apartment. It didn't lead outside, but it did connect to another studio apartment located on the top right side of the café – Doug's apartment.

Amanda locked her apartment and stepped outside into a day that had not yet fully awoken. The morning sky was still relatively dark; however, the glow from the floating halo above the café offered a golden hue that illuminated every step down the staircase.

Amanda used the café key that Bertie had issued her and breezed through the front door. She turned and locked the door behind her since the café didn't normally open for customers until seven o'clock. She closed her eyes and smiled as the angelic chimes welcomed her inside. After only three weeks, this place felt like home to her. She knew that her stay was only temporary, until she got on her feet financially, but she had not felt this safe and secure since her father was alive.

The smell of thick-sliced, pepper bacon and buttermilk biscuits immediately invaded her senses. She opened her eyes and inhaled the simple, yet enticing, aromas of Max's country breakfast. She closed her eyes again, savoring the image of butter melting slowly between the thick, fluffy biscuits. She blushed considerably when she opened her eyes again and discovered Max and Doug grinning at her from the kitchen.

"You're early, as usual," Max laughed. "Come on back here, girl, and fix yourself a plate. I know how you love a good breakfast."

Amanda grabbed one of Bertie's frilly, white aprons off the wall and danced into the kitchen. She lifted the lid off the huge stainless steel pot and closed her eyes. "Aww... I knew it! I knew you would make cheese grits this morning, Max! I love your grits! I don't suppose you made any sausage gravy to pour over them, did you? You know how I like it...a layer of cheese grits, at least two scrambled eggs on top of the grits, and then smother it all with the sausage gravy. Yep, that's the best! Of course, I'll take a couple of biscuits to sop up any gravy that might be left behind..."

Max and Doug shared a smile while Doug teased back, "You love any kind of food, Amanda. I don't think I've seen you turn down anything Max has cooked up here these past few weeks."

Amanda smiled at his good-natured teasing. "I know, I think I've gained five pounds already. Oh, by the way... I know neither of you, or Bertie, are big fans of smoking, so y'all will be glad to know that I tossed the cigarettes this morning. Yep, sure did... flushed them right down the toilet!"

"Well, now," Max nodded his approval. "This is a great start to a great day, I do believe it is. By the way...I did make a small pot of sausage gravy just for you this morning. I may have to add it to the menu, permanently. You've talked about it so much to the customers; they want to know why they can't have some, too."

Amanda filled her plate with the cheese grits, eggs, and gravy. Almost as an afterthought, she grabbed four slices of peppered-bacon. "Hey, Doug, wanna toss me a couple of those biscuits there, please? I'll need some butter for those, too…if you don't mind." She pulled a stool up to an empty counter and began savoring the scrumptious breakfast. She couldn't remember ever tasting food this good. Half-way through the meal, she patted her slim belly and looked over at Max. "Yep, I do believe you're right, Max. This is going to be a great day."

Max turned to look back at her and winked. "That it is, Princess…that it is. Just keep your eyes and your heart open, for whatever awaits you this day…"

Amanda almost choked on the buttermilk biscuit she had just bitten into. Her mouth was full and she couldn't say anything, but when she glanced quickly at Doug she saw that he winked and smiled back at her.

He raised his eyebrows and laughed at her inability to say anything with a mouthful of food. "Ditto…" he grinned and winked again before leaving the kitchen to unlock the front door for several truckers who had just pulled into the parking lot.

CHAPTER 8

Amanda Meets Kris

The Heavenly Grille Café was open for business six days a week, Monday through Saturday, from 7:00 AM to 11:00 PM. Amanda's normal shift at the café was from 7:00 AM to 4:00 PM, with an hour off for lunch. Once she began working this shift, Bertie had changed her own hours, usually coming in around 9:00 AM and staying most evenings till around 6:00 PM. Max was at his stove every morning at 5:00 AM, preparing the day's menu. Amanda never knew what time he actually left the café; she often thought that he worked the entire 7:00 AM to 11.00 PM work day because he always seemed to be there. Doug's shift was usually 4:00 PM to closing time, but he, too, always seemed to be there. She had commented on it to him a couple of times and his response was that he wanted to learn as much as he could from Max so that he could open up his own restaurant one day. Something about his explanation always seemed to nag at her, because Doug just didn't look the type to work in a restaurant, much less own one. Amanda thought he looked more like the mercenary, soldier-of-fortune type, travelling from one country to the next seeking adventure. She often wondered what he would be like if he lost his temper; but, she didn't think she really wanted to be around if that ever happened. Given his obvious physical strength, she felt sorry for anyone on the receiving end of his anger. No, the more she thought about it, the harder it was to visualize Doug flipping pancakes and burgers for the rest of his life.

The day sped by for Amanda. She had lost track of how many customers she had waited on, how many she had stared at and performed her own internal analysis to determine if he/she was the one she was supposed to help that day. Her mother and father, in her dream, had told her to keep her eyes and heart open, that there would be someone today who needed her help.

Amanda checked the large clock, designed in the shape of angel wings, that hung on the wall above the counter. It was 3:45 PM and every stool at the counter was filled, mostly with truckers sopping up their chicken and dumplings with Max's famous southern cornbread. She watched as Bertie flitted around taking care of the customers at the twelve tables and six booths scattered throughout the café. Amanda wondered why she had been hired because it was obvious Bertie could handle a full restaurant by herself, with energy to spare. The sound of Bertie's laughter brought a smile to Amanda's face; she shook her head every time Bertie stopped and punched one of the customers on their shoulder.

"No one..." Amanda sighed, unaware that she had spoken out loud.

Doug was passing by her on his way to the kitchen and stopped. "What did you say, Amanda?"

His deep, masculine voice startled her. "What?"

Doug smiled at her and Amanda thought, not for the first time, how extraordinarily handsome the man really was. It would have been perfectly normal for his good looks to stir more intimate thoughts inside her brain, but for some reason that she couldn't explain, she found that she had never been drawn to Doug in that way. Her attraction bordered more toward genuine affection, almost.... brotherly. She was more than a little surprised at her feelings toward him because she knew he would be a great catch for someone. A really great catch!

"I thought you said something," Doug smiled down at her, placing a hand upon her shoulder.

The sensation was immediate, just like that day in the parking lot when she had tripped over him and he had helped her up. She shivered involuntarily as a wave of emotion shuddered through her at his touch. It wasn't so much a physical reaction to his touch as it was an emotional one. She always felt an immediate sense of calmness when he touched her like that.

She shook her head as she stared at the clock again. "Ummm... oh, I, uh... you'll think I'm crazy."

Doug winked and shook his head. "Too late...I already think you're crazy."

His good-natured humor seemed to settle her brain cells into a weak semblance of normalcy. She smiled at him as she turned to get the coffee pot. "You're probably right. It's just that, well, I had this dream last night. Well, actually, I guess it was really this morning, just before I woke up."

The café was packed with customers, and Amanda knew that Doug was getting things ready to start his night shift. However, she felt the need to tell someone about the strange dream. She needed someone to tell her she wasn't as crazy as she felt - waiting all day for someone to walk through the door...someone who would rush to her and say "You're the one! Help me, please!"

"Want to tell me about the dream?" Doug asked.

Amanda looked up at him and wrinkled her nose. She sat the coffee pot back on the burner. "Yeah...what the heck, you already think I'm crazy, so why not. You see...I dreamed about my mom and my dad. They were together, in Heaven, I think. They're both dead, you know that, but in the dream, they were together, so I figured they must have been in Heaven. Anyway, the last thing they told me was...well, they told me that I needed to keep my eyes, and my heart, open today because there would be someone who needed my help. I've been here all day and not one person has showed up who seems to need my help."

Doug continued to listen but offered no immediate response.

"You know," Amanda went on. "You and Max pretty much said the same thing to me this morning when I first came in. Do you remember? About keeping my eyes and my heart open?"

Doug nodded his head. "I do remember, yes."

"And Max called me *Princess*. My Dad was the only one who ever called me that." Amanda shook involuntarily. "Anyway," she shrugged, "I've been looking at every customer who has come in today, wondering if he, or she, was the one I was supposed to help. How the heck am I supposed to know?" She felt Doug's intense green eyes boring down upon her. She looked up at him and shrugged again. "Well, at least now you have good reason to think I'm crazy, huh?"

Doug put his arm around her. One of his gifts, as an angel, was the ability to bring a sense of peace and order to any situation or surrounding. He knew that his touch did this instantly for Amanda. He could feel her tense muscles relax beneath his touch. "You're not crazy, Amanda." He hugged her to him and grinned. "And…besides, the day's not over yet, is it? There's still time for you to come to someone's rescue. Hang in there, *Princess*."

Amanda watched as Doug made his way back into the kitchen. She saw him leaning close to Max. She couldn't hear what they were saying, but when Max looked up, he was staring directly at her. She saw him smile at her and, once again, that sensation of calmness came over her. She shook the cobwebs from her brain and grabbed the coffee pot again. It was time for one final round among the truckers before calling it a day.

Amanda hung up her apron at 4:15 and was getting ready

to leave when Bertie stopped her.

"Hey there, Princess! I hate to ask since it's quitting time for you, but I need a huge favor," Bertie bellowed while she grabbed Amanda in a bear hug.

"Sure thing," Amanda smiled, trying to catch a breath beneath Bertie's embrace. "There doesn't seem to be anything on my agenda for the rest of the day, so what can I do for you, Bertie?"

"Can you make a quick run to Sam's and get us six large cans of spaghetti sauce? Max has to leave for a few hours and Doug needs to whip up some extra sauce while he's gone. There aren't enough hours left to make Max's special sauce, so we thought we could doctor up the canned stuff and hope that not too many customers will notice the slight." Bertie reached in her apron pocket and handed Amanda a twenty dollar bill. "That should cover it, I think. But we need it PRONTO! I hate to ask. I know it's been a long day and you're probably tired."

"No, actually, I'm not tired a bit, Bertie. I'm a little keyed up right now so the ride will do me good... give me time to unwind and think about some things. You got it, no problem!" Amanda replied. "Just let me run upstairs and grab my car keys and pocket book. I'll be back in a jiffy."

Bertie grinned. "Haven't heard too many young folks use that expression lately."

It was Amanda's turn to grin. "It was something my Dad use to say. Guess it kind of stuck with me."

Bertie nodded in agreement. "Yes, our Father's words do have a way of sticking with us, don't they?" She punched Amanda's shoulder and said, "Thanks a lot, Princess. Now, go... scoot! But drive safe now, you hear!"

The drive to Sam's Warehouse was a relatively short one, less than thirty minutes away, and the drive really did allow Amanda time to reflect on the day. She tried to remain upbeat, but it didn't take long for disappointment to take over her normally happy outlook on life. She sighed and said, "Well, Lord...it looks like nobody needed my help today after all. I tried to keep my eyes and my heart open, really I did, but maybe I missed a sign or something. Maybe whoever it was who needed my help slipped by unnoticed today. I'm sorry if I let you down. .."

Amanda pulled into Sam's parking lot, ran inside, and quickly made her purchase. She had just exited the door and stepped off the curb into the road when one of the sauce cans tipped slightly and fell out of the box she used to carry them. She reached out and tried to stop it with her foot, but it seemed to have a mind of its own as it quickly rolled toward the picnic table where the store employees usually sat during their breaks.

There was presently only one person at the table, a young woman who, from a distance, appeared to be about Amanda's age. She had her back to Amanda so it wasn't until the can of sauce hit her sandaled feet that she turned around and stared at Amanda.

"Watch it, *bitch*..." she said, the last word barely under her breath. She leaned over, picked up the can of sauce, and practically threw it back at Amanda.

Amanda caught the can and managed to balance the remaining cans without dropping them, too. "Thanks..." Amanda began but stopped when she noticed the woman's tear-streaked face. It was obvious that the woman hadn't used water-proof mascara because most of it was smudged beneath her tear-swollen eyes. Amanda took quick notice of the woman's cut-off jeans and a black, tight-fitting camisole-like top. She wore simple, black flip-flops upon her feet. Other than her messy mascara, the woman appeared neat and clean. Amanda inwardly envied her curly red hair that was tied back into a neat ponytail. Her eyes moved quickly over the woman before her stare stopped at her pregnant midsection.

"What are you looking at!" the woman hissed. It wasn't a question. She grabbed her belly in what appeared to be a protective manner. "Get the Hell away from me!"

Amanda's eyes opened wide as she stared back at the

woman. Just as she was about to issue an apology for staring, a distant sound of thunder boomed, shaking the ground beneath her. Amanda knew it was impossible but she had the distinct feeling that the thunder had come from the direction of the Heavenly Grille. It was then that Amanda's heart seemed to skip a beat and she gasped. "It's you... you're the one..." she whispered, smiling back at the woman.

The woman stared back at Amanda as if she had suddenly grown two heads. "Crazy *bitch*..." she muttered as she maneuvered her very pregnant belly up and away from Amanda's outstretched arms.

CHAPTER 9

Kris Meets the Angels of HGC

It was normal for there to be a lull in customers between the hours of five and six, and the employees of the Heavenly Grille appreciated it because it gave them time to regroup for the night crowd. The customers who frequented the café at night were of a different caliber than the construction workers, secretaries, preachers, retired folks, and children who gathered for meals during the day time hours. Word was spreading quickly among the neighboring communities about the great food and service offered at the Heavenly Grille. The majority of the day time customers came for Max's home cooking and mouth-watering desserts, some came because they had heard about the floating halo and wanted to see it for themselves, and some just wandered in the small, out-of-the-way café as if they were somehow, mystically, drawn to it.

On the other hand, the night crowds were more often than not a bit on the rowdy side; this was another reason that Max had specifically recruited Doug for the night shift. Martin had argued against the assignment from day one, concerned that Doug wasn't quite ready for an earthly assignment and had worried whether or not Doug could keep his temper under control in that type of environment. However, Max knew that Doug's physical strength and chiseled physique would help tremendously in taming the café's nightly customers. Max's recommendation had prevailed, as usual, and he had not been wrong. Doug had proven to be a quick learner and he had not shown any weakness in being able to control his temper. In fact, in the three short weeks Doug had been working, he continued to impress and reassure Max that he had been the right choice for the assignment. He assisted Max in meal preparation, he helped Bertie wait on tables, and he had amicably persuaded men twice his size that their reason for stopping at the Heavenly Grille was to enjoy God's meal in a peaceful ambiance. So far, he had not had to use any physical force. His firm hand upon their shoulders had been all it had taken to settle arguments and to ensure a peaceful, albeit sometimes temporary, co-existence with their fellow patrons.

It was now five o'clock and the café was temporarily empty of customers. Three of Heaven's most popular angels sat around one of the tables with their eyes closed and their hands clasped beneath their chins.

"Heavenly Father," Max began in his raspy baritone. "Thank you for allowing us to serve you this day, for sending those to us who were in need of comfort. We ask that, if it is your will, they continue to return to us for whatever help we may provide them. As we begin our work on the night shift, we pray for the strength, guidance, wisdom, and patience to continue the work you have sent us here to do. We ask these things in the name of Jesus Christ. AMEN!"

"Woo-hoo!" Bertie shouted, lifting her right hand in a celebratory fist. "Amen, and amen to that, Lord!" She reached over and punched Doug on the shoulder. "Make sure you remember the part where he requested *patience*, big fella!"

Doug smiled and rubbed his shoulder. "I'm working on

that one, Bertie; and, trust me, with some of the crowd in here at night, well... let's just say, they really do test my patience at times."

Bertie noticed his inadvertent glance at the clock before stretching his neck to look out at the empty parking lot, again. She gave him another good-natured punch as she pushed back her chair and stood up. "She's okay, handsome. Quit your worrying. In fact..." Bertie said, puckering her lips together and tilting her head sideways, "I'd say she should be driving up right about..."

They all heard a car door close outside.

"Now!" Bertie grinned and kissed the top of Doug's head. She ruffled his thick, black hair and laughed out loud. "Oh, I just bet the girls loved you, didn't they! You are just too damn pretty for your own good."

Max grinned at Doug's reddened face. "Now you've gone and embarrassed the man, Bertie."

Bertie looked back and grinned at Doug's obvious discomfort. "Settle down, handsome. Whatsamatter? Nobody ever pay you a compliment before? Why, your ears are so red they look like they just might pop a blister!"

Doug shook his head and grinned at the two senior angels. ""Yes," he thought, *this is definitely going to be an interesting five years..."*

All three of them turned at the sound of a second car door shutting.

"Well, I'll be damned," Bertie said, "Looks like our girl brought company..."

Max looked out the window and whistled out loud when he saw the woman's extremely pregnant belly. "Well, I just hope we won't have to add delivering babies to the menu."

"Yessiree," Bertie nodded, "That girl looks like she's gonna pop any second now, doesn't she?"

Doug was the last to rise from his chair. He watched through the window as the two women made their way toward the café's entrance. He noticed the protective way in which Amanda placed her hand against the woman's back.

He also noticed the subsequent flinch the woman made at that touch.

All three angels said in unison, "She found her..."

When Amanda opened the door, allowing her new friend to enter first, she was caught a bit off guard to find her three co-workers standing just inside the entrance, all of them sporting huge Cheshire-like grins. A strange feeling immediately came over her, causing her to shiver in spite of the hot, July temperature. It was a tingling sensation that she had never experienced before, one that started at the tips of her toes and quickly rushed to the top of her head. She shivered again as the tingling quickly immersed into a complete feeling of calmness that seemed to engulf her very being. She knew now, beyond a shadow of a doubt, that she had made the right decision by convincing the stranger to come back with her to the café.

It had taken Amanda a good thirty minutes to convince the young woman to accept her offer of help. In that short time, Amanda had learned that her new friend's name was Kris DeVone, and that she was twenty-three years old and seven months pregnant.

Kris had reluctantly told Amanda the short version of her story that involved her and her boyfriend stopping at Sam's Warehouse to that Kris could use their facilities. When she had finished, she could not find her boyfriend anywhere. She had wandered around the store and parking lot for nearly an hour before finally settling at the outside table where Amanda had found her. Her boyfriend was gone and so was her car.

"Hey, everyone..." Amanda shrugged sheepishly. "Look who I found... this is... Kris."

Bertie swiftly moved in to offer her usual bear hug to Kris, but found it a bit difficult due to the size of Kris' swollen belly. "Well, come on in, Kris...it looks like you need to take a load off, girl." She glanced back at Amanda, raised her eyebrows, and puckered her lips together. "Well, Princess, I do hope you remembered the tomato sauce!"

Standing before the four smiling strangers, and for the first time in her life, Kris DeVone was absolutely speechless.

CHAPTER 10

Kris' Story

After a momentary and somewhat awkward moment of silence, Bertie laughed out loud and embraced Kris once again. "Come on, shoog; what do you say we get you off your feet and some food in that belly of yours? Looks like you're about to pop that little one any time now. How far along are you, anyway?" One of Bertie's favorite terms of endearment was *shoog*, which was just her countrified abbreviation for *sugar*. Her grandmother had called her *shoog* and Bertie had used the fond expression while caring for her own two young children.

Kris instinctively placed both hands upon her belly and wondered, not for the first time, what she had been thinking when she accepted a total stranger's offer of help. She had never been a very trusting person, but her situation had seemed bleak and she felt she had little choice but to accept Amanda's offer of a ride home. She had no car and no money for a cab. "The baby is due September twelfth," she mumbled as she slid into one of the booth seats, which allowed her a window view of the parking lot.

She noticed that Amanda's Trooper was the only car in the lot, which caused another quick wave of fear to course through her body. She had heard stories about weird sickos who cut babies out of near-term pregnant women. However, all the uneasiness and fear she had felt just moments before dissipated into thin air the moment Max sat across the table from her and placed his massive, black hand atop hers. All her inward trembling and insecurity seemed to cease immediately upon his touch. She stared into his soulful, brown eyes, and time seemed to freeze as the strangest, most unusual feeling of calmness seeped slowly throughout her entire body. Her previously morbid thoughts of abduction and murder immediately quelled; she now experienced an immense sense of total serenity. It was the strangest feeling she had ever experienced. The next thought that popped into her mind was that she knew, without a doubt, that she was safe with these people. She couldn't explain why, but she knew that nothing bad would happen to her here.

Amanda scooted in next to Kris while Bertie followed suit next to Max. Kris looked up at the handsome man left standing beside the table. *"Damn!"* she thought, *"he's hot!"* She was suddenly so entranced with the man's piercing green eyes that she momentarily forgot where she was, who she was, and why she was here. She failed to notice the raised eyebrows and puckered smiles coming from the older woman and the black man sitting at the table.

Doug was totally oblivious of the impact he had on women. He had been watching Kris and Amanda closely from the moment they entered the café. He extended his hand across the table and smiled. "It's very nice to meet you, Kris. I'm Doug. I'm going to get you something to eat; is there anything special you want to drink?"

Kris was still holding onto his extended hand. The first thought that entered her mind was that she never wanted to let it go. Once again, that feeling of warmth, safety, and security flowed through her while Doug's strong hand held her own. Of course, the black man's hand still lay atop her left hand. When both men finally released her hands back into her own custody, she closed her mouth, blinked hard, and shook her head. "Uh... coffee would be good, I guess. No sugar or cream...black is fine."

"That's the way I like it, too. Coming right up," Doug smiled back at her and made his way into the kitchen.

Now that her hands were her own again, Kris' thoughts couldn't help but turn to the rich aromas of food filtering throughout the café. "Something sure smells good."

Bertie laughed out loud. It was her turn to take hold of Kris' hands. "You're safe here, you know, shoog. By the way, don't know where the Hell our manners went. You've obviously already met our sweet Amanda. This gentle giant beside me is Max. He's the owner of the café and he's responsible for all that good food you're about to sink your teeth into. You've met pretty boy back there; he works the night shift with me. Oh, yeah, and I'm Bertie."

Kris took her time looking at each of them. Her initial doubts of getting into Amanda's car seemed dim in comparison to the total peace her mind and body were now experiencing. It was true, she had never been one to trust strangers, but she had a feeling that was about to change. She spent the next forty-five minutes eating the best food she had ever tasted and telling four strangers the story of her life...

Kris had never known her biological father; in fact, she doubted if her mother even knew who the father of her only child had been. There had been so many men in and out of her mother's life, men who always seemed to take priority over Kris. Her mother had somehow managed to get Kris into grade school without causing too much physical damage to the child and in spite of Social Services' constant interventions. By the time she was eight years old, the roles between mother and daughter had been reversed. Kris was essentially taking care of her mother, cleaning up the aftermath effects of the woman's drunken nights, preparing whatever meager meals she could scrape together from the little food kept in the house, and, getting herself to school every day. As bad as life was with her mother and the string of men who frequented their home, Kris was convinced that it had to be better than being shuffled from one foster home to another. Life with Sylvia Devone was, at the very least, predictable; and, that predictability was the only stable factor in Kris' childhood. She was never disappointed because she knew never to expect anything from her mother.

By the time she was fourteen, Kris looked a few years older than she was. She was petite but shapely, her delicate skin was as smooth as fine porcelain, and her vibrant red hair fell nearly to her waist. It didn't escape her that the male population found her attractive, but she was always quick to downplay her looks as much as possible. She instinctively determined that the less attention she brought to herself the safer she would be. However, that all changed one summer night when one of the many men who shared her mother's bed stumbled drunkenly into her room and raped her. It was the night of her fourteenth birthday. Her beautiful long, red curls became wet with the man's drunken sweat, while his grossly obese body weighed heavily upon her own small frame. He mumbled something about *"how good that was, Sylvia"* just before he passed out. That was the first time Kris DeVone ran away from home.

The rape experience changed her in more ways than one. Over the next three years, Kris fell in with a bad crowd. Her experimentation with drugs and sex was all encompassing. If it was made available, she tried it. If she liked it, she tried it again and again. Somehow, in spite of her downward-spiraling lifestyle, she managed to maintain impressive grades, keep Social Services at bay, and to stay out of jail. Life was as good as it had ever been to her but it got even better when she met Mike Stephens and fell in love for the first time in her life.

She was in her senior year of high school and had no real direction of where her life was going. Her goal for the past several years had been to graduate and move as far away from her mother, who by now had added cocaine to her daily addiction, as she could get. She knew it was only a matter of time before the drugs and alcohol killed her mother and she didn't want to be witness to that event. Even though she felt no real love for the woman who had birthed her, neither did she want to stick around and watch the life completely fade from her.

Mike Stephens quickly became her ticket out of Hell. He was as good as Kris was bad, and she had no idea what he saw in her. Nevertheless, he eventually convinced her that he truly loved her and wanted her to move to Georgia with him. He was scheduled to start Basic Training at Fort Benning, Georgia in January 2005 and before he left, he had made Kris promise to meet him there after he completed his six weeks of Basic Training.

Kris made the difficult decision to drop out of school in March 2005. She packed up what little belongings she had, left her mother a brief note, and moved to Columbus, Georgia, where she and Mike had six beautiful months together before he got orders for Afghanistan. Mike did his best to convince her to marry him before he left, but Kris thought they should wait until his tour was up, to give them more time to get to know one another. She knew that he was the best thing that had ever happened to her, but she wanted to give him enough time to realize exactly what he was getting in her, which in her own eyes, was damaged goods.

During the following eleven months, Kris and Mike used email and SKYPE on a daily basis to keep in touch with each other. Mike consistently sent money home for Kris to put into a special savings account for their wedding. Kris made the most of the time that Mike was away. She spent her free time fixing up the small apartment she and Mike had found before he left; she waitressed at a local barbecue restaurant; she earned her GED; and, she enrolled in the local community college to take her basic, core classes. Life in Georgia was good, and their time apart was quickly coming to an end. Mike had less than a month left in his tour to Afghanistan.

The phone call came in mid-August 2006, just as Kris was

leaving the apartment to rush to her Algebra class. The woman identified herself as Irene Stephens; she was Mike's mother. Mrs. Stephens' clipped voice was quick and abrupt when she told Kris that Mike was dead, killed instantly by friendly fire during a routine training exercise. She never hesitated with her words, and her voice indicated no signs of emotion. She concluded the conversation by telling Kris that she, and the rest of her family, would appreciate it if Kris did not attend the funeral and did not ever contact them again in the future. She told Kris that her son had been engaged to a wonderful woman before he met Kris and that she doubted that Mike had really cared for Kris.

Mrs. Stephens' hurtful words turned Kris' life upside down once again. She convinced herself that Mike's mother spoke the truth. By the time she hung up the phone, she knew she could not afford to live alone without the additional money that Mike always sent her, so she did the only thing she could. She turned in her notice, quit her job, dropped out of school, returned to Florida, and quickly fell back into her old routine, complete with alcohol, drug and sexual experimentation. The only difference was that she moved in with an old boyfriend instead of returning to her mother's home. Her mother, like Mike, was also dead and gone. Kris never grieved over the loss of her mother, but she never quit loving Mike and wondering about the life they could have had.

After two years of living her old lifestyle, and with no real direction in sight, Kris met another set of gonads who promised her a better life. She figured she didn't have anything to lose so she dumped her live-in boyfriend and agreed to move in with Danny Raye. Surprisingly, things did seem to improve a bit. Her drug and alcohol consumption decreased, she found a steady waitressing job, and worked long hours to save enough money to enroll in school again. Her life with Danny Raye gradually meshed into a semi-comfortable routine.

That comfortable routine changed on her twenty-first

birthday when Kris found out she was pregnant. She wasn't sure how she felt about the prospect of becoming a mother; Danny, on the other hand, was quick to inform her that he wanted no part of it. He gave her the money for an abortion and told her to take care of the problem. The look in his eye that day left no doubt in Kris' mind that if she didn't take care of the problem, he would. She felt she had no choice. She took his money and aborted the pregnancy.

After the abortion, Kris came to hate Danny with every fiber of her being, but she also knew that she had nowhere to go and no family to turn to. So, she did what she had done all her life. She survived.

Over the next year, Kris put aside every spare dollar she could into her secret savings account – the same account she and Mike had started in preparation for the wedding they never had. Her plan was to leave Danny when she had enough saved and when she had attained her associate's degree. She didn't know where she would go, but she knew it would be far away from Danny and the life they shared. He had never been physically abusive to her yet; however, she was constantly aware that she was probably only one punch away from being hurt by him.

She was finally ready to make her move in January 2011 but something happened to change her plans. She became pregnant again; and, like before, Danny insisted on an abortion. He blamed her for trying to trap him, so the only difference this time was that he told her she could pay for the abortion herself. Kris had never forgiven herself for agreeing to the first abortion and she knew, without a doubt, that she could never go through another one. She knew it would be hard to raise a baby alone, but she had convinced herself she could do it. She waited until later that night when Danny left to meet up with some of his friends. She called a locksmith, had the locks on the door changed, and piled all his belongings on the steps outside their apartment. He never came home that night. She called and told him he needed to come collect his belongings if he wanted them. She even arranged for a policeman, the husband of a friend of a friend, to be with her the next day when he finally came to collect his things.

His hands closed tightly into fists before he bent down to gather his belongings. He looked at her, looked at the cop, and offered a final smirk. "So long, bitch."

Kris was all alone in her pregnancy during the following six months. She went to all her county-sponsored doctor appointments, took her vitamins, ate right, exercised, and was feeling confident that she could be something that she had never had – a good mother. She knew that lots of other single women made it work and she was determined to do the same. There was a brief time during that six-month period that she even considered joining a church, maybe learn to pray. However, she quickly abandoned that thought. She had never been exposed to any type of formal religion and she didn't really believe in God anyway; the last thing she wanted to do was to be hypocritical about that situation. Maybe one day, but not now.

Kris arrived home from one of her night classes three weeks later to find Danny Raye sitting on the steps outside her apartment. Even though he appeared to be clean-shaven and sober, she instinctively moved to get back inside her vehicle when she spotted him.

Danny jumped off the steps when he saw her start to get back inside her car and shouted, "Wait, Kris... please! Hey, I promise I'm not here to hurt you. I just wanna talk to you for a minute. Okay?"

It went against her better judgment, but Kris listened while Danny begged her forgiveness and asked her to take him back. He had thought things over and he wanted them to try to make things work, to be a real family. He wanted to be a father to their baby.

Kris wanted so desperately to believe him, so... she did.

She allowed Danny to move back in and it didn't take him long to quickly lure her into a false sense of security. It was another three weeks later when she exited the bathroom of

Sam's Warehouse to find that Danny Raye had abandoned her, and stolen both her car and purse. She had, unfortunately, confessed to him about the secret savings account. It didn't take him long to convince her to cash in the savings so that they could furnish a nursery and find a larger apartment, away from the crime and drug scenes. She could almost hear Mike pleading with her not to do it, but she knew she had to really begin trusting Danny again; he was, after all, the father of her child. That money had been in her purse. She had wanted to take the purse inside Sam's with her, but Danny told her he would watch it for her, that she didn't need to be carrying it inside since it had so much money in it...someone might steal it...

After telling her story to the four patient and compassionate people sitting around the café table with her, Kris shrugged her shoulders and said. "Well, that's it, I guess. That's my story. Leave it to me to pick the biggest losers, huh?"

Bertie pushed up and away from the table while Doug refilled everyone's cups with steaming coffee. "I think I'll go fetch us all some dessert," Bertie sighed.

Max stood up and looked down at Kris. "I'll go call the police."

Kris watched Bertie, Max, and Doug all walk silently toward the kitchen. She looked over at Amanda, whose eyes were wet with unshed tears. She couldn't remember anyone ever crying over her. It felt really strange, but somehow....comforting, too. Kris offered a weak smile. "I bet you're really glad you stopped to help me, aren't you?"

"Oh, more than you can imagine! You know, Kris, there really is a God," Amanda whispered. "I've known Him all my life and, trust me, He is awesome! If you only put your faith in Him, you'll see that everything is going to be just fine."

Kris rolled her eyes and shook her head. "I learned a long time ago, Amanda, to put my faith in only one person, and that's ME. I'm sorry, I know your faith is real to you, but...I don't believe in your God. I mean, just look at my life, at everything that has happened to me. What kind of God allows people to suffer like that? No, I do not believe in your God."

Amanda watched her new friend turn her face toward the window. She smiled to herself and thought, *"That's okay... you don't have to believe in Him just yet, because He believes in you.*

CHAPTER 11

Heaven
Amanda's Parents Meet Martin

S tephen and Regina Turner stood off to one side waiting patiently for the tall, skinny black man to acknowledge their presence. Each of them had been in different locations when they had telepathically received what they could only perceive to be a summons; so, they had closed their eyes, concentrated on the voice and command they heard, and when they opened their eyes, they found themselves standing next to each other for the first time since Regina's death.

They had not been physically together when Amanda first dreamed about them, but they had joined forces, telepathically, in order to relay the important message to their daughter. This summons by Martin was the first time Stephen had laid eyes on the love of his life in fourteen years; well, fourteen human years, anyway. He had no idea how long he had been in what he now knew was Heaven; sometimes it felt like it had only been a few days, while at others, it felt more like the three years since he had died.

Regina's eyes lit up when she saw her husband. She reached for his hand and squeezed it tightly. "I've been waiting for you for such a long time, Stephen."

Stephen squeezed back, amazed at the sensations that rocked his new heavenly body. He couldn't take his eyes off Regina and, at first, was unable to speak past the lump in his throat. "Regina...oh, my, God...I am so confused." He pulled her into an embrace, never wanting to let her go again. He kissed the top of her head and said, "I know this is the first time we've seen each other, but I could swear you and I were together, speaking to Amanda... in a dream, I think, but how could that be possible? My, God...you look...wonderful..."

Regina smiled back at him. "I know it's confusing, love, but it will all begin to make more sense, eventually...after all, you're still a newbie at all this." She waved her arms to include the vast whiteness surrounding them before continuing. "But, you're right...we were together, sort of. It was the same dream, but we weren't physically together. I have to admit that I still don't understand all the mechanics of how it all works. I doubt if any of us ever will, but it really doesn't matter how things happen here. We just accept that they do happen and that there's always a good reason behind why they happen as they do." She wrapped her arms around his waist and threw back her golden hair. "I'm just so glad to finally be able to hold you in my arms and to see you again. I've missed you so much, Stephen...so very much."

A thought suddenly occurred to Stephen Turner as he stared at the woman he had shared his life with, the mother of his only child. It dawned on him that this woman who had been such an important part of his human life, and whose body he had known so intimately, now held no sexual attraction to him at all. He also knew that these same thoughts and feelings were shared by Regina. The love and the bond they had always shared were still there, stronger than ever, but neither of them experienced any sexual inclinations toward the other.

He ran both hands down his face and shook his head as this final thought sunk in. "I really am confused..."

Martin had his back turned to the couple while he fidgeted with some buttons and switches beside the huge screen with scrolling, black lettering. He decided to give them a few more moments together before acknowledging them. He loved being a part of the *heavenly reunions between husbands and wives, and he smiled now when he heard Stephen's confused thoughts about the lack of sexual attraction toward his wife. This had always been one of the hardest things for the human souls to accept and understand; however, Martin always chuckled when they realized that it was, also, somewhat of a relief!*

"Who is he?" Stephen asked, nodding his head in Martin's direction. "And, where exactly are we? One second I was sitting with a group of people listening to a man explaining to us about the hierarchy of angels, and the next thing I knew I was here, standing beside you. By the way, did you know that you and I aren't angels? I learned that in the class I was attending today...just one more thing to add to my overall confusion, I guess..."

Regina reached up and pushed back a lock of her husband's hair that had fallen down upon his forehead. His spiritual soul, as well as her own, were at the ages of twenty-eight and twenty-six, respectively – not much older than their daughter currently was in her earthly years. She glanced over at Martin and smiled in acknowledgment. "His name is Martin and he's the first assistant to Max. Max is what we humans would call an angel, not to be confused with the real heavenly angels, mind you. Max operates the café where our Amanda is working. But, like I said, neither Max nor Martin are "Heavenly" angels....just as you and I aren't, nor will we ever be Heavenly angels. We'll be more like...well...angel assistants, or spiritual guides. Real angels... Heavenly angels... have never lived human lives."

Stephen squeezed his chin together between his open palms and shook his head. "Gee, thanks for clearing that up for me, dear. Oh yeah... sure... it all makes so much more sense now." He pulled her close to him, kissed the top of her head, and rested his chin there while he watched Martin's back. He couldn't be sure, but by the slight heaving of the man's shoulders, he would have sworn that Martin was suppressing laughter!

The huge white screen suddenly flickered off as Martin turned to face the couple. "Ah, Regina! So good to see you again, my dear! How have you been?"

Regina walked toward Martin and accepted his embrace. She sighed and smiled up at him. "Much better now, thank you." She glanced back at Stephen and sighed. "There's still so much to learn, Martin. After all this time, I still feel like such a beginner in my lessons."

Martin nodded. "Not to worry, my dear. You have plenty of time and you have already learned much more than you may realize." Martin looked over at Stephen and motioned him forward. "Stephen, please come here...join us."

There was no hesitation on Stephen's part. This man exalted trust, honesty, and integrity; it oozed from every particle surrounding him. Stephen trusted him instantly.

Martin welcomed Stephen into their embrace. "I know how happy Regina is to finally be able to talk with you again. She has waited a long time for your arrival, and you're probably wondering why it didn't happen sooner. After all, you have been with us now for three years."

Stephen cocked his eyebrows and nodded in agreement. "I'm actually wondering about a lot of things! For instance, I was fifty-one when I died and, well... this isn't exactly the body I died in, if you know what I mean. And, Regina was only thirty-five when she died, but..." he sighed again as he took a long look at his wife, "Well, she doesn't look any older than she was the day I first met her."

Martin released them both and fluttered his hands theatrically in the air. "Time is truly irrelevant, don't you think? Humans put far too much thought and energy into worrying about time. If only they knew what the two of you have learned since you've been here...ahh...their time on earth would be so much more rewarding for them." He turned back to the large screen and motioned them closer. "Enough of that, come closer...both of you, I want you to see this."

The huge screen flickered on again, and images of the current inhabitants of the Heavenly Grille Café filled it; they were all sitting around a booth. Regina and Steve moved closer and observed an older man and woman sitting on one side of the booth; and, their daughter, Amanda, was sitting on the opposite side of the booth next to a young woman – a very pregnant young woman. A handsome young man stood at the end of the booth filling cups with steaming coffee.

"Oh, look!" whispered Regina, grabbing hold of Stephen's hand.

"There's Amanda! Oh, Stephen, look at how beautiful she is." She looked up at her husband. "You really did a wonderful job of raising her, you know. Thank you for that…"

Stephen smiled down at her. "Well, I'm not sure how much credit I should take in that. I tried not to screw things up too badly, but I have to admit that it was touch and go at times. Let's just say… there were many, many times when she could have used her mother's touch and advice, but she had to settle for her Dad's inane efforts. Do you have any idea how long it takes to master a French braid?"

Martin allowed them to linger their attention on their daughter for a few moments before he interjected. "Amanda is not only beautiful on the outside; she also has a good soul. Even though she is all alone in the world, she still has compassion for her fellow human beings, always on the lookout for someone to help. She seldom allows herself self-pity, does she?"

Stephen shook his head. "Nope, that's just not Amanda's style; I think she gets that from her mother's side of the family. Whenever things didn't go her way, she would just pick herself up and tell me that tomorrow would be a better day. She also had a lot of compassion for animals, especially abused ones. It seems like she brought strays home every week and would keep them until she could find a forever home for them." Stephen nodded at the pregnant woman sitting beside his daughter. "Something tells me that this young lady might just be Amanda's latest stray…am I right? She's the person that Regina and I told Amanda to be on the lookout for, isn't she?"

"In a sense," Martin smiled. "Yes, I suppose you could call Kris Devone a stray. Her life has, indeed, been very similar to that of a stray animal…but…we are hoping that Amanda will be able to help her turn her life around."

Stephen leaned closer to look at the screen and pointed at the older woman sitting at the booth opposite his daughter. "Well, I'll be! Look! It's that actress who played Hazel on television! Look, Regina!"

Regina took a closer look at Bertie. She did indeed bear a striking resemblance to the actress, Shirley Booth, a character actress who had played in the television series, "Hazel." The show had been a *hit series from 1961 through 1966. Stephen was born in 1960 but had grown up watching re-runs of the series and had been Shirley Booth's biggest fan. He had adored everything about the woman. Regina grinned in agreement. "She definitely looks a lot like her, Stephen."*

Stephen was grinning from ear to ear. "What a great actress she was; when I was a kid, I would pretend to be "Sport" – the son of the family Hazel worked for – did you know that she dropped out of school at the age of fourteen to pursue a stage career? Oh, and I even remember an interview she did once, around 1971, I think. She told the person interviewing her that she would rather have affection than admiration because affection was warmer and lasted longer. For some reason, that statement has always stuck in my head…" Steve shook the cobwebs from his brain and grinned at Martin. "What is Hazel doing sitting across from my daughter?"

Martin laughed out loud. "Well, you may be right about her looks. I've never really thought about it, but now that I look closer at her, I do believe you are right. Our Bertie does bear a striking resemblance to Miss Booth. However, since you appear to be such an expert on the actress, then you must know that Miss Shirley Booth passed away… let's see… on October 16, 1992. She was buried in Mt. Hebron Cemetery in Montclair, New Jersey. The last time I checked, that's a long way from Monticello, Florida…"

"Bertie?" Regina and Stephen asked in unison.

"Ah, yes," Martin replied. "Bertie is… how should I say… one of ours."

"She's an angel?" Stephen asked.

"Well," Martin sighed, "She's what you humans might call an angel, but, as you will learn when you return to your study of the hierarchy of angels, there are nine orders of angels. Let's see…it's been a very long time since I taught that particular class, but as I recall, they include the seraphim, the cherubim, the thrones, the rulers, the virtues, the powers, the principalities, the archangels, and…the regular angels. Bertie falls more into the realm of a regular angel's assistant. You see, real angels, the angels that our Heavenly Father created Himself, have never held human bodies and souls; real angels were created by God when he created the Heavens. However, more importantly, real angels are totally and

absolutely without sin, and trust me...our Bertie most definitely does not fall into that category."

"I'm not sure I understand, Martin," Regina said. "Are you saying that Bertie is like us? She was a human...that she lived on earth? Oh my goodness...does that mean that we can return, too?"

Martin placed a hand on each of their shoulders. "I know it is confusing, dear, but yes, Bertie began and lived life as a human. She actually died in 1911, run over by an automobile, she was. Yes, that was a long time ago, but...our Max, he's the one sitting next to Bertie, is also an angel. He, too, lived life as a human, but his time goes a lot farther back than even Bertie's. You see, Max was a true and noble gladiator during the Roman Empire era."

"This is fascinating. I'm almost afraid to ask," Stephen queried. "What about the young man?"

"Oh, yes, indeed! That would be Doug and...bingo...he, too, is one of us. This is actually Doug's first earthly assignment."

Both Stephen and Regina clasped their hands in prayer, hope gleaming in their eyes.

Martin recognized the look immediately and shook his head. "To answer your last question, Regina...no...it is not possible. I am afraid you cannot go back, at least not for quite a while. One of the stipulations for returning to earth on assignment is that you must have been dead for at least fifty years." He fluttered his hands above his head. "But, that's another lesson you'll learn about in due time. The reason I have summoned the two of you here today is to let you know that, even though you cannot return to earth, you will be allowed to interact with your daughter, Amanda."

"I don't understand...what do you mean?" Stephen asked.

Regina looked at Martin as the answer suddenly came to her. She grinned at him and said, "Oh, I think I understand. You're talking about Amanda's dreams, aren't you?"

Martin nodded, pleased at Regina's quick grasp of the situation. "Precisely correct, my dear. Amanda's faith will be tested, for sure, but with the help of the café staff and your appearances in her dreams, we are hopeful that she will become a true friend to Miss DeVone, and be instrumental in bringing the young lady to Christ. It will be a test of Amanda's faith."

Regina beamed with maternal pride. "Well, I have no doubt that

Amanda will excel in this particular test. Miss DeVone is very lucky to have met our daughter today."

"Oh, please!" Martin mused theatrically. "You don't really believe luck had anything at all to do with any of this, do you now?"

Stephen listened and watched while his wife and Martin bantered back and forth. He sighed deeply and whispered..."Oh, I really do have so much to learn..."

"Trust in the Lord with all your heart, and lean not on your own understanding."

-Proverbs 3:5 (NKJV)

CHAPTER 12

Doug and Amanda Discuss Kris

The Heavenly Grille was always closed on Sundays, much to the disappointment of the Monticello, Florida church crowd. Doug and Amanda sat together at the round, oak picnic table situated in the small wooded area behind the Heavenly Grille Café; it was the second Sunday since Amanda had first brought Kris to the café. They sat in amiable silence, enjoying the mid-morning sounds and sights of the array of birds, squirrels, and turtles competing for attention in the woods surrounding them. A large pitcher of Max's delicious, iced lemonade-tea sat between them. The beverage was a favorite of customers and Amanda was a huge fan, too. She had tried to duplicate Max's recipe for the tea, but had yet to perfect the exact measurements that resulted in the rich, robust flavors of tea married with the light, sweet tartness of homemade lemonade.

It was the first week of August and even though the temperature was in the mid-nineties, a cool breeze waffled through the leaves of the old oak trees clustered behind the café. A small white picket fence separated the forty feet that divided the dense wood line from the café; the area between was blanketed with a wide variety of Florida-friendly plants. A celestial arrangement of autumn and holly ferns shared the small space with lavender twin flowers, bugleweed, caladiums, lilies, and Mondo grass. A small brook snaked along one side of the property. Amanda loved this spot almost as much as she had loved the tropical back yard her father had created in their Tampa home. The colorful, serene setting could have been one of the many captivating settings captured in Thomas Kinkade's paintings; he was Amanda's favorite modern-day painter. The more she soaked in the natural beauty surrounding her, the more the peaceful setting actually reminded her of Kinkade's painting, "Beside Still Waters." She had always wanted to own one of the artist's oil paintings but had never been able to afford them; instead, her father had given her a small print of "Beside Still Waters" for her sixteenth birthday. The priceless print was still packed away in her car, along with most of her personal belongings, excluding clothing. She knew her living arrangements at the Heavenly Grille were only temporary, until she could find her own apartment, so she had not unpacked anything yet.

Amanda closed her eyes, listening to the choir of birds perched high above in the old oaks, and stretched out her legs on her side of the bench. "This has got to be the best way to spend a lazy Sunday, huh, Dougie? It just doesn't get any better than this…"

Doug smiled at her. His mother was the only person, besides Bertie, who had ever called him Dougie. "Well, I'm not sure if you're talking about having a day off from your hectic schedule, or whether it's this fantastic tea. Which is it?"

Amanda opened her eyes and grinned back at him. She lifted her hands high above her head and stretched. "All of it! This place… the tea…finding you, Bertie, and Max… EVERYTHING! I just feel so blessed to have ended up here. Hey, and not only that, but did I tell you that I have also found a fantastic church?"

Doug winked at her. He knew that finding a church had been high on Amanda's priority list. "No, you hadn't mentioned that, but I did know you've been looking for one. I'm really glad things are working out for you, Princess; and, I'm really glad you've found a church." He cleared his throat and glanced down at the watch he only wore at Bertie's insistence, after she had punched his shoulder and told him it would make him *fit in*. "Since it is such a fantastic church, maybe you want to explain why you aren't there now?"

Amanda pulled her knees to her chest and laughed. "Probably for the same reason you're not, I guess," she teased. "For your information, I went to the early-morning services. I like those better because then I have even more time to sit outside and enjoy all this! God, it's all so beautiful..."

"I know what you mean, Amanda. It is very serene...very peaceful here, isn't it?"

Amanda nodded and grinned. "Yep, for sure. Sometimes, it seems like...if I can just sit here for a few minutes, then all my worries and problems will – POOF - evaporate into thin air and be solved in no time at all."

Doug nodded and poured them each another glass of tea. "Speaking of worries and problems...what's going on with your new friend, Kris? It sure seems like she's had more than her fair share of problems to resolve. How is she doing?"

Amanda sighed. It had been two weeks since she had brought Kris Devone to the Heavenly Grille. The dream – the one with her parents in it - had led her to believe that someone needing her help would waltz into the café. Instead, she had found Kris a relatively short, twenty-five miles away at Sam's Warehouse in Tallahassee, and brought her back to the café. Max had called the police to report the theft of Kris' car and purse by her boyfriend, Danny Raye; and, Amanda had offered to drive Kris back to her apartment. Amanda had even used part of her own meager savings, against Kris' protests, to pay to have the locks changed on Kris' home. It had taken a couple of days before the police found Kris' car, apparently abandoned, at the Tallahassee Airport; her purse was still inside the car, albeit, void of any monetary contents or credit cards. The police had not yet located Danny Raye.

"You know, considering everything that has happened to her, I think she's actually doing pretty good," Amanda said. "She's a little nervous about things, especially with her due date only six weeks away. We never discussed it, but for a while there, I was afraid that she might be thinking of giving the baby up for adoption, but the more I get to know her, I don't think there is any way she would ever let that baby out of her sight! She's worried about money, too, especially since she had planned on using her savings to finish getting the things she needed for the nursery, and to be able to take some time off after the baby comes. But, you know what? Her boss, the man who owns the coffee house she works at…well, he must be a good man. He's been a HUGE help. He schedules her all the hours she wants to work, and he's told her that he'll pay her salary for six weeks after she has the baby, until she's able to go back to work full-time. Yep, he's a good man, alright."

Doug nodded. "Sounds that way. She's lucky to have him for a boss."

"For sure!" Kris agreed. "We found out that he had a daughter who would have been about our age, I guess. She died a few years ago, some kind of undetected heart problem, I think. I don't know, but somehow, I have a feeling that, by helping Kris, he feels like he's doing what he would have done for his own daughter, if she had lived long enough to have kids."

Doug nodded as he continued sipping his tea. "He really does sound like a good man. You did tell us that Kris has no family, is that right?"

Amanda shook her head. "Nope, she has absolutely no one. Something we seem to have in common. I guess that's why I've been thinking that we might be able to help each other out."

What do you mean?" Doug asked.

Amanda shrugged. "I don't know. We haven't really talked about it, but I've been thinking that day care has got to be pretty expensive, especially on a waitress's salary. I've been tossing around the idea of talking to her about us getting a place together, and work our schedules out to where one of us was there to take care of the baby while the other one worked. Does that sound crazy? I mean, we hardly know one another."

"Crazy? No...but it is a lot of responsibility to sign on for, especially for someone you just met. I commend you for wanting to help. She's very lucky that you came to her rescue. I guess there's no sign of the boyfriend yet?"

"That scumbag? No, he's probably hiding under a rock somewhere, spending all of Kris' savings on booze and drugs. People like that, I don't know... how could he just leave her like he did?"

"I don't know, Amanda, but I do believe that everything that happens to us in our lives is pre-destined, chapters written long before we're even born. There is a reason for everything that happens to us, a reason for certain people to come into our lives. We may question why things happen but there's a good chance we'll never really know the answer. Besides, the answer may not be the most important thing for us to understand."

"What do you mean?"

"Well," Doug shrugged. "Having the answer to why things happen might bring closure to a situation, but it really doesn't change anything that has already happened, does it? So, why should it matter to us WHY things happen? What difference would it make? We can't change the past and we have no control over the future, so we shouldn't expend too much of our thoughts and efforts on the WHY of things."

Amanda stared at him for a long moment before shaking her head. "You know, Dougie, if I still smoked, I think I would have to light one up after that load of malarkey." She stood up and took a final gulp of tea. "But, what's even stranger is the fact that... well, it almost makes sense, what you said. So, with that being said, I'm going to leave you to enjoy all this. By the way, where are Bertie and Max? They must have taken off early this morning for somewhere."

Doug stood up and took her empty glass from her. "They did leave early. They both have, shall we say... out-of-town business on Sundays."

"Which is a nice way of saying that it's none of my business, huh? Okay, never mind, big fella. I'm off to visit Kris. I hate to leave you here all by yourself. Do you want to come with me?"

"No thanks, Amanda. You go ahead, but let Kris know that we are all thinking about her. I've actually got some things to do myself." Doug picked up the tray with the pitcher and glasses and turned toward the café's back door.

"Oh, don't tell me, let me guess," Amanda joked. "You've got some *out of town business* to attend to, right?"

Doug offered a shy grin and winked back at her. "Something like that, Princess. Something like that."

CHAPTER 13

Amanda Meets Officer Hall

Amanda inserted a Patsy Cline CD into her stereo and rolled down her car window. She was definitely her father's daughter because she never tired of listening to the artist's distinctively soulful, country sound. The only other singer who had even come close to the quality of Patsy's voice, in Amanda's opinion, was Leann Rimes. A listener could get lost in the lyrics of their songs and in the melodic symphonies of their voices.

It only took Amanda a few short minutes to reach the famous traffic circle in Monticello, a small northern Florida city established in 1827. One look at the pre-civil, war-styled architecture left no doubt in one's mind as to why the downtown area had been designated a National Historic District. The beautiful tree-lined streets, old antebellum homes, and the 1890 Opera House were a steady reminder of the area's proud southern heritage. The city had become infamous in 2003 when ABC-TV named it the "South's Most Haunted Small Town." The most haunted building in Monticello was thought to be the Palmer House. Some folks even said that Dr. Dabne Palmer, who was a physician as well as a mortician, could still be seen walking around his old office. John Perkins, the founder of the Monticello Opera House, had also been sighted, by credible witnesses, hanging around his famous theater. One of the town's quaint B&B's, the John Denham House Bed and Breakfast, was tagged to be one of the "Top Ten Places to Sleep with Ghosts" by USA Today. No, there was definitely no shortage of ghosts in Monticello and the town's history fascinated Amanda. As much as she had loved growing up in Tampa, she had always wanted to live in a small town, where everyone knew everyone else and nobody was in a hurry to get anywhere. It somehow made her feel less alone.

Amanda slowed the Trooper as she approached the town's Police Department which was located in the very center of Monticello, on Mulberry Street. There was not a single red light in the small town, whose population boasted less than three thousand, more than half of whom seemed to be regulars at the cafe. She recognized a police officer, standing outside the Police Department, as the one who had come to the café to write up the report of Kris' stolen car and purse. She slowed her car even more, honked twice, and waved her hand at the officer who was now looking in her direction. She pulled into a parking space along the curb, turned Patsy's wail on low volume, and leaned out the window. "Hey, there! Officer Hall, isn't it?"

The young police officer removed his sun glasses and walked over to the Trooper. "Yes, Ma'am," he replied, "Can I help you?" The woman's face looked familiar to him and it only took him a minute before he recognized Amanda. "Oh, hello, there. Miss Turner, right?"

Amanda grinned at him and nodded. "You remembered? But, it's Amanda, not Miss Turner."

Officer Dean Hall tipped his hat and flashed a lopsided grin. "I actually finished number one in my photo-memory class. It's good to see you again, and under better circumstances. How is your friend...Miss De...Kris?"

"Hmmm..." Amanda thought, *"He does have a good memory..."* She grinned at him. "She's trying to pick up the pieces, kicking herself for giving that scumbag of a boyfriend a second chance, getting ready to drastically change her life by becoming a single mom... you know... all the usual, every day sort of stuff we girls have to deal with... all in all, though, I'd have to say she's doing pretty good – a lot better than I would be in her situation, for sure."

Officer Hall smiled and nodded at the pretty blonde. "We've actually had a couple of tips on his whereabouts, but so far he's managed to stay one step ahead of us. The last tip we received was that he might somewhere in Georgia. We just have to be patient. His luck will run out sooner than later... it always does."

The officer's rugged good looks had not gone unnoticed by Amanda, but she had a feeling that Officer Hall held more than a professional interest in her friend, Kris. "Well, personally, I don't really care if you find him or not, just as long as he stays far, far away from Kris and the baby. By the way, I'm on my way over to her place now to watch Lifetime movies and pig out on pizza. If you're not busy later... or married... you should stop by and say hi. I bet she would really enjoy seeing you again."

"Well," Dean grinned at her easy directness. "I can't say that I'm a real big fan of Lifetime and, unfortunately, I'm working a double shift today. Do you think maybe I can get a rain check on that offer?"

Amanda laughed. "Well then, I guess that means you're not married either, huh?"

Dean shook his head. "Nope, not married."

"Well okay then...that rain check is definitely on the table. Maybe next Sunday we can order another pizza and watch baseball or racing or something more macho than Lifetime. Although, I gotta say, you don't know what you're missing; you can learn an awful lot from those Lifetime movies."

Dean's deep laugh was genuine and contagious. "Yes, Ma'am, that sounds like a good plan; maybe we can all get together next Sunday. I've got some rounds to make. Drive careful now, and… be sure and tell Miss Devone… Kris… I said hello."

"Oh, you bet I will," Amanda grinned. "I definitely will do that. Don't you work too hard now!"

Amanda's matchmaking thoughts were still swirling inside her head when she pulled into Kris' driveway five minutes later. Kris was outside watering her collection of household plants. She wore white cut-off jeans and a red, form-fitting camisole top that barely contained her womanly attributes. Amanda looked down at her own small chest, void of any cleavage, and shrugged. She waved to Kris as she got out of the Trooper.

Kris raised the hose in welcome, offering an unintentional dousing in Amanda's direction. "Oops! Sorry 'bout that!" she laughed.

Amanda squeezed water out of her ponytail and laughed back. It felt so good to hear laughter coming from Kris that she couldn't get upset about a little water. "Good thing you're pregnant or I'd be chasing you around the yard for some big-time payback! Just for that, I get to order *my* favorite pizza today."

Kris held her belly with her free hand. "We're so hungry we could eat the box right now. What do you mean *order* your favorite pizza? I thought the plan was for you to bring it with you! We could be eating now instead of waiting another forty-five minutes."

Amanda blew out her cheeks and shrugged. "That was the plan, wasn't it? Yep…that was the plan…but I sort of got a little side-tracked back there in town. I ran into that cute officer, you know the one who took your statement about Mr. Wonderful? Well, he's just so darn cute… he has a great smile by the way… that he made me forget all about the pizza. I know this is a small town, but the pizza joints do deliver, don't they? If not, I'll go back in a bit and pick one up. Do you think one is going to be enough or is this gonna be a two-pizza affair today?"

"Well, one's enough for me," Kris joked back. "So... you said you ran into Officer Hall?" She put the hose down and ran her hands through her thick red curls.

Amanda stared at her pregnant friend. It was hard to tell which was bigger... Kris' breasts or her belly. "Yes, I did," she nodded. "As a matter of fact, I even invited him over to watch Lifetime movies with us and eat pizza."

The shocked expression on Kris' face was priceless and made it hard for Amanda to keep a straight face. It wasn't easy to shock Kris Devone, but Amanda had to pat herself on the back because she had managed to do just that.

"Oh my, God! You didn't!" shrieked Kris. She looked down at her ragged shorts and bare feet. She ran her hands nervously through her hair again. "I'm a mess..."

"Calm down, Missy," Amanda giggled. "Besides, he can't come. He's working a double shift today, but... he did tell me that I should tell you hello and that, maybe, if the invitation is still open... that next Sunday he could come hang out with us. We've got to promise to watch baseball or something besides Lifetime, though..."

Amanda watched Kris' strained effort to bend over, without toppling over, and retrieve the hose. She shook her head in protest, knowing instantly what was coming, and laughed as she backed away slowly from Kris' weapon of choice. She threw her hands up in mock defense. "What! Hey, I thought you'd be happy!" She wiped away the first flooding of water from her face and laughed again. "Plus, you might be glad to know that he's S-I-N-G-L-E!"

The second dousing left Amanda totally drenched and doubled over with laughter. She hadn't laughed this hard since before her father's illness had been diagnosed. She had forgotten how good it felt, how cleansing it was to the soul. Laughter really was the best medicine.

Kris shut off the water and turned to enter the small, well-maintained duplex. "Make mine a double pepperoni with the thickest crust they have... and... double cheese!"

Amanda got back into her car and yelled after the woman who was quickly becoming a best friend, a sister she never had. "Some people have absolutely no sense of humor!"

CHAPTER 14

Andrew and Amos Brown

August was usually a slow month at the Heavenly Grille Café, with parents getting ready for back-to-school requirements, and the fact that it was just too darn hot to do much of anything that required extensive movement. It was typical weather for summer in the south, for sure; it was no wonder that the infamous snowbirds made their way back to their respective northern quarters during the South's torrid summer season. The weather was undeniably hot and what little air that did manage to circulate, without air conditioning, was humid, muggy, and just down right miserable. The summer of 2011 was proving to be one of the wettest since the mid-1940s; however, the rain did little to cool things off, and the attitudes and temperament of the customers routinely fell in line with the day's forecast.

Northern Florida towns, especially small towns like Monticello, do not routinely depend on tourism for their survival. Most of the customers visiting the café during Florida's hurricane season, running from June through November, consisted of locals and long-distance truckers who had passed information and directions to the café via word of mouth. However, even the locals opted to stay inside their own air-conditioned homes throughout the month of August, which often proved to be the hottest and most uncomfortable month of the year.

It was the last Monday in August, around two-thirty in the afternoon, and dark clouds once again offered a brief respite and cover from the summer's scorching sun. Thunder and lightning joined forces occasionally but, so far, no rain had fallen. Twin brothers Amos and Andrew Brown, two regular customers, sat on their regular stools at the counter eating generous servings of Max's buttermilk cake. Amos chased his dessert with hot, black coffee, while his brother preferred a cold glass of milk - real milk, not the watered-down, healthier, fat-free version. After all, if one was going to indulge in Max's buttermilk cake, saving a few calories on a glass of milk seemed a bit ridiculous.

Amos and Andrew were two of Bertie's favorite customers and she placed a hand on each of their shoulders as she came up behind them. "How are we doing here, fellas? Y'all managing to stay cool enough in this wretched heat?"

Amos was the older of the brothers, by two minutes, and he never let Andrew forget it. His almost toothless grin widened as he closed his eyes. "Lawd, Miss Bertie, you know fo' sure that it's hotter than a goat's butt in a pepper patch outside, but this here cake..."

Bertie smiled when he opened his eyes and grinned with what she called his "summer" teeth - meaning some are here and some are there. "Looks like you're about ready for another cup of coffee, Amos. I can guarantee you that it's already been saucered and blowed, just the way you like it."

Amos nodded and sighed. "Why, I thanks you...that would be mighty nice of you, Miss Bertie. And you be sure to tell Mr. Max that his cake is even gooder'n his grits, if that's even possible."

Bertie patted the old man on the back again and looked over at his twin. "You're kinda quiet today, Andrew. Are you feeling okay?"

Andrew swallowed a bite of cake and licked his generous lips. "Well, to tell ya the truth, Miss Bertie, I was feelin' a bit poorly when I first came in here... like I'd been chewed up and spit out, if you know what I mean. But this here cake is enough to make a cow want to suck on its own utters... pardon the expression, Ma'am..."

Bertie smiled and hugged them both between her widespread arms. "I know exactly what you mean, Andrew, but as long as you feel better when you leave than you did when you came through that door, well, then... life is good, ain't it?"

Andrew covered his mouth trying to suppress the congested cough that inflamed his cancer-ridden lungs. Bertie knew he didn't have much time left and she knew that Andrew knew it, too. "I'll bring you another glass of milk, Andrew. I'd never say it to Max, but sometimes that cake can be a little on the dry side."

Andrew shook his head. "Oh, no, Ma'am... I loves this cake. It's the best cake I've ever tasted in my life. Sure wish Mr. Max would share his recipe."

Bertie turned and grinned at the old black man, who she suspected would be meeting their Heavenly Father before the year was out. "Now you know that will never happen, Andrew. Y'all sit tight. I'll be right back with your drinks and some more of that cake. It's hard to eat just one slice!"

Mondays were Amanda's regular day off, but she and Kris shared a booth... the same booth they shared the first time Amanda brought Kris to the café. They had watched and listened to Bertie's interaction with the two old men while they downed their own generous portions of buttermilk cake.

Kris shivered. "I'm sorry, but I don't know how she can stand to touch them. They just look so... dirty."

Amanda was getting use to Kris' occasional bouts of rudeness and lack of compassion, but they still managed to shock her at times. She had to remind herself that the two of them had experienced very different upbringings and, as a result, had totally opposite outlooks on life in general. Amanda always saw the glass as being half full, so it was no surprise to her that Kris usually took the opposite view. She had seen a softening of Kris' demeanor over the past few weeks, but sometimes, like today, she would make comments that reminded Amanda of their vast differences in personality. Amanda had grown to love Amos and Andrew and it hurt her that Kris would be so obviously repulsed by them.

"They're not dirty, Kris... they're just poor."

"Poor? Hell, I'm poor, but I still manage to brush my teeth every day. Have you seen their teeth?" Kris grimaced. "Gross!"

Amanda shook her head and smiled at her new best friend. "Well, the way I look at it, they don't really need a lot of teeth now, do they, to enjoy this delicious buttermilk cake." She filled her own mouth with a large chunk, partially to keep herself from saying something that might hurt her friend's feelings.

"Yeah, yeah... whatever..." Kris mumbled.

Amanda watched as Kris fidgeted in her seat. "Are you okay?"

Kris exhaled and grimaced. "I don't know. It's my damn back. I can't seem to get comfortable the past few days. It hurts to stand, hurts to sit. Not pain really... just... hell, I don't know." She exhaled again, closed her eyes, and rubbed her temples. After a few moments, she opened her eyes and smiled at her friend's concerned expression. "It's probably just indigestion. I get it just breathing in air these days. It feels a little better now." She swallowed another bite of cake. "This really is the best cake I've ever tasted. So... have you given any thought to what we talked about over the weekend?"

Amanda smiled. "You mean Dean's suggestion that I move in with you?"

Kris stirred the ice in her Pepsi and took a long sip. "Yeah... I mean... the more I think about it, the more sense it actually makes. I wasn't really looking for a roommate, but you did say that you were just living here temporarily, until you could afford your own place. And Dean doesn't think I need to be alone these next few weeks, you know, so close to the baby's birth and all. It would definitely help us both out if we could share expenses. It makes perfect sense if you think about it."

"You and Dean are getting pretty cozy, aren't you?" Amanda smiled again. She had wanted to discuss this situation with Doug again before she made up her mind, but she hadn't been able to get him alone long enough to do that.

Kris shrugged. "You're changing the subject. Besides... look at me, will you? I look, and feel, like a beached whale. What man in his right mind would even want to get cozy with me right now?"

"Well, beached whale or not, you know I'm right, Kris. It's only been a couple of weeks, but I can tell. That man, as my Daddy would say, is pretty smitten with you."

"Sure he is," Kris snickered as she rubbed her huge belly. "I'm sure he's just dying to jump on this band wagon." She planted her hands atop her belly and looked at Amanda. "He, or any man for that matter, would be crazy to want to get involved with me."

"So..." Amanda teased back. "Maybe the man is crazy!"

"Like I said... you're changing the subject, Amanda. So tell me. Have you, or have you not, thought about moving in with me? Or do you have to run it by Pretty Boy first?"

Amanda turned in her seat so that her back pressed against the window frame. She stretched her legs out across the bench and sighed. "If you're referring to Doug as being Pretty Boy, which he is, by the way, then... yes, I was hoping to talk to him about it."

"Do you two have something going on?" Kris asked.

Amanda almost choked on her drink. "Oh, God! No! Shoot, he's like... well, he's like the big brother I always wished I had, you know. He's so easy to talk to and when we do talk, it's always like the answers to all my problems just sort of materialize; everything sort of falls into place and makes better sense after talking to Doug."

"Uh-huh… so now he's not only pretty, he's a magician, too?"

"Well," Amanda nodded, "I don't know about him being a magician, but good things do seem to happen whenever he's around. You should see him whenever these big, burly truckers start to get out of hand. Just when you'd think they would mop the floor up with him, all he has to do is go to them, put his hand on their shoulder, and… POOF, they become, I don't know… nice guys! Bertie said the truckers were really a handful before Doug started working here."

The door chimes jingled as the café door opened and in walked the purported magician. The rain had finally made its way to the Heavenly Grille and Doug shook the water out of his thick, dark hair at the same time he wiped his feet on the huge welcome mat just inside the door. He nodded to Amanda and Kris who were sitting in the first booth to the right of the door, and he waved at the Brown brothers sitting at the counter. He took a quick inventory of the rest of the café and noticed that the only other customers were a couple sitting at the far end, their heads bent toward each other, apparently deep in conversation. Doug watched them for a moment and shivered involuntarily. Something felt *off* about the couple but he couldn't get a quick grasp on what it might be. He was glad when the uneasy feeling dissipated almost as quickly as it had appeared.

"Well," Kris yelled out in welcome, "Speak of the devil!"

Doug waved to Max and Bertie who stood in the kitchen, their own heads bent toward each other in conversation. They both turned to him at the same time and waved back. He was quick to notice that their expressions appeared serious, in contrast to their normal, happy demeanors. He also noticed the worried look they shared with him when they glanced back at the couple sharing the table at the far end of the café. Doug wondered if they had the same uneasy feeling he had when he first saw the couple. He tried to read their thoughts but got nothing. That same involuntary shiver coursed through him again, but once again, he managed to shake it off quickly. Doug smiled at Kris. "Devil? Not me, not by a long shot! How are you ladies doing?"

Kris scooted over and motioned for him to sit beside her since Amanda was still stretched out on the other bench seat. "Actually, we were just discussing you."

Doug's eyebrows raised in surprise. "I'm afraid to ask; good, bad, or otherwise?"

Amanda laughed and drew her knees up to her chest. "Oh, it was good! Always good, Doug."

Doug took the offered spot next to Kris and stole another quick glance at Max and Bertie. They were both still staring at the couple in the corner, who were now positioned at Doug's back. He didn't want to be too obvious by turning around and staring at them, too.

"Amanda has something she wants to ask you, don't you, Amanda?" Kris grinned.

There was that involuntary shiver again. It ran from the base of Doug's neck down to his toes in a millisecond. He somehow fought the urge to turn around and look at the couple; instead, he turned his attention to Amanda who was, uncharacteristically, quiet. "Is that right? Well... I'm listening, Princess..."

When Amanda either didn't, or couldn't, say anything, Kris was quick to jump in. She wasn't going to let Amanda put off the discussion any longer. "Doug, Amanda wants your opinion on something."

Doug nodded toward Amanda while watching Bertie out of the corner of his eye, as she approached their table with a hot, steaming cup of black coffee – Doug's favorite choice of drink. "What is it, Amanda?"

Amanda finally found her voice and shot a glancing glare toward Kris. "Well...I wanted to talk to you about something, to get your opinion about... well... I wanted to see what you thought about me moving in with Kris. I mean, it would help us both out, you know. We could split the cost of her duplex, which would save us both some money, and I could be there with Kris... you know, the closer it gets to her having the baby and all... what do you think about that idea, Doug?"

Bertie had reached the table and set the cup of steaming coffee in front of Doug. She looked at Doug, offered a sideways glance at the couple in the corner, and nodded her head indiscreetly.

Doug took a sip of coffee, fought off a third stream of the involuntary shudder, and said, "That's a great idea... I think you should do just that, Amanda." He looked up at Bertie, who nodded her head once, looked at the couple again, and walked back toward Max.

"You do, really?" Amanda seemed surprised at his quick response.

Doug looked deep into Amanda's questioning gaze. "Yes, Princess, I do. In fact, the sooner the better. I'll even help you." Doug thought that the last involuntary shudder surely had to be evident to everyone, especially the couple sitting at the rear of the café.

CHAPTER 15

-Heaven-
Max and Bertie Visit Home

*T*hey had spent the day in Heaven, but it was almost time for Max and Bertie to leave and return to their responsibilities on earth. They both always looked forward to their trips Home on Sundays because it gave them each the time they so desperately needed to recharge and regroup. There was no need to come up with a weekly strategy plan because they knew it wasn't their place to do that. Neither of them had the power to change things that had happened in the past or things that might occur in the future. Their duty was to guide and protect the humans in their care with their day-to-day contentions; however, under no circumstances, were they to interfere with God's destiny. Max and Bertie knew exactly where the line was drawn and they had no intentions of ever crossing that line.

"Oh, Max..." Bertie sighed. "Don't you ever feel like turning over the reins to someone else so that you can stay up here? It gets harder and harder every Sunday to leave here and to return to all the rush and fuss on earth. It's just so peaceful here." Bertie sighed again. "Tell me again why we do what we do."

Max had been sorting through data on Martin's large, white screen and looked up when he heard Bertie's exaggerated sigh. "Don't tell me you're growing tired of your assignment at the Heavenly Grille, Bertie? I don't even want to have to think about replacing YOU!"

Bertie stuck out her tongue and laughed. "Not by a long shot, big fella! Hell, you know as well as I do that you'll never find anyone who could replace me." She grinned and relaxed as she enjoyed the easy camaraderie they shared. "But, you know, Max…even though it doesn't feel like it, I have been doing this for fifty years; and, you've been at it twice as long as I have. Don't you ever worry that someone will eventually come along, and who has been living long enough, to recognize you and the café from times past? It amazes me that it hasn't happened yet?"

Martin suddenly materialized beside Max and nodded toward Bertie. "What makes you think it hasn't already happened? Don't tell me you haven't told her, Max?"

Max grabbed the skinny black man and embraced him in a bear hug. "There you are, my old friend! I was beginning to think we might not see you this week."

"Like that would happen…" Martin mused. "I seriously doubt if you could manage an entire week without my input."

Bertie glided up next to her two favorite black men and punched Martin's skinny shoulder. "Oh, no, you don't buster! You can't come shimmering in here like dew on grass, say something like that, and then not explain what you mean. Come on… spill the beans!"

Martin laughed as he welcomed Bertie's subsequent embrace, which was quickly followed by another thump on his shoulder. He looked over at Max and pursed his full lips together. "Well, my friend, do you want to tell her the story or should I? You know she won't give us another moment of peace until one of us…how did she so eloquently put it… spills the beans."

Max nodded and laughed in his deep baritone. "Well, since you're a much more accurate bean counter than I am, why don't you tell her, Martin?"

Bertie plopped her adequate behind on the counter beside the white screen, sitting Indian-style, rested her elbows upon her knees, and cupped her chin in the palms of her hands. "I'm waiting and *you both know that patience is not one of my virtues, so let's get on with it. Besides, I love a good story. Let's hear it, Martin."*

"Well..." Martin began, "It's true... it has already happened. In fact, you've actually met the persons in question, Bertie."

"Really?" Bertie was genuinely surprised. "I've been helping Max for fifty years now. I know I don't have the best memory in the world, but I don't recall ever running into the same person again, once we've moved on to a new location. I figured that's what you were up here doing with all these buttons and gadgets you play with all day long."

Martin cleared his throat and rubbed his hands together in glee. He grinned at Max. "Oh, do you have any idea how much I'm enjoying this? Knowing something that Miss Naughty Angel here doesn't know? Oh, my... that's not a very Christian way of thinking, now is it?"

"No, it's not! Forget all that crap," Bertie commanded. "Come, on, spill those beans, boy!"

Martin exhaled and pursed his lips in a sly grin. "Well, as I said, Bertie, you do know the persons in question. It is the Brown brothers. You know... Amos and Andrew."

"Get outta here," Bertie countered, ignoring his grin. "I'm not following you. I've never met them before we moved to the location we're at now, and, I'm pretty sure I would remember those two sweethearts." She placed her hand over her heart, showing genuine affection for the brothers.

"Let's clarify the story a bit," Max offered. "It was way before your time at the café, Bertie, and it was me who has seen them twice in their life time. You see... I think I first met them around 1941. They must have been what... about seven at the time, right, Martin?"

"It was actually on their seventh birthday, yes," Martin nodded. "Their father worked on a farm in Booneville, Mississippi. Their mother worked as a housekeeper for a moderately wealthy family, and the Browns were allowed to live in a small, two-bedroom shack located on the back forty of the property. The boys' seventh birthday was on a Saturday and their parents wanted to treat them to some cake and ice cream at a new restaurant that had just opened up in town."

Bertie was quick to catch on. "Wait! Don't tell me," she grinned, "Was it called the Heavenly Grill Café by any chance?"

Max guffawed. "Well, of course not. I do change things up every now and then, you know. As a matter of fact, it was called the Heavenly Halo Restaurant back then."

"Still with the floating halo, I suppose?" Bertie asked.

"I see no reason to mess with perfection," Max replied. "I've never understood why people insist on fixing things that aren't broken. When something works, there's no reason to go and change it. The halo has always been a staple of the restaurant, grille, café, and inn... whatever noun we attached to the name."

"Anyway," Martin continued as he fluttered his hands about him, "Back to the story... I love a good story, too... let's see...where was I?"

Bertie raised her eyebrows at Martin and said, "Cake and ice cream... seventh birthday?"

"Oh, yes!" Martin laughed. "Well... the entire Brown family came into the restaurant that day and proceeded to sit down at the only vacant table."

Max turned back to sorting data on the white screen. "We don't have much more time, Martin, so you might want to skip all the gory details and just give Bertie the basic information on what happened that day.

Bertie leaned over and punched Max on the shoulder as his fingers flitted across the screen, scrolling through pages and pages of data. "Oh, poo! Go ahead, Martin... don't listen to him, we have plenty of time."

"Well..." Martin continued, "As you may recall, 1941 was not the best time to grow up black, especially in Mississippi – actually, it still isn't if you ask me, but never mind that. Long story short, the white folks in the restaurant that day began to cause quite a ruckus when the Brown family sat down at that vacant table and opened up their menus. Max was in the kitchen because, even though he has always been in charge, well there have been certain times during the past one hundred years that he's had to act more like just a cook and not the owner. There was another Spirit Guide who helped Max back then, by the name of Charlie Byce. Charlie was a big man, too, like Max, but he was white. Anyway, when

Charlie heard all the fuss being made, he marched out there and told everyone in the restaurant that the Browns were more than welcome to sit at the vacant table and that if anyone didn't like it, well then, they could just leave or deal with him."

"And did they leave?" Bertie asked.

Martin wrinkled up his nose and shook his head. "Not the first one. They all settled down and whispered among themselves for a bit, but they didn't argue any more – not even when it came time for the Brown boys to blow out the candles on the buttermilk cake that Max had sent out to them. Oh how those boys loved that buttermilk cake, yes they did!"

"They still do, but..." Bertie queried, "Are you telling me the boys remembered Max from 1941? They were only seven years old!"

"Oh, no, not the boys," Martin grinned. "It was their Daddy!"

Bertie allowed her head to roll back as she laughed out loud. "You're kidding?"

Max looked away from the scrolling screen and folded his massive arms across his chest. He smiled and nodded. "You met their father, Bertie. It was about the second week after we opened the Heavenly Grille Café at its current location. Joshua Brown and his twin sons came in together for cake and coffee one evening. They said they could see the glow of the halo from their living room window and came to check it out."

Bertie nodded. "Yes... I do remember when I first met them. What a wonderful man Joshua was; but, he passed away just after that, didn't he?"

It was Max's turn to nod. "Yes, he did. But, if you remember, that first night they came in, after they'd eaten their cake, Joshua asked you if he could meet the cook."

"That's right," Bertie nodded. "I remember that. He said he'd only tasted cake that good one other time in his life... oh my goodness, he remembered you from 1941?"

"That he did," Max grinned. "We only met briefly back in 1941. It was after he and his family had finished their cake and ice cream. He asked Charlie if he could meet and thank the cook."

"And..." Bertie confirmed, "Lo and behold, when he met you seventy years later, you still looked the same as you did in 1941!

Bet that was a shocker to the old fart, huh?"

"BERTIE!" Martin exclaimed, looking around him in all directions, praying that no one else had heard her outburst.

"Sorry, your highness... please, please forgive me," Bertie pleaded, albeit somewhat sheepishly. "But I bet neither of you saw that one coming, did you?"

"No, we certainly did not," Max grinned. "There have been a few close calls over the years, but..."

"So, did he ask if you were the same Max he had met back in 1941?" Bertie leaned forward.

"He didn't have to," Martin chimed in. "He knew it was the same person, but he also knew that it wasn't his place to question why things happened the way they did. He was just glad to have been given the opportunity to see Max one more time. He never confirmed his suspicions to anyone... that we know of..."

Bertie laughed out loud, doubling over, and would have tumbled off the counter had Max not broken her fall. "Oh, oh...you don't have to say it. Oh, this is too good! You don't know if Joshua ever told his boys about Max, do you? Well, hey, there's one way to be sure. He's gotta be up here somewhere, right? Why don't you just summon the old f..."

"BERTIE!" Martin sighed, throwing up his hands in defeat.

"Martin, you should be used to her shenanigans by now, my old friend," Max smiled as he used one finger to assist Bertie off the counter.

She floated slowly to the ground. "Oh, calm down, Martin, or you'll be the first angel in Heaven to die twice from a heart attack! Where is old Joshua, by the way?"

Martin threw back his shoulders and assumed his "in control" stance. "Just as Amanda's father is still in the transitioning phase, so is our dear friend, Joshua."

"I see," Bertie pursed her lips. "Well, I suppose I could just come out and ask Amos and Andrew whether or not their Daddy ever told them they had been served by angels on at least two occasions."

Max scratched his head and smiled at Bertie. "That would definitely make some interesting dinner conversation, I dare say. Actually, though, I have to admit, I have been curious to know what Joshua may have told his sons, if anything."

"Well, Hell then, we'll just have to find out, won't we?" Bertie winked and smiled simultaneously, as she grabbed Max's hand.

"BERTIE!!!" Martin yelled after the vanishing spirits. "Oh, that woman is going to be the second death of me yet…"

"A man's heart plans his way, but the Lord directs his steps."

-Proverbs 16:9 (NKJV)

CHAPTER 16

Here Comes the Baby

It was Monday, September fifth, exactly one week before Kris' due date. Once the decision had been made for Amanda to move in with Kris, things had moved quickly. Doug and Dean had worked together to make sure that all of Amanda's belongings had been moved into the spare bedroom. Dean had left to make a pizza run, and Doug had remained behind to help Amanda get settled in her new home. He didn't want to admit how much he would miss having her live next door to him, but he knew that the move to Kris' was the best decision.

"I'm going to hang some of those pictures for you, Amanda," Doug offered. "Why don't you and Kris take a break?" He smiled at them both as he headed in the direction of the small bedroom that would become Amanda's new room.

"You talked me in to it!" Amanda grinned as she watched him leave the living room. She quickly flopped down on the love seat and smiled as she watched Kris trying to get comfortable in the old, well-worn leather recliner.

They both sipped on iced tea, trying to cool themselves after a long day of unloading and unpacking boxes. They were enjoying the comfortable silence, which didn't last long. A loud thump, coming from the direction of Amanda's new bedroom, startled them both.

Amanda thought she heard Doug muttering to himself. She jumped up from the love seat and ran into her room. "Are you okay?" she shouted as she collided full force into Doug's massive chest. It felt like she had hit a brick wall. "OUCH!" she moaned, rubbing her shoulder.

Doug reached out to steady her. "Are you okay? I'm sorry… I guess I'm better at using a frying pan than I am at using a hammer. I keep hitting the wall instead of the nail. I think I hit my thumb a time or two. You might want to check those pictures before I leave. I can't guarantee how straight they might be or if I got them exactly where you wanted them. I have to admit, though; it's looking pretty good in here."

"Yeah, I'm okay." She checked his offered thumb which looked perfectly normal to her. She smiled up at him before kissing the allegedly sore thumb. "Doug, you're the best, you know that? You have no idea how much I appreciate your help in getting me moved in here. I mean, it's Labor Day, and the café is closed. You should be relaxing, enjoying a day off. I'm sure you could have found something a lot more fun to do than this." She spun around looking at her new domicile. "But…I love it! Everything looks great. It's good to finally be able to have my things around me again. I didn't realize how much I missed looking at some of these pictures."

Most of the pictures that Doug had hung on the wall were of Amanda and her parents, at various stages of her life.

"It's one good looking family, for sure," Doug said. "I know how much you must miss your Dad. Your mother was very pretty. You…uh…you look a lot like her, you know?"

"Do you really think so?" Amanda smiled. "That's what my Dad always told me, but I figured he was just saying that. Sometimes I see the resemblance, but…well…I just wish I could have known her better. I can't remember if I ever told you or not, but I was only seven when she died. I mean, I can still remember what she looked like, but I think it's because of all the pictures we always kept around the house."

"How did she die?" Doug asked. "If you don't mind me asking…"

Amanda shrugged. "No, I don't mind. Oh, it was a freak car accident. Daddy always said it should have been him instead of Mama. He had just gotten home from work and was supposed to stop by Walmart to pick up some fever medicine for me. I had the flu or something. Anyway, he forgot to stop and get the medicine. He told Mom he would go get it but she told him to relax and spend some time with me, said she needed to get a couple of other things, anyway. She asked him to keep an eye on dinner…. her specialty was Hamburger Helper and canned biscuits. Daddy said she kissed me on the forehead and him on the lips, and said she would be back in a jiffy."

Doug sat down on the twin bed that occupied half the room and patted the space beside him. "What happened next?"

Amanda sat next to him and glanced at the pictures on the wall, smiling after each one. "Well, she made it to Walmart, got the items she needed and chatted with the cashier who was also our next-door neighbor. Mom left the parking lot and, from an eye witness's account, was second in line at the red light. Doug, she was only five minutes from home." Amanda sighed and continued with her story. "The light turned green, the car in front of her turned right and she followed behind him. We don't think she ever saw the car coming. Some young kid was coming fast from the other direction, looking down adjusting the knobs on his radio instead of focusing on the road, ran the light just as my Mom pulled out. . ."

"I'm so sorry," Doug said as he put his arm around her and pulled her to him. He rested his chin on the top of her head. "That must have devastated your father."

Amanda looked up at him and smiled. "I don't think he ever got over it... he never quit blaming himself for what happened. But, you know...I think when something like that happens, it either rips a family apart forever, or...it brings them even closer than they ever thought they could be."

"I'm glad it turned out to be the latter for you and your father, Amanda."

"Whew!" Amanda sighed. "It always wears me out emotionally when I tell that story. You know, it's been a really long day. It's getting late and I am so tired. I'm sure you are, too, but I am also starving to death. You are staying until Dean gets back with the pizza and hot wings, aren't you?"

Doug stood up and pulled Amanda to her feet. "I would love to, but I have a few things I need to get done at the café while it's closed today. I promised Max I would check out a clog in the kitchen sink. Just between you and me, I think he's been pouring that fat back grease down the drain again."

Amanda laughed. "I'm surprised he would waste any of it by throwing it out. I thought he seasoned everything with that stuff. Did you ever try any of it when he fries it up, though? My, God! The stuff is amazing! I had never really heard of it before working at the café, but Max really does use it to season just about everything! Maybe that's the secret to his good food."

He fries fat?" Doug asked. "I must have missed that lesson."

"Fat back!" Amanda corrected. "It's actually the fat and skin off a pig's back. He buys it in blocks and slices it up. It's been salted down so even after you rinse it good, it still has a very salty taste to it."

Doug's complexion paled noticeably. "And you've eaten that? Pig's fat?"

Amanda's eyes rolled back in her head. "Oh, God, yes! It's so good, Doug! Max said the best way to eat it is to throw a couple of pieces between a slice of white bread. The bread cuts down on the salty taste, and soaks up the grease, but you're still mighty thirsty afterwards."

"I see…well, pizza and hot wings are sounding better and better," Doug groaned. "Maybe I can stay for just a little while…"

"That's great…" Amanda stopped mid-sentence when she heard another loud thumping sound that startled them both. It sounded like it came from the direction of the living room.

They both raced out of Amanda's room when they heard Kris' panicked voice.

"OH, GOD…AMANDA!" Kris screamed.

Doug reached the living room first and stopped dead in his track when he saw Kris slumped back in the recliner, both hands holding her massive belly. He took at the glass of iced tea that had tumbled onto the tiled floor, but had not broken. He noticed the liquid trail that flowed down the front of the recliner; his first thought being that it must be the spilled tea.

"Amanda!" Kris cried out again. "Oh, Jeez…I've pissed all over myself…"

Doug reached her and knelt in front of her just as a quick knock came at the front door.

Amanda ran to open the door and practically dragged Dean inside.

"Dean!" Kris screamed, reaching out to him from the chair.

Doug was already attempting to pull Kris to her feet but feeling ill-equipped to offer any real help.

Dean stopped in his own tracks when he saw the panicked look on Kris' face. He threw the pizza and hot wings to the floor in his wild dash to the recliner.

Amanda appeared momentarily torn between helping Kris and salvaging dinner.

Doug looked at Dean and shrugged his shoulders. "I don't know what's wrong. She just screamed and we came running."

"Oh, damn, this is embarrassing…" Kris groaned, looking down at her wet shorts. "I didn't even really have to pee. I was just sitting here and the next thing I knew…"

The realization of what was happening suddenly dawned on all four of them simultaneously and seemingly in slow motion.

Kris looked terrified as she was the last one in the room to realize what was happening.

"Your water broke!" her three friends exclaimed in unison.

CHAPTER 17

Max and Bertie Discuss Amanda and Kris

The café was closed that Monday for the Labor Day holiday, so Max and Bertie decided to use the extra time to catch up on some general cleaning as well as preparing vegetables and desserts for the next day. They had both enjoyed their day off, the day before, spending it as they did every Sunday, in Heaven.

"Hey, I thought Doug was going to be here to fix that clog," Bertie commented as she used the old straw broom to sweep a lone cobweb from a corner. "You do know it's clogged 'cause you're throwing too much of that fat back grease down the drain, right?"

Max was whistling, out of tune as usual, and grinned back at her. "That fat back grease is what makes my cooking the talk of the county, I'll have you know." He began whistling "Amazing Grace" and stopped in mid-whistle. "But, you know…you're right. Doug was supposed to meet us here and fix that drain. He's pretty handy with things like that.

Anyway, I'm sure he'll be along shortly. Wasn't he helping Amanda move this weekend?"

Bertie slapped her open palm against her forehead. "I'd forgotten about that." She continued sweeping the floor for a few minutes before speaking again. "You know, Max, we haven't talked about it, but I can't get it off my mind. You know what I'm talking about..."

Max swept some chopped carrots into a plastic bag and tied it securely before placing it in the huge, commercial under-the-counter refrigerator. He looked over at Bertie and sighed. "Yes, Bertie, I do know what you're talking about." He shook his head. "I even searched the data base when we went Home yesterday, but..."

Bertie nodded. "I know... that fancy data base only contains information on dead folks; and, that couple that was in here a few days ago, well, they certainly weren't dead. You know as well as I do, Max... well, something just felt off about those two. I can't seem to wrap my head around what it is, though. I couldn't tell if they were good folks or bad folks, but something about them just made my skin crawl. One thing I am sure about, though... the woman is sick. She may not know it yet, but she's really sick."

"Yes, she is," Max agreed. "The husband seemed to be very protective of her, too, which is perfectly understandable." He stood at his full height, which was an impressive seventy-six inches and rolled his shoulders. "Still, something about them... I don't know... I just had the feeling that we needed to protect Amanda from them."

Bertie resumed her sweeping. "I thought it was Amanda, too, at first... that's why I encouraged Doug to convince her to agree to move in with Kris; but... now... I'm not so sure. The connection could have been between them and Kris, rather than Amanda."

"Well, one thing we do know for certain is that the couple isn't related to either of the girls. Neither of them has a single living relative. Even though something felt off about the couple, I did not pick up on any threatening thoughts from either of them, did you?"

Bertie looked at him and shook her head. "That's what was so strange. Usually I can get a quick reading off any human being, you know, as to their nature, whether they're good guys or bad guys... but... it felt blocked this time. I just got that uneasy feeling, knowing in my gut that something just wasn't right about the two of them, even though they seemed perfectly harmless. How much time do you think the woman has?"

Max picked up a few stalks of cleaned celery and began chopping them into large chunks for the vegetable soup on Tuesday's lunch menu. "We're not always privy to that information, you know that, Bertie. Sometimes, like with Andrew Brown, we know, but I think that's just because Andrew is special in our lives."

"What makes him any more special than that stranger?" Bertie asked. "I mean, we're angels! Shouldn't we be able to know something like that about all of them if we can determine it about someone like Andrew?"

"I don't know," Max shrugged. "I don't have all the answers, Bertie. Sometimes I think we both forget that we're not real angels. We're just God's messengers."

"Yeah, yeah, I know all that," Bertie sighed in exasperation. "I just think the man upstairs should let us know if there's something dangerous about that couple, something we need to be on the look-out for."

"Oh, you do, do you?" Max grinned.

Bertie walked over to the counter and punched Max hard on the shoulder. "Don't you go making fun of me, Maximus. You know what I mean. Hell, I know He doesn't have to tell us a damn thing if he doesn't want to. It's His overall plan, right? What will be, will be, and all that philosophical crap."

Max rubbed his shoulder, still surprised that so much strength came from such a little woman. "Yes, Bertie, He does have an overall plan, one written for each and every one of us before we're even born; however, and this is important to remember... He also gave free will to all men. People tend to forget that during difficult times. It isn't God who makes bad things happen to people; it's a combination of Satan's influence and the free will given to mankind... a deadly combination at times."

Bertie leaned her broom against the wall and placed both hands on her broad hips. "Well, whatever His plan is, I'm hoping and praying it doesn't involve our Amanda. I've grown pretty fond of that young woman."

"We all have," Max agreed. "But I really do think it's a good thing that she moved in with Kris. I have a feeling that Kris is in dire need of a true friend. She's been disappointed by so many people in her life. I'm thinking that God may even be using Amanda to convert Kris to Christianity. What do you think?"

Bertie retrieved her broom and moved toward the dining area. "That's going to be a hard sale, I'm afraid. You do know that Kris doesn't believe in God, the church, the Bible, none of that stuff?"

"That's because she was never exposed to it while growing up," Max said. "Her mother was a bad seed, indeed, and there was never anyone else to pull Kris toward those beliefs. I do know that she actually blames God for everything bad that has happened in her life, but, she doesn't know any better."

"That's so sad. Maybe Amanda will be a good influence on her because one thing is for sure. Our Amanda is one of the finest Christians I've ever had the pleasure of meeting, before and after I died!"

Max grinned. "Yes, she is a good soul, indeed she is. She not only believes... she has the faith that will be needed to get her through life, no matter what happens. I wish more young people had her faith."

"Yep," Bertie nodded. "She's not the type to blame God for any of her failures or disappointments in life. She seems so sure about her faith, in spite of everything that's happened in her young life. Hey! Did you get to meet her parents while we were there yesterday?"

"Yes, I did," Max nodded. "They should both be credited for being instrumental in building Amanda's strength and faith. They are very good people...so much love between them."

"Well," Bertie sighed. "Let's just hope Amanda can help turn Kris around before it's too late; and, if that couple comes in again, I'll try to get a better reading on them. That yucky feeling might have just been a false alarm."

"Maybe..." Max agreed, "We'll see. Just remember, it is NOT our place to interfere in any of their lives. That's something we may need to remind Doug of, too."

The front door suddenly slammed open and Doug stumbled inside. Bertie and Max were caught off guard at the normally confident and secure young man who now appeared disheveled and frightened.

"Bertie! Max! You have to come quick! Kris is having the baby!"

Bertie threw down her broom and ripped off her apron.

Max dropped his knife and was beside them both in the blink of an eye. "Well, praise the Lord!" he beamed. "Let's go, boy!"

Although the three of them could have easily and quickly metamorphosed their way to the John D. Archbold Memorial Hospital, they decided to travel the way most humans did, via automobile. All three quickly jumped into the café's van that Doug had borrowed to help move Amanda's boxes. The three angels were so delirious with joy and anticipation that none of them noticed the dark sedan parked amongst the trees across the street from the café.

The couple who had been the subject of Max and Bertie's earlier conversation watched the café employees scurry into the van. They waited a few moments before they pulled the sedan onto the roadway and followed at a safe distance until the van pulled into the hospital's parking lot.

The angels never felt the couple's presence.

CHAPTER 18

Waiting for Baby to Arrive

The trio of angelic messengers rushed into the waiting room and found Officer Dean Hall, out of uniform, pacing back and forth in front of two older men who were sitting in the uncomfortable folding chairs provided. Bertie looked over at the men, who smiled back at her and nodded toward Dean.

"First-time father, eh?" one of the men asked, nodding in Dean's direction.

Bertie knew that Dean had been spending some Sunday afternoons with Amanda and Kris, but she was still surprised to see him there. "Goodness, no!" she exclaimed while quickly scanning the area for Amanda. "He's not the daddy."

The other man took one look at Doug, who was still flushed and sweating from his quick run from the hospital to the café and back to the hospital. "Must be that one, then. He looks more nervous than a whore in church if you ask me."

Bertie resisted the urge to ask the man if he knew many whores who frequented his church; instead, she nodded toward the towering black man by her side. "Don't recall asking you, but…no, this is her Daddy, so you may want to take your assumptions down the hall and use them to wipe your…"

"BERTIE!" Max turned toward her sharply. "Please try to behave…"

The two men looked at each other and then looked back at the giant black man standing beside the little spitfire of a woman. "Lord help you, sir. Sure looks like you've got your hands full today."

Max shook his head and guided Bertie forward by the elbow. "You have no idea…I've got my hands full every day, trust me."

The mood inside the treatment room was a lot calmer than it was in the waiting room. Kris sat atop a table, with her legs dangling over the side. She pressed both hands hard upon the table as another contraction took its' turn.

Amanda stood beside her, rubbing her back. "The nurse said you should lie down."

Kris made a slight grimacing sound before exhaling. "That one wasn't so bad. I don't want to lie down, Amanda. I feel like I need to get up and walk around. Help me?"

"But the nurse…"

"I don't give a rat's ass about the nurse!" Kris hissed as she scooted to the edge of the table. "Are you going to help me or not?"

"Okay, okay!" Amanda said, "Just be careful, please."

Once she achieved a full-standing position, Kris exhaled deeply and actually smiled. "Whew, that feels better on my back, anyway. God, where are they with that that epidural? So far, it hasn't been all that bad, just some cramping, but I don't want to feel anything worse than that if I don't have to. Bring on the drugs!"

"I think you're doing just great, Kris. Much better than I would be, I'm sure."

Kris began walking slowly, in a large circle, around the room. She stopped for a moment and looked over at Amanda, who walked by her side every step. "Did I ever tell you that I considered giving the baby up for adoption?"

"No..." Amanda whispered, "I never knew you were even thinking along those lines."

Kris nodded. "Well, I was, especially the first few weeks after Danny left me stranded at Sam's. The same day I met you. All I could think about was the fact that I was alone, without much money, no real education, and no family to help out. I just thought the best thing for the baby would be to let someone else raise it, to give it everything I couldn't."

"What changed your mind?" Amanda asked.

Kris stopped as another contraction began forming, inhaled deeply and exhaled slowly. She felt another sharp pain in her lower back. She allowed it to pass before moving back toward the table. "Well, actually... it was meeting you that changed my mind about things."

Amanda helped her friend back up on the table. "Me? How did I change your mind? We never even talked about your options after giving birth. I just always assumed that you would raise the baby on your own. You're one of the strongest women I've ever met, so I've never had any doubts that you could do it."

"Well, you had more confidence in me than I did myself, and, don't let it go to your head, or anything, but..." Kris lay back on the table, drawing both knees up until her feet pressed flat on the table. "I...well...the truth is, I didn't feel so alone after I met you. You became more than a friend. You became the sister I always wished I had. And then there's Doug, Bertie and Max. It just felt like all of a sudden I had my own little support group, you know?"

Amanda offered a sheepish grin. "And don't forget about Officer Hall."

Kris closed her eyes and held her open palms against them. "Oh, God...how could I forget him? He saw me piss all over myself. He's seen me fat and grumpy; he's seen me abandoned; he's seen me eat an entire meat-lover's pizza by *myself!*"

Amanda smiled and nodded. "And yet... he's still here,

isn't he?"

"Is he?" Kris asked, "Really?"

"Oh you couldn't move him with an electric cow prod!" Amanda laughed. "He's pacing the floors out there like a true expectant father. Doug went back to the café to tell Bertie and Max. Sit still and I'll go out and see if they're here yet."

Kris grabbed Amanda's arm as she started to leave. "Amanda... I, uh... it's not easy for me to say, but... I just want to say thanks. Thanks for being here with me. I don't think I could do this by myself."

Amanda turned back and gave Kris a long hug. "I think... no, I'm sure... that we came into each other's lives for a reason, Kris. There is no place I'd rather be right now and I'm not going anywhere. After all, I'm about to be an aunt! I'll be back in a sec, okay?"

The nurse entered the room just as Amanda was leaving. "Who's ready for an epidural?" she asked.

Kris raised one hand while the other hand supported her lower back. "That would be me!"

"Well, young lady," the nurse replied, "You're doing just great. You're already at six centimeters and moving along nicely. I need you to lie back now. I need to prep you and give you an enema. Someone will be in to give you that shot real soon."

"An enema? Oh, that sounds like loads of fun," Kris groaned.

The nurse laughed and said, "Oh, you don't know the half of it, sweetie. The fun is just beginning!"

Kris' collage of friends rushed toward Amanda the moment she exited the treatment room.

"How's she doing?" Bertie asked, reaching her first and embracing her in her typical bear hug.

"Well," Amanda grinned, happy to see that everyone was there, "I certainly don't know anything about birthing babies, but from what the nurses are telling us, everything is going great, no complications. They said if she keeps going at the rate she's going, it won't be a long wait for any of us. Hey there, Max!"

It was Max's turn to embrace Amanda. As usual, she felt the strength flowing from his body into her own. She took a deep breath, feeling suddenly refreshed. "I'm so glad you all came."

"Well, it's a good thing it's a holiday and the café was closed," Max said, "Or else, we would have a room full of customers serving themselves right about now."

"Is she really doing okay, Amanda?" Dean asked, looking more like a nervous first-time father than anyone else in the room. "You're not just saying that?"

"Yep, she's really doing okay, Dean. It's going to mean a lot to her to know that all of you are out here."

"Well, we're not going anywhere till that precious baby gets here," Bertie said. "Now, Dean, why don't you and Doug make yourselves useful and go get us some coffee and something to snack on. I'd be willing to bet that none of you have eaten much today, have you?"

Dean shrugged, "Well, I think there might be some pizza and hot wings on the floor of Kris' living room."

Max wrinkled his nose. "I think some black coffee and a Danish would suit me just fine." He reached in his pocket for money. "I never have acquired a taste for pizza."

Dean held up his hand. "I've got this, sir. We'll be back as soon as we can." He looked back at Amanda. "You'll let her know that I'm still here, won't you?"

Amanda nodded. "You bet I will!"

Bertie and Max led Amanda to the overstuffed sofa and the three made themselves as comfortable as the sagging springs allowed.

Doug and Dean waved at those they left behind in the waiting room and made their way to the elevators.

"I think the cafeteria might still be open," Doug said.

"Well, if not, we'll just raid the vending machine, and hope they've got a Danish in there," Dean said. He turned his head from side to side, working out the kinks and tension. "Man, this is nerve-wracking, isn't it?"

"I'm sorry?" Doug queried.

"You know...the waiting, and not being able to do anything for her. I mean, they won't even let me go inside because we're not related, I'm not the baby's father..."

"Maybe you should have thought quicker on your feet, like Amanda did," Doug smiled. "The nurse actually thinks they're sisters."

Dean shrugged again. "I just wish I could be there with her, that's all." The tension seemed to suddenly dissipate from his neck and shoulders when Doug placed his hand on his back.

"She's going to be just fine, Dean; and, she knows you're here. I'm sure that means a lot to her right now. She needs all the friends she can get."

They had reached the cafeteria just in time; the kitchen was about to close. Dean ordered hamburgers and fries for everyone, as well as coffee and soft drinks. He even found a day-old Danish for Max. He paid for the order and gave Doug half of it to carry. They were almost out the door when Doug said, "Forgot the straws. Go hold the elevator and I'll catch up." He turned back to the condiments counter and grabbed some straws and napkins. Just as he turned to leave, a strange, tingling sensation crept up and down his spine. It was the same sensation he had experienced several days ago when he and Bertie exchanged glances at the couple in the café.

"Oh, no..." he whispered under his breath as he turned slowly and surveyed the small cafeteria. He had initially thought it was empty when he and Dean first entered, but he had been wrong. Tucked away in a corner booth, their faces turned quickly away from him when he looked sharply in their direction.

The same couple that had unnerved him several days ago at the Heavenly Grille was now sitting in a booth at the John D. Archbold Memorial Hospital's cafeteria. Why were they here? Doug wanted more than anything to approach them and ask them that question, but he could hear Dean calling out to him from the lobby.

The couple's gazes lifted and the three of them stared at one another for a long moment before Doug turned reluctantly to leave. His spine stiffened as he walked away and he turned to give the couple what he hoped was a final, warning look. He exhaled deeply as he approached Dean at the elevator.

"Thought you'd gotten lost," Dean teased as he stepped inside the elevator.

"No," Doug replied absently. "Thought I saw someone I knew."

As the elevator doors began to close, Doug leaned forward and saw the couple leaving the cafeteria. The woman looked back at him and offered a thin, waning smile. The man stood protectively behind her and stared blankly at Doug.

The tingling sensation, once again, crept throughout Doug's body as the elevator doors closed.

CHAPTER 19

A Warning Dream for Amanda

Amanda's alarm went off at its usual time, five-fifteen, on the day after Labor Day. Her shift at the café didn't start until seven but she wanted to get there early, have some breakfast, and catch Max up on the status of the new mom and her baby. However, she decided another ten minutes of sleep would be a great way to start the day, so she fumbled in the dark for the snooze button. She fell quickly back to sleep and immediately began to dream...

"Wake up, Princess..." Stephen whispered.

"We don't have much time..." Regina chimed in.

In the dream, Amanda opened her eyes and smiled broadly when she saw her parents' faces floating above her. "Well, hey there...so good to see you two again. Oh no, please don't tell me there's someone else who needs my help today?" she quipped. One look at the serious expressions on her parents' faces brought Amanda to an upright position in the dream.

Regina looked at Stephen and nodded for him to continue.

"Princess, we really don't have much time in these dreams, but

you do realize that we are real, don't you? That this is much more than just a dream, right?"

"I'm beginning to," Amanda answered back, "But what I really want to do is to be able to reach out and hug you both, to just talk about us, how much I miss you, how happy I am that you're together again...stuff like that."

"Hopefully, there will be plenty of time for that in the years to come," Regina smiled, "But your father is right; we don't have much time today."

"Okay, gotcha," Amanda tilted her head sideways and yawned.

"Princess," Stephen began, "It's very important that you keep your eyes open at all times over the next few months. Stay as close as possible to your new friend and her baby."

"That baby girl is just precious, by the way," Regina added.

Amanda grinned wide. "I know, isn't she? Kris hasn't picked out a name yet. They'll be coming home tomorrow, you know." She watched her father's serious expression while she talked with her mother about the baby. "Sorry, Daddy...go on with what you were saying. You said I need to stay close to them. Why? Is something going to happen?"

Stephen shook his head. "We don't know exactly what's going to happen, Amanda. We just know that if anything does, it is very important for you to be there."

"Well, that sure sounds vague and cryptic. No offense, Daddy, but that's not much help. How about giving me a who-what-when-or-where?"

Regina chuckled and glanced at her husband. "She sounds like you, Stephen." She smiled again and looked down at Amanda. "I'm afraid it doesn't work that way, Amanda. We're not sure about the who-what-when-or-where. All we can tell you is that you need to be on your guard, especially for the remainder of the year. I wish we could tell you more, but that's really all we know ourselves right now."

"Hmm... maybe I should quit waitressing and join the police force," Amanda quipped.

"You joke, Princess," Stephen smiled down at her, "But, actually, that might be a good career choice for you to consider."

"I WAS joking!" Amanda laughed back at them. "Me? A cop?

Really, Daddy?"

"Something to consider..." Stephen whispered.

Her parents seemed to look behind them at something, or someone, who Amanda could not see or hear. When they turned back to her, their images were already beginning to fade.

"No! Don't go yet!" Amanda yelled out.

Her own voice awakened her. She sat up in bed and rubbed her eyes. "Well, okay then. Stay close to Kris and the baby... that shouldn't be a problem since I'll be living in the same house with them." She jumped out of bed, showered and dressed, and was out the door by six o'clock.

Although the café normally did not open until seven in the morning, Max would frequently open the door early for any trucker who might be waiting in the parking lot. He knew most of them were on tight schedules to deliver their loads and he enjoyed the part he played in their lives by filling their bellies with good food and their hearts with good thoughts. Some of them may have entered the café in down or sour moods, but they always left with their emotional loads feeling much lighter than the truck loads they transported.

Yes, Max had a soft spot for the truckers. He always felt that their occupation was greatly under-rated and, even more, under-appreciated.

Three truckers sat at the counter on Tuesday morning after Labor Day.

Bertie was behind the counter filling their mugs and thermoses with strong, black coffee. Max was in the kitchen, whistling the chorus of "He's Got the Whole World in His Hands." The tune was contagious and it wasn't long before Bertie joined in singing the words, almost as out of key as Max was whistling them.

The three truckers looked at one another and shrugged. "What the Hell," one of them said. They all put down their forks and began singing along with each new verse...

"He's got the little bitty babies, in His hands..."

"He's got the wind and the rain, in His hands..."
"He's got everybody here, in His hands..."
"He's got the whole world in His hands!"

Amanda walked through the front door just as the trucker choir finished up the last verse and chorus. She clapped her hands loudly and whistled through two fingers.

The three truckers stood up and took exaggerated bows. One of them grinned before sitting back down. "Damn! That felt good!"

"Well it sounded pretty darn good, too," Amanda laughed. "Hey, Bertie! What are you doing here so early?"

Bertie walked over to Amanda and gave her a big, good morning hug – the kind of hug that only Bertie could give. "Well, to tell you the truth, Princess, I didn't expect to see you here this morning. You didn't leave the hospital until after midnight. I thought you might want to sleep in a bit before heading back to the hospital."

"Oh, that's sweet of you, Bertie," Amanda smiled, taking in the calm strength that flowed from Bertie's hug.

"Who's in the hospital?" one of the burly truckers asked.

Amanda paused for a moment before answering. "My…umm… sister had a baby girl last night!"

"That's great! Is the baby okay?" another trucker asked.

"Oh, yes!" Amanda beamed. "The baby is absolutely perfect. Seven pounds, two ounces, eighteen inches long, and a head full of red hair just like her mama."

"What about the Daddy?" the third trucker asked. "Is he in the picture?"

Bertie punched the third trucker on the shoulder as she moved behind the counter once again. "Well, now, ain't you the nosy one, Joe!" she teased back at him. "But to answer your question…no, that gem of a man actually abandoned the mother while she was pregnant…in a damn parking lot, no less!"

"Son-of-a-bitch," the first trucker whispered under his breath. He knew Max didn't appreciate cursing in the café.

"Well, then…" he looked at the other two truckers who were nodding their heads in silent agreement about something. "Bertie, you happen to have an extra mason jar somewhere?"

Bertie produced one from under the counter. "Just so happens, I do." She plopped it on the counter, already reading the truckers' intentions.

Each of the truckers reached into their wallets and tossed a ten-dollar bill into the jar. "That should get the baby fund started. You just leave that jar on the counter, Bertie, and we'll get the word out to the other truckers. Amanda, you'll see that your sister and her baby get the money, right?"

Amanda stared in awe, momentarily speechless at the trucker's generosity and what it would mean to Kris and the baby. "Oh, yes…" she said, unable to stop a tear from rolling down her cheek. "Thank you all, so much… you don't know how much this will mean to her." She gave each of them a hug as they threw more money on the counter to pay their tabs.

"You take care now, little girl," the largest of the three truckers said. "We've gotta roll now, but we'll stop back in on our turnaround and see how that jar is holding out."

"Drive safe, boys!" Bertie yelled after them as they left the café.

"Wow!" Amanda said. "Can you believe that? Those guys are just awesome. I can't believe it. What a nice thing to do."

Bertie was already making a sign for the jar. When she was finished, she placed it by the cash register. "Would be nice if we could put the baby's name on the jar…"

Amanda laughed as she hugged Bertie again and made her way to the kitchen for a quick bite of breakfast. "Kris has promised to decide on a name today. I'll be going to the hospital as soon as my shift is over."

"You go any time you want to, Princess. We've got things covered here," Bertie offered, following close behind her.

"Thanks, Bertie," Amanda sighed as she remembered her father's warning in the dream to stay close to Kris and the baby. "You know...maybe I will leave a little early today." She didn't see the worried look that passed between Max and Bertie.

"I think that's a really good idea," Bertie said as she and Amanda entered the kitchen.

"Something sure smells good," Amanda said as she went over and gave Max a quick hug. "Oh, look, Bertie! He made S-O-S this morning! This is Kris' favorite breakfast!"

Max nodded and smiled at the young woman who had captured a forever place in his huge heart. "That's exactly why I made it. Thought you might want to run up to the hospital this morning to...check on things...and take Kris some real food to eat."

Amanda wondered if it was her imagination, but Max sounded as cautious with his words this morning as her father had sounded in the dream. "You know, I think that's probably a good idea," she said pressing her lips together. "I should get up there and...check on things..."

Max and Bertie shared another look over Amanda's head.

"By the way," Amanda said, "Were the truckers the only customers this morning?"

"So far," Bertie nodded. "Why do you ask?"

Amanda poured a large cup of coffee into the Styrofoam cup. "Well, there was a dark sedan in the parking lot when I got here. There was a couple sitting inside it, but I didn't know if they were coming in or leaving. Hmm...must have been leaving since they're not here now."

Max and Bertie shared one final glance at each other before Max began preparing the take-out breakfast for Amanda and Kris.

"What do you say we get you on the road now, Amanda?" Max smiled. "I think you should just take the entire day off and spend it with Kris and the baby. It'll do all of you good to be together."

"But..." Amanda stuttered.

"No, Max is right," Bertie said. "I've got your shift covered and Doug will be in later to help out, too. I think it's important for Kris to know that she's got someone there for her."

Bertie walked to the front door and looked out onto the empty parking lot. She shivered involuntarily as a squeamish uneasiness quelled inside her.

"Well, if you're sure it's okay...I'd love to spend the day with them," Amanda laughed.

Max quickly loaded her arms with the take-out breakfasts.

"Okay, I'm loaded down with goodies," Amanda laughed again she made her way to the front door. "Are you sure about this, Bertie?"

"Oh, I'm more than sure, Princess. You go ahead now and feed our new mama. She's going to need her strength." Bertie gave Amanda a quick hug before shooing her out the door. "Drive safe now, you hear?"

Max walked to the front door and stood beside Bertie. They watched while Amanda waved and drove off.

"What the Hell is going on, Max?" Bertie whispered, laying her head against his massive forearm.

"I wish I knew, Bertie," Max sighed. "I wish I knew..."

CHAPTER 20

-December 15-
The Kidnapping

Charlotte Grace Devone had ruled the roost since the day she was born on Monday, September 5, 2011, at 11:58PM.

She had all the adults in her life twisted around her tiny, perfect fingers from the moment Kris and Amanda brought her home from the hospital. She was a very undemanding baby who captured the hearts of anyone who came in contact with her.

At the ripe, old age of three and a half months her favorite person at the moment seemed to be Doug. Her brilliant blue eyes twinkled in obvious delight every time he picked her up. The two of them had formed an immediate connection and bond. Charlotte was especially fond of Doug's thick dark hair and twisted it around her tiny fingers at their every encounter.

No one was more surprised than Doug at his bonding with the baby. He had absolutely no experience with babies, yet Charlotte felt so good and natural in his arms. He knew he would do anything and everything in his power to always keep her safe. For the first time since he arrived in Monticello, he dreaded the five-year limit of his assignment at the café. He wasn't sure if he would be able to leave Charlotte Grace behind when the time came. He wanted more than anything to watch her grow up, to watch her become the beautiful, self-confident person he felt she would become.

Kris and Amanda, with the help of their mutual employers, had been able to work out a schedule where one of them was always with Charlotte. Kris was home with the baby during the day and Amanda took care of Charlotte when Kris worked the night shift at the coffee shop. Their combined meager incomes would not have been enough to provide everything the baby needed; and, if it had not been for the truckers' baby fund, Kris would have needed to seek aid from the county. However, the trucker fund had continually supplied her with an extra one hundred dollars a week, more than enough to care for Charlotte Grace. She had thought the contributions would have dwindled by now, but they remained consistent, week to week.

In fact, the truckers' baby fund had actually begun increasing during the Thanksgiving holiday. Christmas was only ten days away and the truckers were now leaving presents for Charlotte Grace, in addition to extra money.

The last three months had passed quickly and everyone was settling into something of a routine with the baby being at the center of all their attention. Charlotte Grace was always within someone's sight and well protected.

Dean Hall had become a regular visitor, stopping by many times during the week to check on his "girls." Kris was more than cautious about getting involved with any man, especially now that she had her daughter to care for, but she soon found herself looking forward to Dean's visits, more than she cared to admit. She knew that having Charlotte Grace was the best thing that had ever happened to her. She hadn't done any drugs in over a year and she never thought about taking a drink, even though she was always worried that she could easily become the alcoholic her own mother had been. She never wanted Charlotte Grace to experience the childhood she herself had endured.

Max and Bertie had gradually begun to relax. Neither of them had seen a dark sedan nor the couple that had raised the hairs on their arms several months ago. They knew Doug had seen the couple at the hospital cafeteria, but after three months, they were beginning to think that the couple had moved on. Since they knew the woman was ill, Bertie believed it was even possible that the woman had died by now.

Regardless, life had mellowed out for everyone. Tensions were low, happiness was high, and Christmas was just around the corner.

Life was so good; at least, it was good until Thursday, December fifteenth.

Kris had gotten the night of December fifteenth off so that she and Amanda could do some final Christmas shopping. Bertie had offered to watch Charlotte Grace for them while they drove to Tallahassee to shop, but Kris wanted to take the baby with her. She was hoping to get Charlotte's first picture with Santa Claus at the mall.

Kris walked into the café with Charlotte strapped securely in her baby carrier. It was four o'clock and she was already thirty minutes late picking up Amanda. They had planned on driving Kris' new, used car since the back seat was already situated to accommodate the baby's car seat. Amanda was planning to purchase a separate car seat for her own car so that they wouldn't have to continually swap the car seat from car to car.

The only customers in the café at the moment were Amos and Andrew. They still looked dirty and unkempt to Kris but she didn't think twice or flinch when Amos came over and tickled the baby's chin. Andrew looked too weak to kneel down to the carrier, so Kris placed it on the counter before him so that he could see Charlotte. Andrew didn't touch the baby, but his eyes watered with tears when Charlotte cooed at him and offered him a smile. Kris couldn't help thinking that it wouldn't be long before Charlotte had more teeth than either Amos or Andrew combined!

Doug and Max were in the kitchen and Bertie was behind the counter.

"Hey there, you!" Amanda waved. "I'm almost finished, won't be but a sec, okay?"

Kris waved back. "No rush, we've got plenty of time, but we're going to hit all that off-work traffic if we don't get out of here soon."

Amanda untied her apron and tossed it to Bertie who caught it quickly in mid-air.

Bertie came from behind the counter and gave Charlotte Grace a sloppy kiss on the cheek.

Max and Doug waved from the kitchen.

"Why don't y'all stop back in here on your way back," Max called out. "I'm making garbage cake for dessert tonight. I know that's one of Kris' favorites!"

Kris waved back. "We may have to cut our shopping short then!" She laughed as she picked up the carrier. She and Amanda made their way out the front door.

Amos and Andrew waved to the two women and went back to their supper of chicken and dumplings. Amos ate his with gusto, while Andrew pushed his around in the bowl, hoping his brother wouldn't notice his loss of appetite and energy.

Nobody could anticipate the terror that was about to unfold.

Kris opened the back door of her car and sat the carrier on the ground while she moved some bags from the back seat to the floor board. She tossed the keys to Amanda and said, "Here, you drive, okay. I'm going to sit back here and give Charlotte a bottle so that she won't be so fussy when we get to the mall."

Amanda caught the keys in mid-air. "Okeydokey!" she laughed. "Oh, shucks! I forgot something."

"What?" Kris said lifting her head from the back seat.

Charlotte Grace was watching both women with what appeared to be patient enthusiasm. She lifted her arms toward Amanda.

Amanda bent down and kissed the baby's cheek. "I'll be right back, I promise, sweetie. The jar is full again, Kris, and I thought it might come in handy tonight."

"Oh, okay, but hurry back. I really don't want to hit all that traffic." Kris yelled back.

The next series of events all happened so quickly, while at the same time, seemingly in slow motion.

Doug met Amanda at the front door. He was holding the jar of money. "I thought you might need this."

Amanda grinned and gave him a hug. "Aww... thanks, Doug! You're an angel..."

Kris' piercing scream echoed from the parking lot, startling them both. The money jar crashed to the floor, splattering splinters of glass everywhere. They both turned at the same time and witnessed the horrific scene unfolding in the parking lot.

Kris had been pushed head-first onto the pavement. A small trickle of blood was flowing from her nose and a cut on her forehead.

A figure - presumably a man - dressed in black pants, a black hoodie, and a black ski mask paused momentarily, after having pushed Kris to the pavement, and quickly snatched up the baby's carrier. He lifted it with one hand and immediately took off running toward a dark sedan, parked across the street.

The sedan's engine was idling. There was a second person, similarly dressed, behind the wheel. The back door of the sedan was open.

The man quickly shoved the carrier onto the back seat, jumped in after it, and yelled, "GO!" to the driver.

The speed at which Doug moved would have impressed Superman himself. No one would have thought it humanly possible for him to have narrowed the distance between the café and the sedan so quickly. He was at the sedan's back door the moment the man yelled, "GO!" He grabbed the man's foot as the car began speeding away, the back door still open.

Doug stumbled but held onto the man's foot as he was dragged another one hundred feet before the man gave one hard, final shove into Doug's face. Doug rolled away from the car, and bounced against the pavement much harder than Kris had. He held the man's black running shoe in his hand. The last thing he heard as the car door slammed shut and the sedan's tires squealed their successful escape, was Charlotte Grace's soft coo and laugh – the same coo and laugh she gave every time she saw him.

He had come so close but, in the end, he had failed to protect the baby girl that had come to mean so much to him. Doug pushed himself up on his knees and looked toward Heaven. He dropped the man's shoe and covered his eyes. His strong, muscular body shook with raw emotion and quickly crumbled as reality slowly sank in.

Charlotte Grace was gone.

CHAPTER 21

-The Kidnappers-
Jack and Susan Peterson

The sky was still blue.

The birds still sang.

The breeze still swayed.

The evening meal still simmered on the stove.

Kris was still screaming and being restrained by Doug by the time every available law enforcement officer in the county arrived within the next thirty minutes.

Amanda was tucked between Max and Bertie, who were trying their best to console and reassure her.

Andrew and Amos were both on their knees, in prayer.

Officer Dean Hall was the first police officer to arrive. He had been on his way to the café for a quick cup of coffee when the call from dispatch came in over his radio. When he heard that a baby had been kidnapped from the parking lot of the Heavenly Grille Café, the contents in his stomach turned sour and he thought he would be physically sick. Somehow he knew in his heart that the baby involved was Charlotte Grace.

The first thing he saw when he swerved into the parking lot was Kris kneeling on the pavement beside her car. He saw that Doug kneeled behind her, holding onto her with a firm grip. He saw Max, Bertie, and Amanda standing just outside the café door. The only other vehicles in the parking lot were Amanda's Trooper, the café's van, and a vintage 1963 Dodge pick-up truck belonging to the Brown brothers.

Kris choked on a scream when the police car screeched to a stop. She shook herself from Doug's hold and took off running into Dean's open arms. She was crying and heaving so hard she couldn't catch her breath. She grabbed him around the waist before her legs defied her.

Dean held on to her as she crumbled back to a kneeling position. He kissed the top of her head and looked at Doug who was quickly approaching them, as was Amanda. Dean took Kris' face between his two hands and waited until she opened her eyes. Her tormented expression broke his heart. "Kris, come on. Let's go inside. You've got to tell me exactly what happened."

Three more police cars poured into the parking lot and began securing the area as Dean led Kris inside the café.

It was four thirty-five in the afternoon and Kris' nightmare was just beginning.

By four forty-five in the afternoon Jack and Susan Peterson had driven the dark sedan inside a deeply wooded area and switched vehicles. Jack had removed the license tag, any trace of the vehicle's identification number, all personal items, and had wiped the car clean of any fingerprints. The only thing he left behind was Charlotte Grace's baby carrier and a note inside it that read: WE WILL NOT HURT THE BABY. WE WILL LOVE AND TAKE CARE OF HER ALWAYS. WE ARE SO VERY SORRY, BUT SHE IS BETTER OFF WITH US.

Jack was sweating profusely as he maneuvered their switched vehicle south onto the interstate. Susan sat in the back seat with the baby. Charlotte Grace cooed and smiled, and held onto Susan's extended finger.

"Oh, my God... I can't believe we got away with it..." Susan whispered hoarsely. She turned her head away from the baby as a coughing spasm began deep in her chest. She reached in her jacket pocket for the inhaler she always kept close by.

Charlotte Grace must have thought the inhaler was a toy. She wiggled her little fingers toward it and cooed again.

"She's such a happy baby," Susan said as a stream of tears began flowing down her cheeks. "Oh, God...Jack...what have we done? Quick, turn around! We've got to take her back. We can't do this..."

Jack Peterson tried in vain to steady hands that were trembling so bad he had trouble holding onto the steering wheel. He took two deep breaths and said. "It's too late for that, Susan; you know that...we've taken this too far now. We have to stick with the plan. It will work. You'll see... and the mother? Well, she's young and healthy. She can have more children. No, my love, we have no choice. We have to stick to our plan. You know what you have to do now, so do it quick before we run into any road blocks."

Knowing that Charlotte Grace's red hair would have made her more distinguishable than most babies, Jack and Susan had come prepared with temporary hair coloring – black like their own – in a spray container. Susan searched through the duffel bag that sat on the back floor board and found the container. She put on a pair of latex gloves, shook the can, sprayed the contents onto her hands and began working it through the thin wisps of hair on Charlotte's tiny head. She was careful not to rub the spray onto the baby's scalp.

The sudden change in the baby's appearance was remarkable.

Jack pulled into a rest area and Susan changed the baby's wet diaper and removed her clothing. She gave them to Jack who put them into a plastic bag and dropped them into a nearby garbage container. Susan rummaged through the duffle bag again and took out a pink shirt with the name "KELLY" embroidered across the front, along with matching pink pants, socks, and shoes. She gathered Charlotte's thin locks of hair together and secured them with a pink and white hair clasp.

"Well, don't you look pretty... *Kelly*..." Susan whispered as she held the baby up for Jack's inspection.

The baby held up her arms to Jack.

Jack took the baby and held her close. He looked at his wife, whom he loved more than anything in the world, who was dying, and had only months to live. He closed his eyes, and thought, *"Dear, God, I am so, so sorry... please forgive us for what we have done."*

Before they left the rest stop, Jack threw one more item into the trash bin – a single, black running shoe.

Susan gave the baby a rattle to play with and she moved to the front seat alongside her husband of sixteen years. She placed her hand over his as he backed out of the parking space. "I know it's wrong and that we've done a terrible thing, but... it's going to be okay, Jack. You'll see..."

Jack sighed deeply and smiled at his wife. "It has to be, Susan. You're right. We have done a horrible, horrible thing today, one that God may never forgive us for, and...that's why it's even more important that we do everything in our power to make it up to this little girl."

It was Susan's turn to sigh. "Jack... you keep avoiding the issue and we haven't really talked about what will happen after... well, you know..."

"After you die?" Jack confirmed.

Susan swallowed hard and nodded.

"Well, I can't really just give her back then, can I?" he attempted to be light-hearted about the situation. "So, I'll do the only thing I can do. I will continue to raise... Kelly... as our daughter, and will provide her everything she needs in life. I will show her pictures of her mother and tell her every day how much her mother loved her... how much her mother hated to leave her..." His attempt at light-heartedness failed and a sob escaped from his throat.

Susan touched his cheek with one hand and wiped away

a tear from her own. "Thank you, Jack. Thank you for letting me do the one thing I've always wanted...to be a mother. I never thought I would get to hold my baby in my arms."

Jack looked over at his wife, her face so pale and her body growing frailer every day. "Why don't you try to get some rest, love? We still have several hours before we reach Tampa. We'll stay in a hotel tonight and meet the movers at the new house tomorrow. Then the Peterson family can begin their new lives. Go on now; close your eyes and rest."

He glanced in the rearview mirror at the tiny baby who was already resting peacefully in the comfortable pink car seat. "Kelly has beaten you to it. See? She's already dreaming sweet thoughts about her new mommy."

He looked over at his wife, whose purple-tinged eyelids had already closed. *"I'm going to Hell for this..."* he thought as he slowly merged with the flow of traffic headed south on I-75.

CHAPTER 22

-Heaven-
The Angels Pray for Charlotte Grace

B *ertie, Max, and Martin formed a circle among themselves and bent their heads in another silent prayer. So many prayers had been said since Charlotte Grace had been abducted three days ago; today would be the fourth day that Kris had mourned over the loss of her baby. Everyone who knew Charlotte Grace was tormented by the absence of the baby's laughter and the twinkling blue eyes that seemed to follow you from room to room.*

Prayers are a powerful form of support on earth, so one can only imagine the impact they have in Heaven; however, even angels cannot alter destiny's path. Only one person has the power to do that, and Bertie, Max, and Martin all knew that it was not their place to question the destiny that God had chosen for Charlotte Grace Devone. Their prayers, instead, centered upon the baby's safety and continued good health. They prayed for Kris, but they also prayed for the couple who had ripped Charlotte from her mother's loving arms.

The three Godly messengers lifted their heads at the same time and looked upward. Almost on cue, dozens of brilliant rainbows filled the space above them. They were made up of the most beautiful and indescribable shades of blue, yellow, green, and red. Bright rays of illuminating white and gold filtered through the rainbows. There was so much happiness, love, and joy in Heaven that it was impossible to feel sadness or disappointment; yet, the three angels all shared a deep void and heavy burden within their hearts and souls.

Bertie exhaled deeply and looked at the two black men before her. Skin color was totally irrelevant in Heaven, and she had never really paid any attention to the color of their skin, but she had to admit to herself that they were indeed two of the blackest men she had ever seen. She sighed again and said, "I think the young people would say that this whole situation really sucks!" A pout began forming on her pursed, quivering lips. She wiped a tear from her eye, almost daring it to reappear. "Hell, I didn't think angels were supposed to cry. Hell, I didn't think there was supposed to be any more pain or sadness once we died and made it here. What gives?"

Martin placed a hand gently upon her shoulder and started to speak. "Bertie, it's not our place to…"

Bertie shoved his hand away and punched his shoulder in return. "Don't say it, Martin! Don't you dare say it! I don't want to hear how this is not God's doing, that it's man's free will; that's just a bunch of sh…"

"B-E-R-T-I-E!"

Bertie jumped because she knew immediately that, this time, the deep, melodic voice had not come from either Max or Martin. It was not a threatening voice, but Bertie knew beyond a doubt that she was walking on thin ice in Heaven today. She threw caution to the wind, though, threw up her hands, and shouted as loudly as she could, "BUT, WHHYYYYY…" She didn't really expect an answer so she wasn't really surprised when she didn't receive one. She flashed a sheepish grin toward Max and Martin. "Guess that was pretty stupid of me, huh?" She wiped away another tear.

Max smiled and nodded. "A little…yes. You might want to try to temper and maintain better control of your emotions, especially here at Home." He kissed the top of her head and pulled her into a side embrace.

Martin joined in their circle. We can't question why this

happened. We just have to believe that it has happened for… whatever reason. We don't have to accept and understand the reason, but we do have to help those involved to get through it. No matter what happens… no matter how it ends."

Bertie nodded. "I know… I know… and, I'm sorry for my outburst." She looked upward and placed her hands together in prayer. "I truly am sorry, Lord. It's just that…well, I just feel so helpless. I mean, why can't we find out who these people are? What good are all our powers and Godly connections if we can't even find them?"

Max and Martin shared a look that Bertie, being more than a foot shorter than both men, missed.

"Bertie… we do know who they are," Max answered, at the same time, holding her at arms' length and looking deeply into her eyes.

Bertie searched his dark chocolate eyes and immediately knew the answer. "It's that couple, isn't it? The two that gave us the willies that day in the café? The ones who raised the hair on our arms? The ones Doug saw at the hospital? It's them, isn't it? She didn't give Max a chance to answer back. "I knew it…I could feel something evil about them."

Max shook his head. "They are not evil, Bertie."

"The Hell they're not!" Bertie shouted.

"B-E-R-T-I-E!"

Bertie raised both hands in surrender. "I really am sorry… again, Lord! Old habits die hard."

"In your case," Martin harrumphed, "They continue into eternity…"

Bertie ignored Martin's criticism of her old habits. "Okay, Max, I'm listening. You say they're not evil? Then, what? Are they poor lost sheep trying to find their way back to God, are they confused, misdirected? What? Please…share with me what excuse you have for these two people. I'd love to know."

Max smiled patiently. "Are you ready to listen, or do you want to get something else off your chest?"

Bertie closed her eyes and took another deep breath. "No. I really am sorry, fellas. I don't know what's come over me. I've never had this reaction before regarding any of our earthly assignments. It just all seems so… what's the word they use today… surreal - even for angels."

She opened her eyes and stared at Max's warm, comforting presence. "Okay, really…I'm ready to listen now. I know I need to settle down and come to grips with this situation, or I'm not going to be able to help Amanda and Kris get through whatever happens."

Every inhabitant of Heaven had their own individual mansion but there were no real "rooms" in any of the common areas - just lots and lots of wide open space. Max led Bertie to a small corner area to the right of the space they currently occupied. "I'm glad you recognize that fact. Come over here, Bertie, and watch this."

There was a large white, round table in the corner, with a glass top that resembled a television screen. The three angels encircled the table and Max waved his hand slowly across the top.

"Oh, my God!" Bertie gasped when an image of Charlotte Grace appeared on the glass top. Bertie recognized her immediately, in spite of the baby's darker hair. Bertie knew that it was Charlotte Grace being diapered and sang to by the woman Bertie had seen in the café – the woman who Bertie had been sure was dying.

"You see," Martin smiled. "The baby is fine. She is safe."

Bertie's eyes were glued to the screen. She continued to watch as the woman picked Charlotte up and danced around the room with her. Bertie's eyes filled with tears when she heard the baby laugh and coo with every twist and turn.

Bertie looked at Max, her expression full of questions, but she was powerless to speak. No words escaped her trembling lips.

Max nodded in understanding. "The couple is Jack and Susan Peterson. They have taken the baby to their new home in Tampa, Florida. I am assuming it is not just a mere coincidence that the foreclosed home they just purchased and moved into is the same home that our Amanda grew up in. Regardless, you were right about Susan. She is dying. She has never smoked a cigarette in her life but she was exposed to second hand smoke during her entire childhood and life at home. She is dying from non-small cell lung cancer."

"What? Are we supposed to feel sorry for her now?" Bertie fluttered her hands in front of her face. "Forget I said that." She took a deep breath as she continued watching Charlotte Grace. Bertie reached out to grasp the little fingers that were reaching toward Susan Peterson. "So, I'm guessing the cancer is terminal?" she asked. "I never realized non-smokers were at risk for lung cancer."

"Actually," Martin began in explanation, "Ninety percent of all lung cancers are caused by smoking; of the remaining ten percent of lung cancers not caused by active smoking, as many as twenty-five percent of the tumors are caused by second-hand smoke."

Bertie looked at him and almost grinned. "Well, aren't we just a fountain of medical knowledge..."

"Well," Martin continued, "The sad truth is that we have far too many souls among us who could have lived much longer lives on earth had it not been for the effects of smoking. Nasty, nasty habit, I say; never did understand the attraction of filling our lungs with polluted smoke...nasty, nasty habit..."

"Okay, okay, you've educated me about lung cancer," Bertie motioned with a bit of impatience creeping into her voice. "Now, tell me more about Jack and Susan Peterson. Will they be caught? Will we get Charlotte Grace back? And what the Hell have they done to that child's hair?"

"B-E-R-T-I-E!"

"Jeez!" Bertie whispered under her breath. "What am I supposed to do? Super glue my lips together?"

"Now that's an intriguing idea..." Martin mumbled.

Max and Martin looked at each other and suddenly began to laugh – something none of them had done much of during the past three days.

Max shook his head. "You know we don't have the answers to those questions, Bertie; just as you know that we cannot, and will not, share any of this information with the humans back on earth. I merely showed this to you because I was concerned about your own spirituality. You needed to be reassured that God truly does know what He is doing. You, also, needed to be reminded that it is NOT our place to question His decisions."

Bertie pouted for only a moment before nodding her head in agreement. "I know all that, I do...but...that doesn't make it any easier to bear."

Max smiled back at her. "It might also give you more discomfort to know that we do not know WHY the Petersons took the baby."

He pulled his broad shoulders back and lifted his chin. "At least not yet."

Bertie grinned at Max. It was so easy for her to envision the gladiator that he was in his human life when he threw back his massive shoulders the way only he could do. "So...do we know how long Susan Peterson has to live?" Bertie asked. "That might give us some hope about when Charlotte Grace might be returned to Kris."

Martin shook his head. "No, Bertie... that is not for us to know... it is between her and God."

"Are they Christians?" Bertie asked, naturally assuming there was no way that could be possible.

"As a matter of fact, yes... they are." Max answered back. "They are good people who made a very bad decision. We can make assumptions all day long about why they did what they did, but in the end, all we can do is wait and to be there to help Kris and Amanda through this."

"So what you're really saying is that there's no way to tell if this is going to have a happy ending?" Bertie looked back and forth between her two mentors. "Oh, for God's sake, please tell me there's going to be a happy ending..."

"That, too, is not our place to know. We can only pray that there will be," Martin replied.

"Then what the Hell are we waiting for?" Bertie practically shouted. "Get on your knees, fellas, on your knees!"

"B-E-R-T-I-E..."

This time, Bertie was almost sure she detected a chuckle in HIS voice.

"Behold, happy is the man whom God corrects."

-Job 5:17 (NKVJ)

CHAPTER 23

One Week After the Kidnapping

A series of events transpired during the week following the baby's kidnapping: the police had interviewed dozens of people; hundreds of tips had been reported through the National Center for Missing and Exploited Children hotline; Danny Raye had been found sitting in an Atlanta, Georgia jail cell and eliminated as a person of interest; Kris had done three television interviews, begging the kidnappers to return Charlotte Grace; and, Andrew Brown had passed peacefully, in his sleep, into the loving and welcoming arms of His Father.

Kris' employer, Al Jernigan, had told her not to worry about her job and that she should focus on her daughter. He even continued to pay her basic salary but it really wasn't needed because the truckers' jar at the Heavenly Grille had tripled its normal weekly currency. Every trucker who frequented the café had spread the news about Kris and Charlotte among themselves; and, every trucker was keeping an eye out for a little red-haired baby, wherever their travels took them.

It was six o'clock in the morning of Friday, December twenty-third. The two roommates were watching Kris' latest television interview on the local early morning news when their cell phones rang simultaneously. They both jumped, grabbed their phones, and moved to opposite ends of the room, hoping...dreading...that one of the calls would bring news about Charlotte Grace.

Dean was on the other end of Kris' call.

"Dean! Any news? Please tell me you've found something... heard something... anything."

It broke Dean's heart to hear the total desperation in Kris' voice. "Kris, I'm getting off work in a few minutes and will be over then; but, I wanted to let you know that the Tallahassee police did find something last night."

"What?" Kris asked with a dreaded tone, pressing the phone closer against her ear. Surely if it was something bad, Dean would have waited and told her in person. *"Just, please... don't tell me they've found a baby's body..."* she couldn't help thinking.

"Well, it seems that some kids were horsing around in a rest stop just off I-75, near Tallahassee, and knocked over one of the trash bins. Evidently the county waste collectors didn't do a good job of collecting all the trash last week. The bin was full, but something caught the parents' attention. They had seen your interviews on television so they became suspicious when they saw the soiled diaper, baby clothes, and...a man's running shoe."

"Oh...my...God..." Kris' hand flew to her mouth and she slid down to the floor, drawing her knees in to her chest.

Amanda had been talking to Doug, but hung up her cell phone and rushed over to where Kris crouched. She kneeled down beside her best friend and asked, "What? What's happened?"

Kris' wide eyes stared back in shock but she held up her hand to quiet Amanda. She blew out a deep breath and put the cell phone back to her ear. "What else did they find, Dean?" She was almost certain she didn't really want to know the answer to that question.

Dean recognized the fear in her cracking voice and was quick to reassure her. "Easy, Kris. There was no sign of Charlotte Grace. And we don't know for sure if the clothing and shoe are related, but we're pretty confident they might be. The reason I'm calling... Kris... they need you to see if you can identify the clothing. I'm sorry... I wish you didn't have to do this."

Kris nodded and barely suppressed the sob threatening to escape her throat. "No, it's okay... I can do that."

"Good," Dean responded. "I'll pick you up in about an hour and take you to the police department in Tallahassee; I don't want you driving there by yourself... if that's okay with you?"

Kris choked on a sob. "That's more than okay, Dean. Thank you...so much. I'll be waiting, but...please hurry." Kris ended the call and stared into Amanda's questioning face. "They, uh...they think they may have found Charlotte's clothing, and the man's shoe... at a rest stop off the interstate near Tallahassee..."

"Tallahassee?" Amanda whispered. "Well, that's good news, isn't it? I mean, the police have been speculating that the kidnappers, most likely, headed north, out of Florida."

Kris shrugged her tired shoulders. "Yeah, maybe, I don't know. They've been focusing their search in Georgia and Alabama. Of course, by now, who knows? They could be anywhere." Kris shook her head. "I don't understand, though...why haven't they been able to find the car?"

Amanda sighed. "I don't know... so... did I hear you right? Dean is coming over?"

Kris pushed up to a standing position and wiped away her tears. "Yeah, he's taking me to the Tallahassee Police Department, where they're keeping the items for now. They need me to identify the clothing." She attempted, but failed, to choke back another heart-wrenching sob.

"Then, I'm going with you." Amanda said, folding her friend's hands into her own.

Kris shook her head. "No, that's okay, Amanda… really. One of us needs to stay here in case something else comes up. Besides… I know you need to get ready for work… and today is Andrew's funeral. I really wanted to go to that."

Amanda nodded. "Yeah, the café will be closing at two o'clock so that everyone can attend."

Kris looked at Amanda. "I feel so bad about the things I said and thought about Andrew. I don't know how long this trip will take, but if we finish up in time, I'll ask Dean to bring me to the funeral."

"We're all meeting back at the café after the funeral for a… celebration of Andrew's life," Amanda reminded her. "If you don't finish in time for the funeral, then maybe you and Dean can stop by the café."

Kris only nodded as she made her way to her bedroom to change clothes.

Amanda watched the woman who had become like a sister to her turn around and walk into the bedroom. It broke her heart to see Kris' slumped shoulders but she knew that her friend would never give up looking for her baby, no matter how long it took. It was Amanda's job to make sure that Kris never gave up hope. Her parents had told her that in another dream the day after the kidnapping. They told her that it would be up to her to instill faith and hope in Kris – a tall order, especially since Kris was more down on God than ever since the kidnapping. Amanda had tried to get Kris to pray with her on several occasions, but Kris had not wanted any part of a God who would allow something like this to happen to an innocent baby.

Amanda's cell phone rang. It was Doug calling again. Amanda told him about the phone call that Kris had received from Dean. They spoke for a few minutes before Amanda hung up, showered, and dressed for work. She took a change of clothing for the funeral. On her way out the door, she glanced down at her Bible laying on the end table beside the love seat. She had highlighted one of her favorite passages the night before, Isaiah 41:10… "Fear not, for I am with you;

be not dismayed for I am your God. I will strengthen you, yes I will help you, I will uphold you with my righteous right hand." Amanda closed her eyes in a quick, silent prayer, *"Please be with Kris, today, and Lord… she needs your strength and your love more than she knows. Please… help me… show me how to help her…"*

Kris came out of her own room just as Amanda was about to close the front door.

Amanda turned to her and said. "I love you, Kris. Call me as soon as you finish."

Kris offered a weak smile and nodded. "I will…"

Kris stood just inside the doorway and watched as Amanda drove off. She closed the door and sat down on the love seat while she waited for Dean's arrival. She lowered her head into her open palms and took a deep breath. When she lifted her head, her eyes were drawn to Amanda's open Bible and the passage that was highlighted in yellow. She read the passage, shook her head, and allowed the tears to flow. "When have you ever been with me… and where are you now?"

She heard a car door shut and knew Dean had arrived. She looked at the Bible and closed it slowly. She did not know how to pray, but she had seen Amanda do it often enough. Something deep inside her wanted to reach out to Amanda's God; however, something equally as strong was preventing her from doing so.

For now, the latter feeling prevailed.

CHAPTER 24

Andrew Brown's Funeral

Dean held Kris securely in his arms as they stood in the parking lot of the Tallahassee Police Department. The harder she cried, the harder he held onto her. Every gulp of air she took tore into his heart and he knew without a doubt that he was falling in love with this woman. He stroked her hair and lifted her chin so that they looked into each other's tear-drenched eyes. "We are going to find her, Kris. I promise you that. I will never stop looking for Charlotte Grace…"

Kris shook her head and looked back at him, the agony and despair evident on her face. She tried to smile. "Maybe you shouldn't make promises like that, Dean." She blew out her cheeks and took a step back from him. "That was her outfit, Dean; that was my baby girl's outfit…"

Dean's shoulders dropped. "I know."

Kris took another deep breath. She knew she had to hold herself together. She used both hands to wipe away her tear-soaked cheeks. "Okay… I'm okay. So… what happens next?"

They walked to the passenger side of Dean's car. He

opened the car door for her and waited while she buckled her seat belt. He closed her door, walked around to the driver's side, and got in. He smiled back at the brave face she projected. "Now, they'll send the outfit to the lab for testing. There didn't appear to be any sign of any trauma to the clothing, so we have to assume that the kidnappers simply threw them away. It was a pretty careless thing for them to do, though. I can only guess that maybe they just didn't want to take any chances of having Charlotte's own clothing in the car with them in case they were stopped at a check point."

"What about the man's shoe?' Kris asked.

"They've already compared it to the one that Doug held onto that day and have confirmed it is a match. They'll be doing extensive DNA testing on it, but without a suspect to compare the DNA results against, we're still up against a wall. More and more tips are coming in every day. It's just a matter of time, Kris."

Kris looked at the young police officer who was melting the hard place that had formed around her heart. They had not so much as kissed yet but she knew she was beginning to have strong feelings for him, and that scared her. Every time she loved something or someone, she either lost them or they left her. "I really want to believe that… Christmas is only two days away." Her eyes began filling with tears again. "My little girl's first Christmas…"

Dean reached across and unhooked her seat belt. He held her again as loud, great sobs erupted from deep inside Kris. He wanted to promise her more than anything that her baby would be home for Christmas, but with each additional day that passed, he knew that this was one promise he could not, and would not, make. He held her in his arms for another ten minutes until her sobbing began to subside.

Kris took a deep breath and looked up at him. "There's nothing more we can do here, so…if you think we can make it… well, I'd really like to be at Andrew Brown's funeral.

Dean looked at his watch. "We can make it. What do you say we get you hooked back up in that seat belt?" He reached across her, hooked the belt, took her head between his hands, and kissed her softly on the forehead. "Yeah... we can make it."

Andrew's funeral had been everything that he would have wanted, complete with lots of singing, praise, joy, and laughter. The church had been filled with every living person Amos and Andrew had ever known.

Everyone had gathered at the Heavenly Grille by four o'clock, and Max wasted no time in serving all of them southern fried chicken, potato salad, biscuits and gravy, and plenty of Andrew's favorite dessert – buttermilk cake. Bertie, Doug, and Amanda filled coffee cups and tea glasses while they chatted with everyone who had stopped by to help celebrate Andrew's life.

Amos sat in his usual spot at the counter. The seat next to him, where Andrew always sat, remained empty. Nobody even thought of sitting there even though it was standing room only in the café for the next two hours.

The last of the well-wishers had left the café by six-thirty. The only ones remaining were Amos, Max, Bertie, Doug, Amanda, Kris, and Dean.

Amos looked exhausted and...lonely. He looked at Max and smiled. "I wants to thank you, Mr. Max for everything you done today. It was mighty nice of you and Miss Bertie, yes sir, mighty nice... Andrew would've been right proud at the turn-out. It was a fine turn-out, indeed..."

Dean and Kris came up behind Amos and Max. Dean put his hand on Amos's shoulder. "Yes, it was a good turn-out, Mr. Brown. Andrew had a lot of friends, that's for sure. You know, sir, if you're ready to go, I'd be happy to drive you home."

Amos glanced back at Max and unspoken words seemed to pass between them.

Max said, "That's okay, Officer Hall. I'll see to it,

personally, that Amos gets home."

Amos touched the officer's hand that was still on his shoulder. He patted Dean's hand and said, "Thankee... that's mighty nice of you to offer, but I think I'll be ridin' home with Mr. Max. He looked sideways where Kris stood beside the officer. He nodded and smiled at her. "Andrew and I been prayin' for your baby, Ma'am. The Lord... He's watchin' out for her. She gonna be jes fine and she'll be comin' home soon. You'll see..."

Kris was so touched by the genuine warmth that emanated from the old black man. She no longer felt repulsed by his toothless grin, but she still surprised herself when she moved closer to Amos and wrapped her arms around him. She felt him shudder beneath her slight embrace and knew he was crying. She whispered in his ear so only he could hear. "I hope you're right, Amos. I hope you're right. Thank you..."

Bertie had been watching, and listening to their conversation. She wiped away a tear of her own and told Amanda. "Why don't you go home and get some rest too, Amanda? We're closing for the rest of the evening and we can manage the clean up here."

Amanda looked tired. She had been trying so hard during the past week to keep Kris' spirits and hopes up that she had not gotten much rest herself. "Are you sure, Bertie? I don't mind staying at all."

Bertie shook her head. "No, you go on now. It won't take us long to clean things up. Doug and I can do that while Max takes Amos home. It's been a long day and I think all of you need to get some much needed rest."

"Okay, then," Amanda nodded. "I am a little pooped." She smiled at Kris and Dean. "Kris? Do you want to ride with me?"

Kris almost agreed until she felt Dean squeeze her hand tightly. It hadn't been lost on her that he had been holding on to it most of the day. She shook her head and smiled at her roommate. "That's okay, Amanda. Thanks, but... Dean can drop me off. We'll be right behind you."

After Amanda, Kris, and Dean had left, Max looked at Amos and said. "I'm going to box you up some of these leftovers to take home, Amos. Finish your coffee."

"That's mighty kind of you, Mr. Max." Amos slurped the strong coffee while he ran his hand across the empty stool beside him.

Bertie and Doug began carrying dishes to the kitchen.

"That really was a good turn-out," Bertie said when Max walked in and began boxing leftover chicken and biscuits into a box.

Max opened a cupboard and took down an entire buttermilk cake and wrapped it in tin foil. "Yes it was." He saw Bertie's half grin while she watched him wrap the cake. "Saved this one just for Amos," he smiled. When he finished boxing up the leftovers, Max looked at his fellow angels and shook his head. "It never gets any easier, does it? Saying good-bye, I mean."

Bertie walked over and punched him lightly on his shoulder. "Nope, it sure doesn't, but we all know that Andrew is in a much better place now. No more pain…"

Max nodded. "His transition should be an easy one, for sure. I've never met anyone more ready to meet his maker. The hardest thing for him was leaving Amos behind."

"I think it's always hardest for those left behind," Doug agreed. "Dying seems to be the easy part; but, letting go of a loved one? Well… that's never easy."

"But at least they both knew it was coming," Bertie said. "They had time to be together, to do things they wanted to do together, even if it was just sitting on those stools out there, drinking coffee and milk, and eating buttermilk cake."

"That is true," Max agreed. "So many people don't get the chance to say good-bye to their loved ones. I think it's harder for them to let go because they never saw it coming. Denial is a strong force to combat."

Bertie watched as Max placed everything in two large bags. "Why don't you go ahead and take Amos home now? Doug and I can finish up here. You stay with him as long as you need to, Max."

"You know I will," Max said. "You know I will."

Three hours later, sitting on the old floral couch inside Amos and Andrew's small, but tidy, trailer, Max laughed at yet another story Amos told of his and Andrew's younger years in Mississippi.

"I bet you boys kept your Mama and Daddy on their toes, for sure," Max laughed.

Amos wiped away a tear of laughter and nodded. "Yes sir, we did, Mr. Max. We sure did."

He chuckled again and looked deep into Max's dark eyes. "Yes sir... we laughed lots with Mama and Daddy. Matter of fact... why, I even remember, not so long ago, how's we laughed so hard we practically peed our pants. That was the day Daddy told us all about you, Mr. Max. If I remembers correctly, it was last year, right after you first opened the café. Mama had passed on a couple years before, but Daddy was still with us then."

Max's own chuckle stopped in his throat. "About me?"

"Yes sir, Mr. Max. Amos and I got plumb tickled when Daddy started talking about you, said he knew a secret about you. We's laughed even harder cuz we really thought he was teasin' us... you know...'bout you being an angel and all."

Max scratched the back of his neck. He hadn't seen this coming...and it wasn't easy to catch an angel off guard. He silently chastised himself for not finding out sooner exactly what their father had suspected about him.

Amos laughed out loud. "You look like you done been caught with your hand in the cookie jar, Mr. Max. You jes sit tight for a spell; I be's back in jes a minute." He was still laughing when he went into one of the bedrooms.

Max was still wringing his hands and wondering what he should say, what he should admit to, when he saw Amos coming back into the room. He was carrying a wooden box about the size of a large shoe box. "What do you have there, Amos?" Max asked, but not really sure he wanted to know.

Amos sat down on the couch beside Max and said, "Well sir, inside this here box, I have somethin' my Daddy left us. Andrew and me, well, we's didn't find it till a few days after Daddy died. When we seen it, well... we might be just simple country folk, but we knew what it meant."

"I'm not sure what you mean, Amos," Max replied, still grasping for ideas.

Amos smiled, totally unaware of the discomfort he was causing the man sitting beside him. "When you first arrived here in town, Daddy used to joke with us that you was an angel, 'cause you owned a café with a halo and all. After he done died, Andrew and I found this here box under his bed. He never showed it to us while he was livin' but... well, sir... we figured things out purty quick for ourselves, yes we did."

Max remained silent and kept his hands pressed together hard.

Amos lifted the box lid and removed an old black and white photograph, still in remarkably good shape - considering it was taken in 1941, at a Mississippi restaurant called the Heavenly Halo. There were five people in the photograph. One very large black man, looking to be in his mid-forties stood in the middle. He had an arm around a black couple, the man on his right and the woman on his left. Standing in front of the man was one twin boy; standing in front of the woman was another twin boy. Both boys held up a plate piled high with Max's famous buttermilk cake.

Amos remained quiet when he handed the photo to Max.

Max stared at the photo for a long time.

Amos was patient, rocking slightly to and fro, waiting to see what Max had to say.

Max sighed and looked over at Amos. He didn't even try to deny it or offer up an alternative explanation for his presence in the picture. He finally smiled awkwardly and said, "I can't believe I forgot about this photo..."

Amos' eyes lit up with laughter and happiness. He

touched Max's shoulder and said. "You hasn't changed a bit, Mr. Max…no, sir, not one little bit."

Max grinned and shook his head. Maybe it was best if he didn't say anything.

Amos grinned his trademark toothless grin, "That don't surprise me none, Mr. Max, 'cause Daddy use to tell me and Andrew lots of stories 'bout angels. I's remember him telling us one thing in particular… he told us that angels… that they don't age." He grinned again. "I guess Daddy was right about that, wasn't he now, Mr. Max?"

Max shook his head and rubbed the bridge of his nose between his thumb and forefinger. *"Oh…Bertie is going to love this…"* Max thought as he slowly embraced the old black man sitting beside him.

CHAPTER 25

-Christmas 2011-
The Visit to Tampa

Amanda awoke Christmas morning from another dream. During this dream, her parents had wished her a Merry Christmas and told her that she should try to persuade Kris to attend church with her. Amanda told them she had been trying to get Kris to go to church with her for months but that she would continue to try. Her parents told her that it was very important that she not give up on that quest.

Amanda was dressed and ready for church when Kris walked into the kitchen, empty coffee cup in hand.

Kris looked at the clock over the microwave and said, "You're still here? Aren't you going to be late for church?"

Amanda shook her head. "I'm not going to the early service this morning. I... uh... thought if I waited a bit, I might be able to change your mind about coming with me." Amanda smiled as she got up to refill Kris' coffee cup. "Come on, sit down... have a cup of coffee with me."

Kris exhaled and raised her eyebrows. "We've been

through this so many times, Amanda. I told you. I am not going to church with you or anyone else for that matter. How many times do I have to tell you that I do not believe in the church?"

"But how can you say that, Kris? You've never even been!" Amanda laughed. "How do you know you wouldn't love it?"

Kris looked at Amanda and shook her head. "You just don't get it, do you, Amanda?"

Amanda shrugged her shoulders. "What?"

"How very different we are," Kris said. "I have never stepped foot in a church. My mother never took me; I never had any relatives or friends to take me. I've never read the Bible. I don't know any of the Bible stories you're always talking about, and, well, look at the things that have happened to me in the past six months! What kind of a God allows people to suffer like that? Never mind, don't answer that, or you WILL be late for church."

Amanda smiled. "I know what a hard time…"

Kris shook her head. "No, that's just it, Amanda. You don't know! You have had a fun, carefree life. You had parents who loved you; a wonderful Dad who raised you; a nice home to grow up in; lots of friends; a good education. I doubt you've ever really known any kind of heartache, except for losing your Mom and Dad. So, please, spare me… don't tell me you know how I feel…because you don't. You cannot possibly know how empty I feel without Charlotte Grace in my arms. She was the only good thing that has ever happened in my life and now… well, here it is, Christmas Day… my baby's first Christmas… and I have no clue where she is, who she's with… whether she's alive or dead…"

Kris couldn't continue when her body wracked with her tormented sobs.

Amanda wrapped her arms around her and held her tight until the sobs evolved into short gasps.

After several minutes, Amanda wiped away her own tears and said, "Okay, then, you win; you don't have to go to church with me."

Kris wiped her eyes and attempted a smile. "Thank you..."

"But..." Amanda said, continuing to stroke her friend's head. "If you're not going to church with me, then you have to promise me that you'll get dressed and be ready to go when I get back home."

"Go where?" Kris asked.

Amanda grinned, confident that her idea was a good idea. "Tomorrow is my day off and, well, it is Christmas, so I thought I would ride back home to Tampa to visit my parents' graves. We could spend the night, I could show you a little bit of Tampa, and then we could head back here around two o'clock. What do you think?"

Kris was ready to say no. She had intended to spend her Christmas in bed with Charlotte's favorite stuffed toy, a white teddy bear with angel wings. Dean was working a double shift today so that another officer, who had children, could spend the day with his family. She thought she wanted to be alone, but it suddenly occurred to her that she didn't – not today of all days. She nodded and whispered, "Okay."

"Okay?" Amanda clapped her hands. "Yes! Okay, then. I'll be back by twelve-thirty. Pack a small bag and be ready to go. We should be in Tampa before seven and we'll have a nice Christmas dinner some place, splurge on a decent hotel room, and get up early tomorrow morning to visit my parents' graves and do a little shopping. If we have time, and I think we will, I'll even show you the house I grew up in!"

The roommates made it to Tampa by seven o'clock Christmas night. They had dinner at the Hard Rock Café, played a few slot machines, and were back in bed at The Holiday Inn Express by eleven o'clock.

The hotel was about as nice a hotel as Amanda's budget warranted, but it was comfortable and offered a free continental breakfast to its guests. Amanda and Kris sat at one of the hotel's small tables at seven o'clock Monday morning, sipping coffee, and eating huge sticky, cinnamon buns.

Amanda was eating her bun with gusto, as usual, while Kris was pushing hers around on the paper plate. "You're not hungry?" Amanda asked between bites.

"No, it's a little early for me," Kris replied. "Food and I don't really connect until about eleven or so. Coffee's fine, that's all I need."

"So...you're not going to eat that cinnamon bun?" Amanda asked peevishly.

Kris pushed the pastry toward her roommate. "Help yourself. I swear, I don't know how you stay so small. You eat enough for three people."

Amanda began pulling apart the offered bun. "I have my Dad's metabolism. He was always thin, not skinny, mind you, but thin. He could eat anything he wanted and never gained weight. We used to have contests to see who could eat the most."

Kris smiled back as she watched her friend devour the second bun. "That should have been interesting to watch."

Amanda licked her fingers and stood up. "He always won. I never even came close to winning. Come on, let's get a refill and get out of here. The gates to the cemetery should be open by the time we get there. I want to stop at Walmart and get some artificial flowers to put on the graves, okay?"

Kris stood up. "Hey, you're driving. I'm just along for the ride, remember? Lead the way, Tonto!"

Amanda felt good that she was doing her part in keeping Kris' mind off the kidnapping, even if only for a few hours. "Okay... Garden of Memories... here we come!"

The two roommates had paid their respects to Amanda's parents and were back on the road by nine o'clock. For the next three hours they rode around downtown Tampa while

Amanda showed Kris some of her favorite stores and shops.

Kris closed her eyes as they crossed back over the Howard Frankland Bridge and enjoyed the cool breeze blowing in through the opened windows. She opened her eyes and stared in awe at the massive amount of water surrounding them. "It's absolutely beautiful here, Amanda. I can't imagine why you would ever want to leave this place."

Amanda nodded. She never tired of the amazing view offered during the seven-mile jaunt across the bridge. "I know. I didn't realize how much I missed it until now."

"Do you think you'll ever move back?" Kris asked with a bit of hesitation evident in her voice.

"Oh, I know I will... someday," Amanda beamed. "Tampa will always be my home."

Kris was quiet for a few moments before she continued. "I'll miss you... if you leave."

"Well then," Amanda quirked, "I guess you'll just have to come with me. I tell you what. When they find Charlotte and bring her back home, and they will... why don't we think about moving back here?"

"What?" Kris asked with surprise. "You'd want me to move back here with you?"

"Not just you!" Amanda was quick to reply. "You and Charlotte! Oh wait... we may have to bring whats-his-name with us, too."

Kris looked over at her friend and laughed her first genuine laugh since Charlotte's abduction. "You are too much, girl... too much!"

"Well, you don't think Dean is going to let you out of his sight for very long, now do you?"

Kris shrugged. "He's a really nice guy, Amanda. Actually, he told me a few weeks ago that he wants to transfer to Tampa one day. He has a brother who lives here and is on the Tampa police force, I think. You know, I'm not used to really nice guys, but I've got to admit, I like having him around, but..."

"Not high on your list of priorities right now, I know,"

Amanda said.

"No, not really," Kris muttered. "Okay, well...enough of that. So, where to now?"

"Well, we don't have long before we need to get back on the road, but, I really did want to show you where I grew up. It's not far from here. If the traffic cooperates, we should be there in about thirty minutes or so. The house is probably still empty so we could peek into the windows and look around the yard. Oh...Kris, the back yard is to die for! It will be so good to see that house again."

"Then lead the way," Kris smiled and closed her eyes, trying not to feel guilty about enjoying the cool breeze blowing against her cheeks.

Susan and Jack Peterson decided to enjoy the pleasantly warm day after Christmas sitting outside on their screened lanai. It had been a quiet holiday, with just the three of them, and Jack was enjoying what he knew might be his last Christmas with his wife. Their new baby daughter, Kelly, was napping in the play pen beside them.

All the boxes were unpacked, with Jack doing the majority of the work, and he was ready to begin his new accounting job the following day. He worried about leaving Susan and Charlotte alone so soon after the kidnapping, but he knew it was important that they resumed a normal lifestyle as quickly as possible. He didn't want to draw any unnecessary attention to his family, especially since the daily news still aired pictures and updates of the abduction of Charlotte Grace Devone.

The couple held hands and enjoyed the peaceful afternoon.

"They found the car this morning," Susan whispered, her eyes closed.

Jack wasn't sure if she had heard the morning update or not. "I know..."

"I was hoping it would take them a little longer to find it,"

Susan said, opening her eyes now and looking over at her husband. She squeezed his hand with what little strength she could. It still amazed her that the man sitting beside her had sacrificed so much in order to make her dream of being a mother come true.

"There's nothing in the car to link them to us," Jack reassured her and returned the squeeze.

"They didn't say anything about the note," Susan said. "I wonder why."

Jack shrugged. "Sometimes police keep some information to themselves." He was quiet for several moments before continuing. "You know, Susan... I can't promise that they won't eventually find us."

"I know that, love... but maybe it will take them long enough..."

Jack knew what she meant. "Maybe," he sighed, squeezing her hand again, trying to be careful with the touch. "Maybe..."

The ringing of the doorbell interrupted their conversation. His hold on her hand tightened but he didn't notice the slight wincing of pain in her eyes.

"Jack..."

"Stay calm, Susan. I'll get it. You stay here with the baby. It's probably just one of the neighbors."

Susan closed her eyes, too weak and weary to worry about "what-if" situations.

Jack made his way slowly to the front door. If the scene had been in a movie, Jack's moves would have been captured in slow motion. His breathing increased and became more labored with each step he took toward the door. He saw two silhouettes outside the glass frame of the door. His hand moved forward and stopped when he grasped the handle. He took one more deep breath and opened the door.

Two young women stood before him. The blond woman was smiling. The red-haired woman looked lost...and so very sad.

Jack Peterson recognized the two women immediately,

and prayed with everything in him that he did not do or say anything to raise their suspicions about the nervous man who stood trembling before them.

CHAPTER 26

Face-to-Face With the Kidnappers

Officer Dean Hall was sitting at a counter seat of the Heavenly Grille Cafe at the exact moment Amanda rang the doorbell to the house in which she had been raised. He had worked a double shift on Christmas day, and had been about to leave the station when word was received that the kidnappers' dark sedan had been found.

Dean had waited at the station until the towed car arrived at the Monticello Police Department. A lump formed in his throat when he saw Charlotte's car seat in the back and read the note that the kidnappers had left behind. His first instinct had been to call Kris right away and tell her about the discovery, but he knew that she was in Tampa with Amanda. He hoped the time away would be good for her and he didn't want to interfere with her one day away from the nightmare she had been living for the past eleven days. So, in the end, he had decided that the information could wait until her return later that evening.

"Penny for your thoughts," Bertie said while she refilled his coffee cup. "Never mind, you don't have to say anything.

It's been all over the news this morning. We heard they found the kidnappers' car."

Dean nodded as Doug came out of the kitchen to join them.

The two men shook hands and Dean told them what he could about the discovery. He did not tell them about the note, however, since the police had decided to keep a lid on that bit of information. He would tell Kris about it but would ask her to keep the information to herself for the time being.

"Yes, they did," Dean confirmed. "No immediate prints, no tag, and the Vehicle Identification Number has been scratched off. There's really not much to go on, but having the car seat as confirmation, we are glad to have finally found the vehicle. That tells us the kidnappers must have had a second vehicle close by, or somebody assisting them. It also tells us that it couldn't have been a random, spontaneous kidnapping. This was something that had been carefully planned out by them."

"I wish I could have gotten a better look at them that day in the parking lot," Doug said. He was still beating himself up over the fact that he had his hands on the kidnapper and had not been able to hang on. "I was so focused on Charlotte that I didn't pay as close attention to them as I should have."

"It's not your fault, Doug. It was just good planning on their part," Dean said. "You did everything you could have done... plus some. You know, I still can't believe you didn't get a scratch on you after being dragged like you were on the pavement."

"Yes, I was lucky," Doug nodded. "I had a few bruises, though," he lied, "And, I was pretty sore for a few days, but, yes... I guess I was lucky. Things certainly could have taken a different turn. I wasn't thinking about what I was doing, though... just reacting."

Bertie punched Doug lightly on the shoulder and left to wait on two truckers who had entered. She gave each of the truckers their own friendly shoulder punch and sat them at one of the vacant booths.

Dean watched her for a minute before turning back to Doug. "Did you really have any bruises?"

The question caught Doug momentarily off guard. "Yes, mostly on my lower legs. Jeans covered them and they cleared up in a few days."

Dean didn't lose eye contact with the man before him. "You were kicked in the face, Doug, and dragged almost a hundred feet. I gotta tell you... a lot of us talked about it down at the station. What are you... some kind of Superman?"

Doug appreciated and returned the direct eye contact. "Well... let's just say, I come from a family of extremely fast healers. It takes a lot to wear us down."

"Is that a fact?" Dean asked, not really expecting an answer. He wasn't disappointed.

"So..." Doug continued, pressing his lips together and blowing out his cheeks. "What do you say to a piece of pie to go with that coffee? Max just whipped up the biggest lemon meringue pie I've ever seen. I think he even calls it his mile-high meringue pie."

Dean didn't respond immediately; instead, he continued to make eye contact with Doug. After a few moments, he decided to let it go. He doubted he would ever get any answers about Doug's miraculous recovery from being dragged a hundred yards on asphalt. "No thanks," Dean replied. He decided to change the subject. "By the way, have you heard from the girls since they left?"

Doug's head jerked up and he stared hard at Dean. "What are you talking about? Since they left for where? Today is Amanda's day off, but she didn't say anything about going anywhere."

Dean shrugged and sipped at his coffee. "Well, I'm not sure it was really pre-planned, but it would seem that Amanda talked Kris into riding to Tampa with her yesterday. They're due back some time tonight."

A silent alarm triggered inside Doug's head. He had overheard Bertie and Max talking last night after they returned from visiting Home. They had said something about knowing who took Charlotte Grace, and that they knew the baby was alive and safe... in Tampa. Doug admitted to them that he had eavesdropped on their conversation and asked to know more about the baby's whereabouts. Max did not offer any further details; he had simply reminded Doug that they were not, in any way, to interfere with the lives of the mortals they encountered.

"Well..." Doug said, forcing a smile. "I'm sure it did them both good to get away for a couple of days. There's really not much they could do here other than to worry and wait for more news. Kris will be happy to know the car was found."

Dean nodded and thought, *"Yeah... wish I could say the same thing when she hears about the note that was left behind."*

Two hundred and fifty miles away, Amanda and Kris stood outside the front door to the house Amanda had shared with her father.

Kris shuffled her feet, suddenly nervous and hesitant about being at the house. "Amanda, maybe we should just go. It's obvious someone is living here now. Hell, it could be a serial killer for all we know. What if we get inside and never get to leave?"

"Oh, poo!" Amanda laughed. "You've been watching too many CSI re-runs. Besides, there's a car parked in the driveway. I'm pretty certain that serial killers always park their vehicles in the garage, hidden from view, and..." she grinned at the same time she pushed the doorbell, "It's too late now... I can hear someone inside."

Kris shuddered as a negative sensation surged through her. She couldn't explain why she felt the way she did, but her thoughts immediately turned back to Charlotte Grace. She was feeling guilty about leaving Monticello and felt with sudden certainty that she should return there as quickly as possible. She was about to turn around and head back to the car when the front door was opened by a middle-aged, average-looking white male. She made brief eye contact with him before looking down at her sandaled feet. She wasn't sure but she could have sworn that the man paled visibly when he looked at her. Maybe he thought he might be opening his door to serial killers.

Amanda, on the other hand, was busy being her typical pleasant self. When the man opened the door, she put on her friendliest smile and stuck out her hand. "Hi there!" she said. "My name is Amanda Turner and this is my best friend, Kris Devone. We were visiting Tampa for the day and I wanted to show Kris the house where I grew up... this house. I know it may seem terribly rude to ask, but I was wondering if you would mind if we just looked around for a few minutes before we head back home to Monticello. I promise it will only be for a few minutes."

The pretty blond had a firm handshake, which was a blessing since it helped snap Jack Peterson out of his stunned silence more quickly. "Oh... well... I don't know about that. I mean, you are strangers, and... my wife is..."

Amanda was about to reassure the man of their honesty and integrity when she heard a woman's voice in the background.

"Jack? Who's there?" Susan's weak voice sounded from the lanai.

"I know we're strangers, but I promise we won't be a bother," Amanda rushed on. "We'll be in and out in ten minutes, really."

Kris' gaze had slowly moved from the ground back up to the man's surprised stare. Her first thought was that he appeared to be afraid of them. She took Amanda by the arm and said, "Maybe this isn't a good idea, Amanda. Maybe we should get back on the road... it's getting late."

Against his better judgment, Jack suddenly found himself mumbling a response. "No... I mean... if you promise to be quick, I suppose it will be alright. It's just that we, uh... we just put the baby down for a nap and..."

Kris' head jerked back up. "You have a baby?" she asked. She wasn't sure that she could be around any baby other than Charlotte Grace right now. She looked at the man, who still had that deer-in-the-headlights look about him and said, "Why don't you go in, Amanda, and have a quick look. I'll wait in the car."

Amanda grabbed Kris' arm when she turned to leave. "But I wanted you to see the house and especially the back yard, Kris!" The back yard is the absolute best part about the house. It's like a small paradise… well, at least it was the last time I saw it." She smiled back at the man.

Some color had returned to Jack's cheeks and he almost smiled. "It still is," he agreed. "It's the main reason we wanted this house so badly. That… and, the neighborhood; we thought it would be a good place to raise our child."

Amanda clapped her hands together and beamed. "Oh, it really was a wonderful place to grow up! My father and I shared so many happy memories here."

"Your father?" the man asked. He looked in the direction of their car, a stricken look of fear reappearing upon his face. "Is he with you?"

"Oh, no," Amanda explained. "Daddy died a couple of years ago. "I tried to hang onto the house after he died, but…"

"Oh…I see," the man said. "Well then, if you'll return my hand to me, I suppose it will be okay for you to come in… for a few minutes."

Amanda burst out laughing, unaware that she had been holding onto the man's hand all this time. "Oh, I am so sorry. Thank you so very much. I promise we'll be quick. Come on, Kris. You've got to see the back yard."

Kris exhaled deeply and, against her will and better judgment, followed Amanda into the foyer.

The house was average in size, around seventeen hundred square feet, but it looked larger due to the open layout design. The floors were tiled and the great room was furnished with typical, Florida-themed items. The kitchen looked out into the great room, and sliding glass doors opened onto a very large screened lanai that ran the entire length of the home.

The first thing that Kris noticed when she walked onto the lanai was the play pen and the precious, dark-haired baby sleeping peacefully on its stomach, its tiny butt raised in the air. A lump formed in her throat and tears threatened to escape her green eyes, so she took a deep breath and immediately focused all of her attention on the beautifully-landscaped yard beyond the lanai.

The next thing that Kris noticed was the frail-looking woman reclining next to the play pen.

The woman turned her head when the trio walked onto the lanai. She smiled pleasantly and said, "Hello... we weren't expecting company..." She ran her hands through her thinning hair. "I must look a mess..."

Susan attempted to get up but Jack gently placed a hand upon her shoulder and said, "No, love... you need to rest while the baby is napping."

He looked at the two young women standing beside him, hoping and praying they would not connect the baby in the play pen to the one that had been filling the airways for the last ten days. He was inwardly trying to decide if he and Susan had been found out and whether these women were here to take back the baby. His muscles relaxed when the red-haired woman didn't immediately rush to pick up the sleeping baby, and he knew instinctively that their secret was safe... for now.

"I don't believe we introduced ourselves," he said. "My name is Jack and this beautiful woman is my wife, Susan." He nodded toward the play pen. "This is our baby, Kelly. She's such a handful that I insist that Susan rest whenever the baby is sleeping."

Amanda held out her hand again and smiled broadly. "Well, it's very nice to meet you, Jack." She then held out her hand to Susan and noticed how thin and cold the woman's touch was. "It's nice to meet you, too, Susan. Thank you both so much for letting us look around. Your baby is beautiful.

Is it a girl or a boy?"

Kris noticed the slight hesitation and the quick glance that passed between the Petersons. She couldn't explain the sharp tingle that shivered quickly up and down her spine. She glanced back down at the sleeping baby.

"It's a girl," Susan whispered. "A beautiful, baby girl… just what I always wanted."

Kris allowed her eyes to drift away from the infant, a little girl like her Charlotte Grace. "How old is she?" she asked, directing her question to the woman.

Jack knew that the medications his wife took often made her drowsy and incoherent. He also knew that they made her conversations ramble at times. A feeling of urgency swept over him; he knew he had to get the two young women out of the house before any connection to the kidnapped baby could be made. He moved toward the play pen and looked down. "She's small for her age; she was born premature, but she'll be five months old next week."

Jack looked back at Susan, who appeared ready to say something. "You need to get some rest, love. Amanda used to live in this house and has asked to see it one more time. I'll show them around. I want you to rest and listen out for… Kelly, until I get back."

"Kelly…" Susan lisped. "Oh, that's such a beautiful name, don't you think? Much better than…" Her eyes closed.

Jack motioned Kris and Amanda back inside the kitchen area. "I'm sorry, but what I didn't tell you is that my wife is very sick and heavily sedated right now."

"Oh, I am so very sorry…" Amanda said. "Maybe it would be best if we left?"

Jack shook his head and offered a weak smile in return. "No, you're here now, so please, take a look around. Show your friend the house. I'm sure you want her to see the back-yard paradise that your father worked so hard to create."

"Thank you, Jack," Amanda smiled, taking his hand again. "We'll be out of your hair in no time."

"I don't know what's happened to my manners," Jack

sighed. "May I offer you ladies something to drink? We have iced tea, soda, water…"

"No… but thank you," Kris replied quickly. "We'll just have a quick look around and be gone. We really do need to get back on the road."

"Well, okay then. Let me know if you have any questions or if you change your mind about that drink," Jack offered. He stepped aside and allowed Amanda to act as tour guide for her friend. He watched Kris closely, wondering what she was thinking, how she was feeling about seeing a baby, wondering if she had any idea that she was within inches of her missing child. He knew how he would have felt if his child had been kidnapped. He couldn't help but think that she must be wonderfully resilient if she were out and about sight-seeing, less than two weeks after her child had been kidnapped. *"Maybe we did that baby a favor,"* he thought. *"Maybe we aren't such horrible people after all…"*

CHAPTER 27

-Heaven-
Stephen and Regina Revel in Heaven's Beauty

S tephen and Regina Turner walked along a golden-bricked path, holding hands and enjoying their own private, quiet moment with God. Each of them was in silent prayer with their Heavenly Father; and, each of them was praying the same thing – for the daily protection and safety of their only child, and for the safe return of the infant, Charlotte Grace Devone.

A variety of birds flew above them, while others perched upon bloom-filled dogwood trees. The birds all flew or sat together in groups, as mixed species, rather than singling out their own individual kind. An extraordinary array of bluebirds, doves, eagles, magpies, owls, quails, sparrows, toucans, and woodpeckers created an unexpected, yet beautiful, melody of sounds. A clear, flowing stream off to the right of the path provided a fun-filled meeting place for dozens of avocets, flamingos, geese, and peafowls.

The blissful quiet was suddenly disrupted. An excited bark caused Stephen and Regina to smile and open their eyes from prayer.

"Oh...my...God...I don't believe it!" Stephen laughed as he released Regina's hand and ran to meet the shiny, black Labrador/pit mixed-breed that was running just as fast toward him. "Sam!" Stephen shouted while he ran.

The pet that had shared his and Amanda's life for ten years flew into his open arms when they finally reached each other. Sam barked with joy and licked the tears of happiness from Stephen's cheeks.

Stephen held on to Sam, over-joyed to learn for certain that the pets we loved and cared for on earth really did share a place with us in Heaven. He looked back at Regina who had caught up with him and was smiling broadly. "We got him a few months after you died, Regina. You don't know how much he helped me, and Amanda, cope with your loss." He ruffled the dog's strong neck and embraced him again. "Such a good dog... yes, you are!"

Sam barked happily in apparent agreement.

Regina laughed and bent down to rub Sam's back. "I know...and I'm so glad he was able to help with that. He was a good companion to you both."

"But I don't understand..." Stephen muttered. "I've been here for almost three years and this is the first time I've seen him... or any of my pets for that matter."

Regina nodded. "It's all part of the transitioning phase. If you think about it, you'll probably realize that you've been so preoccupied with... this place... and focusing on Amanda's well-being... that your beloved pets have not been your number one concern."

Stephen smiled and hugged Sam again. "I guess that's true, but I hope Sam doesn't realize that! Plus, even though it's been three years, most of the time it seems like I've only been here for a few weeks. The whole concept of time gets a little lost, doesn't it?"

"That's because time is not a priority for us here, not like it was on earth anyway. On earth we were always rushing to get everything done on time, to get somewhere on time... to prove something to someone or to ourselves... that we often forgot to stop and just enjoy the time that we were in at the moment. Unfortunately, once that time is gone, well... it's gone. We can't get it back, can we?"

Stephen stood up and pulled Regina along with him. "You're talking about all the time you missed out on with Amanda, huh?"

Regina looked at him with all the love she had for him still. "Not just Amanda…" she smiled. "I regret not making more time for us because… well… I thought we had forever together. It's true what they say, you know… that you really don't know what you've got till it's gone, do you?"

"Hmmm…" Stephen smiled. "Wasn't there a song with that line in it?"

Regina grinned back at him. "Probably, but you know what I mean."

Sam barked again and ran toward a couple of peafowls spreading their colorful feathers.

"Sam!" Stephen yelled after him, afraid of what the dog might do to the beautiful birds.

Regina placed her hand on his forearm. "Don't worry, dear. He won't hurt them. That's just another one of the beautiful things about Heaven. You'll see creatures and species of all types just… hanging out together. It's no longer survival of the fittest."

"Amazing…" Stephen said, shaking his head. "There's so much to learn and take in."

"Well, trust me," Regina said. "I've been here a lot longer than you and I haven't even scratched the surface yet. I have been so raptured with just being in God's presence and feeling his eternal love that it's hard to tear myself away from that feeling to… explore the rest of what Heaven has to offer."

"Then I'm glad I have you as my tour guide," Stephen joked. He whistled for Sam and took his wife's hand. "By the way, just how long does this transitioning phase last? And what happens next?"

Regina laughed as Sam jumped between them, barking happily before running ahead of them. "It's different for everyone, Stephen. There's no set time, no tasks or quests to accomplish in order to complete it. It's really hard to explain, but you'll know it when it happens because you'll feel it in here." She placed her free hand over her heart. "If you think you feel joy now just being here in Heaven, you won't know what hit you when the final feeling of transition comes over you. It's really indescribable. Words alone don't do it justice, but trust me… you will definitely know when it happens for *you. As to what happens next… well, that's not for us to say, is it? We are simply blessed to be here and to be a part of it all. The best is yet to come…"*

"Wow…" Stephen shook his head, thinking about all she had said. *"You know… there's something else that I've been meaning to ask."*

"Go ahead," Regina said. *"I may not know the answer but I'll try."*

"Well, it's this feeling I have toward Amanda. You're going to think I'm crazy, but it's like, well, you know how much I love her…"

"Yes, I do…" Regina squeezed his hand.

Stephen laughed nervously. *"I mean, she was my life, my sole reason for living after you died, Regina. So… wouldn't you think I would be more… well… worried about her than I am? Or did I do enough of that while I was living?"*

Regina stopped walking, turned to face him, and placed both hands upon the broad shoulders of the man she had loved for so many years, and would continue to love now throughout eternity. *"That's an easy one, love. There are no worries in Heaven, Stephen. It simply will not happen here. There truly is no pain, no worry, no hardship, no strife, and no tears…other than tears of happiness, which you have already experienced with Sam."*

"So that's really true, then? All the stories we heard about Heaven… they weren't just fiction?"

"The Bible is anything but fiction," Regina reminded him. *"If more people realized and accepted that fact, then their earthly lives might run much more smoothly and they wouldn't have to wait until they got to Heaven to experience happiness and bliss."*

Stephen looked down at his wife. *"We experienced happiness and bliss on earth."*

"We also did our share of worrying, didn't we?" she asked. *"As much as we both believed in God, you more than I… there were still so many times that we doubted Him and didn't trust him with our lives, weren't there?"*

Stephen looked ashamed, recognizing the truth in what she said. *"I always loved God with all my being, except when He took you from us."* He bowed his head. *"I hated Him then, truly hated Him."*

Regina lifted his chin and looked deeply into his eyes. "No you didn't, love. You were angry at Him. There's a fine line between hate and anger. That's perfectly understandable, but you never truly hated Him and He knew that. You made sure that Amanda grew up knowing Him, trusting in Him, and loving Him. Look at what a wonderful job you did with her. She is absolutely remarkable, Stephen, and that was YOUR doing. You couldn't have done that had you truly hated God."

Stephen looked around him and whispered. "He's listening, isn't he?"

Regina laughed out loud and ran after Sam. "He hears EVERYTHING!"

"The Lord is good, a stronghold in the day of trouble; and He knows those who trust in Him."

-Nahum 1:7 (NKJV)

CHAPTER 28

The Holy Spirit Reaches Out to Kris

The songs and melodies of Patsy Cline had kept Amanda sole company on the drive back to Monticello. She had attempted to draw Kris out from within her shell; however, after a couple of hours of responses ranging from grunts to mere nods, she decided to give Kris the space she obviously needed. Amanda guessed that seeing the sleeping infant had disturbed her best friend, and she had thanked God that the baby had been sleeping while they were there. Amanda never doubted that a bouncing, laughing baby would have been too much for Kris to handle.

They were within a half hour from Monticello when Amanda asked, "Do you want to stop at the café and grab a bite to eat before we head home?"

Kris looked over at Amanda, and then glanced out at the darkness that had crept upon them without her realizing it. "We're here already?" She glanced down at her Timex and pressed the illuminating light. "Wow, it's almost eight o'clock. Did I fall asleep?"

Amanda shook her head. "Not really, but you have been

in your own little world since we left my old home." There was a slight hesitation before she continued. "I'm really sorry about that, Kris. I wasn't thinking, I guess. If I'd known there was a baby inside, I never would've put you through that. It just felt so good to be in the old neighborhood again, and once I pulled into the driveway, the house pulled me like a magnet. I just had to be inside, one more time. I really am sorry."

Kris waved her off. "Not your fault, Amanda. You had no way of knowing they had a baby."

Another quiet moment passed between them before Kris continued. "That baby was small for five months, don't you think?"

Amanda saw the glow from the café's halo up ahead. "Well, Jack did say that she was a preemie. Preemies are smaller than normal babies, right?"

Kris nodded but didn't respond.

"Café's up ahead," Amanda said. "You hungry or do you want to just go home and fix something there?"

They were in front of the café's parking lot when Kris pointed with the first excitement she had shown all day. "Look, isn't that Dean's car? Let's stop here and get something to eat. Maybe he's heard some news about..."

"You got it!" Amanda grinned as she whipped into the parking lot.

It was the day after Christmas so Amanda wasn't surprised to see only a couple of cars at the café. Dean's car was parked up front, closest to the door, and Amos Brown's pick-up truck was parked next to it. The café van was parked beneath an old oak tree.

The angel chimes sounded when the two women entered the front door. Amanda couldn't shake the feeling that the chimes always made her feel as though she had come home. That's what the café felt like to her, especially now that she didn't really have a home to call her own.

The first sound the women heard when they opened the door was Max's out-of-tune whistling. Even though the whistling was horrible, Amanda recognized the tune immediately and ran forward to join the small group who smiled and beckoned them over.

Amos began singing and the tone of his deep baritone sent tingles of joy and excitement up and down Amanda's spine. He sang the first verse while the others clapped and hummed along. *"I was standing by my window, on a cold and cloudy day, when I saw the hearse come rollin', for to take my mother away..."*

Amanda had rushed to join in but Kris remained by the front door watching them. She thought they all looked absolutely radiant, even Dean, who stood up during the chorus and made his way over to where she stood. He took her by the arm and led her to a vacant stool.

Kris listened attentively while they all sang the chorus a second time, lifting their heads and hands upwards. *"Will the circle be unbroken? By and by Lord, by and by; there's a better home a-waitin', in the sky, Lord, in the sky."* It was a beautiful, uplifting song and Kris, quite unexpectedly, found herself wishing that she knew the words so that she could join in. She had no idea from where that thought came! She grew more entranced with each new verse. She found herself clapping tentatively when Amos got to the last verse. *"We sang the songs of childhood, hymns of faith that made us strong, ones that our mother had taught us, hear the angels sing along."*

By the time the group was ready to sing the last chorus, Kris knew the words and joined in. It was the first time she remembered ever singing along to a song... any song.

Over the next hour, and in between bites of grilled meatloaf sandwiches and garlic mashed potatoes, Dean recounted the events of the day involving the finding of the dark sedan. The vehicle had been towed to the Monticello Police Department, initially, but had immediately been taken to the Tallahassee Crime Lab. Dean had a copy of the kidnappers' note in his pocket and intended to show it to Kris later tonight.

"We've got Mississippi Mud Pie for dessert," Max beamed at the collected group. "Best I ever made if I must say so myself."

Amanda held her belly, which was full after two huge meatloaf sandwiches and an extra-large serving of mashed potatoes. "Oh, that's one of my favorites," she droned, "but I'm stuffed, Max. Is there any chance of getting some of that to go, maybe? I'm so tired... I just want to climb into bed right now. It's been a long day."

"So you made a trip back to Tampa, I hear?" Doug asked Amanda, who had moved into the kitchen to help Max prepare the desserts to go.

She turned excitedly toward him. "Yep, sure did, and it was GREAT! I took Kris to my old neighborhood and was even able to show her the house I grew up in."

"It was vacant, I take it?" Doug asked, avoiding Max's hard glare.

"Oh, put some extra fudge sauce on my piece, will ya, Max, please?" Amanda's attention was focused on dessert but she had heard Doug's question. "Nope, as a matter of fact, there was a couple and their baby living there. Now that I think about it, I don't remember their last name; I'm not sure if they even told us... but their first names were Jack and Susan – really nice people. They even allowed me to give Amanda the grand tour of the place."

"You said they had a baby?" Doug asked, once again managing to ignore the hard stare coming from Max's direction.

"Yep, a little girl, about five months old. Head full of black hair; such a cute little thing, from what I could tell. She slept the whole time we were there. I don't trust my memory, but I think I remember them saying her name was Kelly."

The next question came from Max. "And how did Kris react to that?"

"It may have been the straw that broke the camel's back," Amanda answered; she was totally unaware of the worried look that passed between the two men.

"How's that?" Max asked as he placed the two desserts into a take-out bag. "Careful you don't spill that extra fudge sauce; it's right on top."

"If it spills, I'll lick the bag clean," Amanda joked. "Anyway, Kris was totally quiet on the ride back. I couldn't get her to say two coherent words. I think seeing that baby unnerved her. It was probably cruel and heartless of me to put her through that, but...I wasn't thinking, I guess. But, hey, that's really good news about them finding the sedan, huh? Maybe they'll be able to get some prints or something now... at least have something to go on."

"Dean told us there was a partial print on the baby's car seat and they've already run it through the database," Doug offered. "So far, nothing has popped up."

"So, I guess that just means that the kidnappers aren't registered criminals," Amanda interjected. "That's a good sign, right?"

"Criminals or not, they still kidnapped a child that did not belong to them," Max sighed. "That just makes it harder for the police to narrow down the suspects."

"They have suspects?" Amanda asked hopefully.

"No..." Doug said, shaking his head. "They have nothing, absolutely nothing other than hundreds of erroneous leads coming in every week. Everybody and their uncle have sighted the baby, from here to Timbuktu."

Max placed a hand across Amanda's shoulder. "We'll continue to pray," he smiled down at her. "Prayer is a very powerful tool, indeed."

"I believe that," Amanda nodded. "Now if I could only get Kris to believe in it, too."

"Don't give up on her," Doug said. "You came into her life for a reason, Amanda. You may be the key that turns her life around."

"Well, I don't know about that," Amanda smiled up at Doug. "That's a pretty tall order, but you can bet I won't give up on her. I just know in my heart that Charlotte Grace will be found soon."

When they walked back into the dining room, Bertie and Amos were deep in conversation at the counter. Dean and

Kris were sitting side by side in the booth closest to the entrance. Dean had taken the opportunity, while they had some time to themselves, to tell her about the kidnappers' note. He told her it was up to her whether or not she wanted to share that information with her friends.

The first thing Amanda noticed were the tears streaming down Kris' cheeks. "What's wrong?" she squealed as she slid into the booth opposite the couple. "Dean? Kris? Somebody say something…"

Kris used the back of her hand to wipe away the fresh tears and looked at the woman who had become such an important part of her life - the sister she had always wanted, the best friend she never had. She shook her head and lifted her brows in defeat. "The kidnappers left a note, Amanda. They don't intend on ever giving her back. There will never be a ransom demand, or any other demand… they have taken my baby to raise as their own."

Everyone was within hearing distance of their conversation and Bertie gasped, "Sweet, Jesus!" She looked at Max who shook his head and lifted his shoulders. Even though she and Max knew about the couple who had taken the baby, they did not know why they had done it.

They had all assumed that Charlotte Grace would eventually be returned safe and sound, but after hearing about the kidnappers' note, they were no longer so sure there would be a happy ending to Kris' nightmare.

Amos slid off his stool and ambled over to where the group had gathered; Bertie followed him. He placed one long arm across Bertie's shoulder and the other over Doug's. He looked at all of them and smiled. A sudden sense of peace filled the room when he closed his eyes and said, "Let us pray…"

Kris watched as, one by one, every occupant of the Heavenly Grille Café bowed their heads in prayer. A sudden tightness clenched her chest and she gasped for air; it came quickly enough, and when she finally exhaled she shivered as a new, different sensation began moving deep within her chest. This new feeling wasn't tightness; instead, it felt like something extremely heavy being lifted off her chest - almost a fluid sensation spreading inside her with every intake of air she breathed. The feeling that had begun as a tremulous tightness had loosened, and was replaced with a warm, tingling sensation that moved across her chest, down her arms, and into her fingers. She couldn't begin to explain it if she had to, but it seemed that every breath she took brought her closer to a sense of oneness with something...or someone. She did not know what was happening to her, but...she liked it. The former frantic, panicky feelings were leaving her body, and were immediately replaced with those of peacefulness and calmness.

Kris DeVone bowed her head in prayer for the first time in her life. She had no clue that the Holy Spirit had just touched her very soul.

CHAPTER 29

–New Year's Eve–
Kris Agrees to Church

The last few days of December went by too slowly for Kris. She received daily updates from Dean on the progress, or lack of progress being made with her case. She also returned to work, thinking the distraction would give her mind, and her heart, a temporary reprieve from the constant aching, desperation, and utter aloneness she felt. It amazed her that she was able to feel so alone even though she was constantly surrounded by people, usually Amanda.

Her customers at the coffee house had been especially supportive, and Kris was still uncomfortable in accepting their prayers and blessings. She wasn't sure she was deserving of so many prayers, especially since she had always scoffed at the existence of God and His church. She knew that Amanda had a lot to do in her subtle relinquishing of some of those particular barriers.

Her shift was coming to a close and Kris was wiping down the last of the tables when she heard the shop's front door open. She had her back to the door and didn't immediately turn around. Instead, she yelled out, "Sorry, but we're closing in five minutes..." When she didn't get the response she expected, she turned sharply toward the door, instantly aware that she was working all alone in the coffee shop. Her relief was obvious when she saw Dean standing inside the doorway. Her hand flew to her mouth and she smiled. "Dean!"

Her heart was beating fast against her chest. She wasn't sure if it was from the momentary fear she felt when no one answered her comment about the shop closing, or if it was from the fact that a man she was growing to care deeply about now stood before her, holding a dozen red roses in his hand. She took a quick glance at his clothing, pressed khakis, white shirt, and a black windbreaker, and thought how even more handsome he looked out of uniform. His hair was neat and he appeared to be freshly shaven.

Dean held the roses out to her for inspection, smiled, and said. "Hey, there, Kris. It's... uh... well, it's New Year's Eve and I thought you should start the New Year off with a little color."

Kris wiped her hands on her apron and tucked a loose curl behind her ear. She made her way hesitantly toward Dean and offered a weak smile. She managed to blink back the unshed tears and said, "No one has ever brought me flowers before..." She took the offered roses and inhaled their seductive, yet pure, aroma. "They smell so good. What a nice thing to do; thank you, Dean... thank you very much..."

He placed both hands in his pockets and rocked back and forth. "Hard to believe no one has ever brought you flowers."

Kris smelled the flowers again. "You're sweet..." She couldn't help but smile at his obvious nervousness. "What? What is it?"

Dean removed one hand from his pocket and ran it through his hair. He thought that things had been good between him and Kris since they first met, and he knew that her life was in a complete turmoil at the moment. However, he needed an answer to something that had been weighing on his mind for some time. He needed to know if Kris was experiencing any of the same feelings toward him as he did her. He was afraid to ask her, especially with Charlotte Grace missing, but he knew that he was going to do everything in his power to return the baby to her mother – and when that happened, he needed to know if Kris had any feelings, other than friendship, toward him. "Listen, Kris, I know this is a pretty lousy time in your life, not knowing where Charlotte Grace is and all..."

"Lousy would be a huge understatement," Kris said. She walked over to the counter. "Come on over and have a seat. Do you want some coffee while I finish up here? I'm closing tonight and I want to make sure I get things locked up before any late-night celebrators decide they want to come in here to sober up."

Dean plopped down on the stool. Maybe now wasn't the best time to get answers to his questions. "Sure... coffee sounds good. Why don't you give me the keys and I'll lock the door for you and pull down the shades?"

Kris pulled the keys from her apron pocket and placed them on the counter. "Thanks! You come in pretty handy sometimes, fella. I'll get that coffee for you, but I've gotta warn you... it is the bottom of the pot, so it might be pretty strong."

"I like strong coffee," Dean grinned as he took the keys, locked the door and pulled down the sage and cream-striped shades. He flicked off the outside lights, which also automatically triggered the inside lights to dimmer mode. Dean grinned to himself. "Hmmm... yeah... I guess a little ambience couldn't hurt the situation."

"Did you say something?" Kris asked from the kitchen.

Dean sat down at the counter where Kris had laid the dozen roses. "Nope, sure didn't."

Kris brought him the last cup of coffee which did, indeed, appear to be extremely strong. "If I was a betting woman, I'd be taking bets on whether or not you'll be able to drink this." She laughed softly as she slid onto the stool next to him, lifted the roses, and inhaled slowly. "These really are beautiful, Dean. Thank you, again."

Dean took a large sip of the coffee and almost gagged. "Oh, God! This stuff is awful!"

Kris 'smile became a smirk. "I warned you that it was the bottom of the pot. I could make you a fresh pot if you like."

Dean cleared his throat and looked down the front of his shirt. "Damn... that stuff is strong enough to put hair on a man's chest."

Kris grinned. "I was serious. I'll be glad to put on a fresh pot..."

Dean pushed away the cup of coffee. "Well, actually, that wouldn't be a bad idea, but do you think we could have it at your place instead of here? I mean, it's New Year's Eve and I... well, I didn't know if you would want to be by yourself tonight. If you do, that's okay, I understand..."

Kris stood up and took the cup into the kitchen, rinsed it, and came back to stand beside Dean. "Well, you know... actually, I wasn't going to be by myself. The Heavenly Grille is open all night and Amanda is ringing in the New Year there. She wanted me to stop by on the way home, and I was going to, but now that it's gotten so late... I really don't feel like being around a crowd right now."

"I didn't think you would," Dean smiled at her, thinking for the hundredth time how pretty she was. He loved the way her thick, curly red hair framed her perfect, smooth face that was covered with a few fugitive freckles racing across her nose and cheeks. He reached out and tucked a loose curl behind her ear. "Why don't you call Amanda and tell her know you're not coming, but be sure to let her know that you won't be all alone on New Year's Eve?"

A shiver raced through Kris' body at Dean's touch. She looked up into his dark eyes and felt the genuine warmth that radiated from them. It was the most sincere look she had ever seen on a man's face. She looked at him for another long moment before nodding her agreement. She picked up the roses and said, "I think that sounds like a great idea. Come on, officer, you can follow me home."

"Lead the way, ma'am!" Dean grinned back at her.

The Heavenly Grille was full of its regular customers who had chosen to ring in the New Year with Max's country ham, stir-fried green beans, bacon-macaroni and cheese, hot buttermilk biscuits, red-eye gravy, and his famous seven-layer, fresh coconut cake for dessert.

No alcohol was allowed on the premises, but the café's regular customers didn't seem to mind. They were all there more for the food, singing, and camaraderie than anything else. There was a mixed array of customers spread throughout the café; everyone from the preacher to ditch digger was there, as well as about fifteen of the regular long-distance truckers that frequented the establishment.

Max was in his second Heaven, whistling away in the kitchen.

Doug would stop in the kitchen periodically to help Max with the mounting orders, but most of his time was spent helping Bertie keep up with the seventy customers who packed the place.

The café was almost at its legal capacity for customers; however, the fire chief was one of those customers tonight, and he looked the other way when Bertie and Doug found seats for an extra ten truckers who had stopped by to celebrate.

Although Amanda wasn't scheduled to work the evening shift, she was glad to pitch in and help Bertie and Doug by keeping coffee and drink cups filled to the brim. She loved catching up with all the locals, but her favorite customers had always been the truckers. They all felt like father-figures to her and she knew they genuinely cared about her general well-being. She glanced over at Kris' contributory jar and couldn't believe that it was overflowing, AGAIN! She had already emptied it three times tonight.

Bertie came up behind her and asked, "When is Kris coming? It's almost midnight."

Amanda slapped her forehead. "Oh! I forgot to tell you, Bertie. She called a few minutes ago and said she was going straight home... said she didn't really feel like being with such a big crowd tonight."

"No! That girl can't be by herself, not tonight!" Bertie shook her head.

Amanda laughed. "That was my first thought, too, Bertie; but, don't you go worrying too much about Kris. It turns out that she's not going to be by herself tonight. It would appear that the good and kind Officer Hall has taken it upon himself to, not only bring her roses, but to also make sure she gets home safely tonight."

Bertie's loud laugh filled the café and she punched Amanda's shoulder. "Well, I'll be damned! Heh, heh! I knew I was right about those two. I don't think either one of them really knows it yet, but there is something gonna happen between them, just you wait and see."

Amanda rubbed her shoulder and grinned. "I hope you're right about that, Bertie. Heaven knows that Kris could use someone like Dean in her life."

Bertie punched Amanda's shoulder again and winked. "Oh, sweet, girl, you'd be surprised just how much Heaven knows!"

Kris and Dean sat side by side on the sofa, coffee mugs in hand. She had placed the roses in the only container she had, an acrylic cylinder-shaped one that had recently stored spaghetti noodles. They watched television, listening to Ryan Seacrest, and waited for the ball to drop in Times Square.

"This has been a tough year for you, Kris." Dean held his coffee mug up to hers. "Here's to smoother sailing in 2012. I'm hoping for nothing but good things to happen in your life..."

Kris smiled and clinked cups with him. "You know, I do believe this is the first New Year's Eve that I've welcomed in being... sober."

"Really... the first?" Dean asked incredulously, but smiling.

Kris raised her eyebrows and nodded. "I began drinking at a very young age, Dean. It's all I knew for a long, long time. Alcohol, drugs, and yes... lots of illicit sex, too. Are you sorry you decided to welcome in a new year with someone like that?"

"That may have been who you were once, but...that's not the Kris I know," he said lowering his gaze. When he looked back up into her eyes, he smiled and said. "I don't care about your past. As far as I'm concerned, it only served to make you stronger, to make you into the person sitting beside me now. The person I know is quick-tempered and sharp-tongued, yes, but she's also kind, loving, and compassionate."

"Are we talking about the same person?" Kris laughed. "I don't think I've ever been described using those words, especially compassionate."

"Oh, you're compassionate, Kris, and it started showing more and more after you had Charlotte Grace."

Kris nodded. "Yeah, that little girl definitely made me look at life differently, that's for sure. If you had asked me six months ago, I would've bet you a month's salary that I didn't have a maternal bone in my body. You don't know this, Dean, and I... am so ashamed to say it out loud now... but I was considering giving Charlotte up for adoption so that she could have a better life, a better mother. I don't know what happened, but..."

"You are a wonderful mother, Kris. Charlotte is lucky to have you."

Kris put her cup down and sighed. "That's nice of you to say, but... she doesn't really have me, does she, Dean?"

Dean put his cup down and moved closer to Kris.

She held her breath, not sure of what was happening... not

sure of what might happen in this room tonight.

Dean cupped her face between his hands so that she was forced to look into his eyes. "She will always have you, Kris... always, and I promise you... we will find her soon. She will be back home where she belongs... in her mother's arms."

"I won't hold you to that promise, Dean," Kris sighed again. "I appreciate everything you and the other officers have done. I know they are all doing everything in their power to find her. I'm even beginning to believe something that Amanda is always telling me."

"What's that?" Dean asked, still cupping her face within his palms.

"Something about the power of prayer," she replied.

Dean released her face and nodded for her to continue.

Kris proceeded to tell him about her spiritual experience at the café the day after Christmas. "I don't know how to explain it, Dean, but these past few days I have felt so much calmer and, well... for the first time since this nightmare began, I actually have hope that Charlotte Grace *will* be found."

"You've learned to pray?" Dean beamed and pulled her to him in a light embrace. "That is wonderful, Kris." He held her back slightly and asked, "Would you like to try it again... now?"

"Really... are you serious?" she asked.

The television counted down the last seconds of 2011... five, four, three, two... ONE!

The unexpected kiss caught her completely off-guard, but Kris had to admit that it felt good to be held and kissed by Officer Dean Hall.

"Happy New Year, Kris," he grinned. "What do you say we start it off right?"

Kris tensed up, automatically assuming he was hinting at what every other man in her life expected from her. She was dumbfounded when he, instead, pushed the coffee table away and got down on his knees, pulling her down with him.

She watched in awe as he propped his elbows on the coffee table and looked over at her, nodding for her to follow suit.

The couple folded their hands in prayer and closed their eyes.

"I hope you're listening, God..." Kris prayed silently. *"Please take care of my baby. Let them be kind to her, but please let them do the right thing and bring her home to me."* Kris opened her eyes and saw Dean beaming at her.

"How did it feel?" he asked.

"A little strange," she smiled back at him. "I mean, I have no idea if I'm saying the right words or not, but when I prayed just now, I got that warm feeling in my chest again. Do you think that means He heard my prayer... that He really heard me?"

"Oh, I know He heard you, Kris. In fact, you may not be ready to believe it just yet, but He has heard every word you've ever spoken."

Kris covered her face with her hands and shook her head. "Oh, let's hope that's not true," she grinned. "Some of my words have not been too kind and loving and... what else did you say? Oh, yes... compassionate."

Dean took her face between his hands once again. "He loves us all, unconditionally, Kris. He died for us, for our sins."

"I have so much to learn..." Kris shook her head.

"Well then," Dean said as he pulled her to a standing position and embraced her again. "Why not come to church with me tomorrow and let those lessons begin?"

Amanda had asked her so many times to attend church, but Kris had always declined. She didn't want to say no to Dean. "I think I'm ready for that... yes, I will go with you."

As the couple shared their first real kiss... fireworks erupted on television and throughout the neighborhood.

Kris laid her head on Dean's chest and closed her eyes. She couldn't help but wonder if the ensuing fireworks display outside was God's way of showing his blessings and approval.

CHAPTER 30

–Ida Brooks–
Neighbor to the Petersons

Jack and Susan Peterson had managed to settle into a strained routine with their new baby, Kelly. It was a constant, daily struggle for them both. On one hand, they tried their best to enjoy the bliss and unity that a new baby brought to their lives; while, at the same time, they also felt like they were looking over their shoulders to see if anyone suspected them of the horrible crime they had committed. They talked about the situation, occasionally, but not enough to weigh the scales in either direction.

Jack's new firm was very pro-active in allowing its employees to work from home two days per week, a situation that worked well to Jack's advantage. It gave him the opportunity to be home with Susan and the baby four out of seven days a week. Once Jack confided to his supervisor the truth about Susan's condition, the company had been even more lenient and accommodating with the twice weekly benefit of working from home.

Jack had also told his supervisor the story that he and Susan had concocted about how they came to be parents of a five-month old. His supervisor had been sympathetic when he heard that Jack's brother and sister-in-law had been killed in a car crash three months ago, leaving behind their infant daughter, Kelly. His supervisor commended him and Susan for adopting the baby, being her only living relatives, in spite of Susan's dire chance for survival.

Jack's normal work schedule was to work in the firm's office on Mondays and Wednesdays, and to work from home on Tuesdays, Thursdays, and Fridays. He performed the majority of his work at night time, after Susan and the baby had retired for the night. This allowed him to bear most of the daily care routine involved in raising an infant. They were both reluctant to hire someone to help with the baby on the days that Jack had to go into the office, but, so far, Susan had been able to manage on her own.

Even though the neighborhood was friendly, most of their neighbors were young, working couples who were not there during the day time; or, they were retired folks who spent most of their time indoors. The only neighbor that Jack and Susan had allowed themselves to become friendly with was Mrs. Ida Brooks, who lived in the small, but tidy bungalow-style home next door.

Ida had lived in her home for the past forty-seven years. It was the first, and only, home she and her husband, Herman, had ever lived in. She couldn't bring herself to sell it when he passed away seven years ago.

It was Wednesday, January eighteenth, and Ida Brooks stood at the Peterson's front door holding a covered casserole dish. She adjusted her cardigan and rang her neighbor's bell for the second time. Their car wasn't in the driveway, but Ida knew that Mr. Peterson worked on Wednesdays, so she assumed that Mrs. Peterson must be home alone.

"Oh, dear," she thought to herself. *"Maybe the poor woman is napping..."* She had convinced herself that nobody was going to answer the door and, just as she was about to leave,

she heard a slight scuffling from within. She peered through the beveled-glass window on the front door, and could make out Susan's tiny frame.

Susan opened the door only wide enough to poke her head out. "Oh, it's you, Mrs. Brooks. It's so good to see you." She opened the door a bit wider. "How are you today?"

Ida paled when she saw how much Susan Peterson's appearance had deteriorated since the family moved into the old Turner home. "Oh, I'm just fine and dandy," Ida smiled. She noticed that Susan carried the baby in the crook of her arm. She smiled and said, "My goodness... I can't get over how big... and so pretty... she's getting."

Ida almost dropped the casserole dish when it appeared that Susan's left arm was weakening beneath the weight of the baby. "Oh, my! Why don't we switch, dear? Here, you take this hamburger casserole I made for you and your husband, and let me hold that sweet bundle for you. Is that alright?"

Ida couldn't be sure, but it looked like relief that quickly spread across Susan's face.

Susan reluctantly offered the baby to her neighbor in return for the lighter casserole dish.

Her response was weak. "Well... maybe for just a moment. Please... won't you come inside, Mrs. Brooks? It's a little cool out today."

"Well," Ida smiled back at her. "The weather man said it was sixty-seven degrees, so you might get some argument on that from all these snowbirds in the area."

Once inside, Ida took the casserole dish from Susan and sat it on a side table in the foyer. She adjusted the baby in her arms and walked behind Susan into the great room.

Susan motioned toward a comfortable looking, overstuffed rocking chair. "Please, Mrs. Brooks... why don't you sit there with the baby? She loves to be rocked."

"Why, thank you dear," Ida smiled as she sat down and readjusted the baby into the crook of her left elbow.

Charlotte Grace cooed and smiled up at Ida Brooks. She

reached out and held onto the old woman's offered finger and began sucking on it

"Just look at this precious angel," Ida beamed. "I think she's hungry, dear. Is it time for a feeding?"

Susan had turned back to the foyer to retrieve the casserole dish. She turned and looked around absently, almost in a daze. "Feeding?"

"Why, yes, dear. I think she's hungry. If you'll show me where her bottle is, I will be more than happy to feed her. You look like you could use a break."

Judging from the concerned look on her neighbor's face, Susan could only assume that she looked as tired as she felt. She placed the casserole on the counter and retrieved a bottle from the refrigerator. She glanced at the clock on the microwave. It was already two o'clock. She usually fed the baby around noon, but for the life of her, Susan couldn't remember if she had missed the feeding or not. She shook her head and squeezed her eyes hard enough to see stars. "I don't know where the day has gone. Yes, she probably is hungry. Thank you so much for your help, Mrs. Brooks," she mumbled as she handed her neighbor the bottle and sat down on the adjacent love seat.

Charlotte reached out eagerly for the offered bottle and Mrs. Brooks smiled down at her. "Why she's guzzling it right down." She smoothed the baby's dark hair out of her eyes. "I do believe this baby has the blackest hair I've ever seen on an infant," she said, more to herself than to Susan.

The comment about the baby's hair immediately arrested Susan's grogginess. She realized that she must have dozed off before Mrs. Brooks' arrival. The baby's disgruntled cooing had shaken her awake. It suddenly dawned on her that not only had she missed the baby's noon feeding, but she had also missed taking her own noon prescription doses. It seemed to her that all she wanted to do these days was to sleep, and she wondered if it was the cancer or the medication causing it.

"You look so tired, dear," Mrs. Brooks clucked. "You

189

know, it's very important that you get some rest whenever the baby is sleeping. I was never blessed with children of my own, but I helped my sisters plenty with their own broods, and I babysat quite often with the little girl that used to live in this very house. I had more energy back then, but I know how much the little tykes can wear you down."

"You mean, Amanda?" Susan almost slurred her words.

Ida looked up in total surprise. "Why, yes! Her name was Amanda. How did you know that?"

Somewhere in Susan's drugged brainwaves, a warning flashed to her that she was talking too much. She pushed a strand of thin brown hair away from her face. "I... I... don't know," she lied. "I must have heard it from someone in the neighborhood..." Susan brushed her hair away again and suppressed a gasp when she saw how many loose strands remained in her hand. She lowered her hand, nonchalantly, to the floor and shook off the loose hair. Jack had told her more than once how important it was that they keep her sickness a secret for as long as possible. She looked up and smiled at her elderly neighbor. "Yes, you're right... the little ones can definitely wear us down... but, they are worth it."

Ida smiled at the obvious love the woman had for her child, at how her tired eyes lit up when she talked about the baby. "I'm sure it is," Ida agreed as she picked Charlotte up and held her against her shoulder. The baby soon released a soft burp. "There we go... such a good baby," she grinned.

Susan watched Ida play with the baby for several more minutes. She knew that she should take the baby and put her in the playpen, away from Ida's watchful eye, but the loveseat felt so comfortable. She felt such a sense of reprieve in having someone else assuming responsibility for the baby's comfort and safety.

Feeling the need to make conversation, Susan cleared her throat and said, "Thank you so much for the casserole, Mrs. Brooks. That was very thoughtful of you."

Ida nodded, still playing with the baby. "Well, dear, I thought it might be a nice break for you, not having to worry about tending to the baby and fretting on what to serve for dinner tonight. Besides, I always make too much; I still haven't learned to cook for only one person. My freezer is full, so I thought I would bring you the extra casserole. I doubled the recipe without even realizing it."

It was a small, white lie on Ida's part. She just felt sorry for the frail-looking woman and the baby. "Is there anything else I can do for you while I'm here?"

Susan had closed her eyes momentarily. She wished she could sleep for twenty-four hours; surely by then she would have the energy she needed to take care of the baby while Jack was away at work. Instead, she swung her feet slowly to the floor and smiled. "You've already done too much, Mrs. Brooks. Thank you, again." Once she found herself in a standing position, the room began a slow spin, and Susan wobbled unsteadily and almost lost her balance. She caught the edge of the end table to steady herself.

Ida had jumped up and reached out to Susan with her free hand. "Susan, dear... what's wrong? My... but... you don't look well at all, dear."

Susan exhaled and stood as erect as her frail, petite frame allowed. It was easier to breathe when she stood erect, but more often than not, she simply did not have the energy to push her body to do so. She made a fluttering motion with her hands. "It's nothing, really, just a winter cold I get every January... saps all my energy..."

Ida looked down at the now contented baby in her arms. "I know what you mean, dear. Colds affect me the same way." She rocked the baby in her arms. "Her eyes are fighting to stay open. Where would you like me to put her down?"

Susan motioned to the playpen in the corner of the room. "Over there will be fine. Thank you, Mrs. Brooks."

Ida placed the baby on her stomach and covered her with a light blanket. "She should be fine for another couple of hours. What time does your husband get home from work, dear?"

Susan's conception of time was totally disoriented. "Oh, he should be here within the hour," she lied. "We'll be fine. Maybe I'll even take your advice and take a nap along with Kelly."

"I think that's a fine idea, dear," Ida nodded. "Why don't you go ahead and lie down? I can let myself out. I noticed a pad on the kitchen counter. I'm going to write my number down for you, and I want you to be sure to call me if you ever need any help at all, you hear?"

Susan was already horizontal on the couch, her eyes closing. "Thank you…"

Ida wrote her number on the pad and made her way to the front door.

Once outside, she looked upward at the darkening clouds forming above. A storm was coming.

A shiver suddenly passed over Ida. She pulled her cardigan tightly around her. "Lord, please keep that little baby safe," she whispered, "And her mama, too."

The loud, booming thunder made her jump and the subsequent, brilliant flash of lightning that ripped through the afternoon sky made her hurry across the lawn to her own home.

Torrential rain flooded the neighboring streets for the next two hours while Ida kept a lookout for Jack Peterson's car. She saw the Peterson car pull into the driveway at four-thirty. Ida sighed and exhaled deeply. "My, goodness, but the angels in Heaven are shedding a lot of tears today," she muttered as she finally closed her blinds and made her way to her small kitchen.

Another flash of lightning lit up her entire living room, causing her to jump. "And it looks like they're not finished yet…"

Yes, indeed… a storm was coming.

CHAPTER 31

Max Reveals His True Identity

Amanda awoke from another dream with her parents. It had been an especially pleasant dream because, for once, they weren't trying to warn her of anything. Instead, she felt like she was running along beside them as they chased one another through the most colorful, flower-filled meadow Amanda had ever seen. There was nothing on earth to compare to the glorious color that filled the meadow.

Amanda was thrilled when she saw her old dog, Sam, running alongside them one minute, and bounding in front of them the next. Arthritis wasn't slowing old Sam down in the dream; his hips appeared to be youthful and completely free of pain – unlike his final days before they had to put him down.

She wanted nothing more but to remain in the dream forever, to be reunited with her parents and her dog – what more could anyone want?

Sam's barking was growing fainter, as was the laughter between her parents. Amanda tried to get back to the meadow, but the dream was ending. Amanda reluctantly opened her eyes, stretched her arms above her head, and glanced sideways at her alarm clock. "It should be going off right about... NOW!" she grinned as she reached over and hit the off button. "Good morning, Lord!" she smiled as she stretched again. "I hope you gain lots of recruits today and your disappointments are few."

Amanda made her way to the kitchen; she thought she might put a pot of coffee on before she jumped in the shower. She was surprised to find the kitchen lights on and Kris already awake and sitting at the kitchen table. "Well, hey there, you! Whatcha doin' up so early?"

Kris ran her fingers through her hair and smiled back at Amanda. "Actually, I haven't been to bed yet." She nodded toward the coffee pot. "I just put on a fresh pot."

"Oh, bless you!" Amanda grinned as she searched for her favorite green, travel mug. It was as old as dirt, but it was the only cup with a lid that never leaked. It was also her very first coffee mug, and had been a gift from her father. They had shared a cup of coffee every morning from the time Amanda turned fifteen until the week before her father died. Amanda poured her coffee and returned to the table. She was shocked, and pleasantly surprised, to see her Bible lying open on the kitchen table.

Kris had been reading Amanda's Bible.

Amanda took a deep breath and offered up a quick, silent prayer of thanks.

Kris knew that Amanda was trying to hide her look of surprise, but she saw it immediately on her friend's face. She glanced down at the Bible and back up at Amanda. "I hope you don't mind. I was all keyed up after getting off work last night. Dean came over and we sat around for hours talking about some new leads that have come in. He helped me get my thoughts together about the next public announcement I'll be making next week. Anyway... after he left, I just couldn't get to sleep so I put on some coffee and tried to watch television. I read every magazine in the house, dusted all the furniture..."

"Sounds like it was a productive night for you," Amanda grinned.

Kris stared at her best friend for a long moment before continuing, "Today's the second of February, Amanda. It's been almost two months since my baby..."

Amanda walked over to Kris' chair and put her arm across her friend's shoulders. "I know... but they're going to find her, Kris. I feel that with every fiber of my being. You've got to stay strong and keep believing that she is coming home."

Kris nodded. "Yeah, well... I'm working on that. I have to admit...my faith in her coming home to me is stronger today than it was a month ago." She patted the open Bible with her fingertips. "I think this is helping..."

"I'm so glad, Kris." Amanda was trying not to let her emotions get the best of her. "Have you been praying, too?"

"Are you kidding?" Kris laughed. "Ever since that first Sunday I went to church with Dean, I've been down on my knees every day, talking to God... not so much for myself, because I'm still not sure he's all that concerned about my well-being... but, more along the lines of Him just keeping Charlotte Grace safe and healthy. Kris paused for a long moment before she said, "There is one thing I haven't been able to do, though..."

"What's that?" Amanda asked as she pulled her chair around to sit beside Kris. She glanced down at the Bible and noticed that it was turned to the Book of Psalms.

"Forgiveness..." Kris replied, shaking her head. "Amanda, I don't know if I'll ever have it in my heart to forgive these people for what they've done. How do you forgive someone who has completely turned your world apart, ripped out your very heart... how?"

Amanda nodded toward the Bible. "Through the grace of God, that's how. You're reading my favorite book in the Bible, Psalms. Why don't you turn to Chapter 30, verse 5, I think..."

"Leave it to you to have the damn book memorized," Kris smiled. She flipped over a few pages and found the chapter and verse. She looked over at Amanda.

"Go ahead," Amanda nodded. "Read it out loud."

Kris shrugged. "Okay, if you say so." She took a deep breath before continuing. "For His anger is but for a moment, His favor is for life; weeping may endure for a night, but joy comes in the morning."

Amanda smiled and nodded. "Now go to chapter 118, verse 6."

Kris flipped through several more pages and read, "The Lord is on my side; I will not fear. What can man do to me?"

"Amanda, what..." Kris began.

Amanda put her finger to her lips and shook her head. "Okay...just one more that I've memorized over the years. Go to Ecclesiastes, Chapter 12, verses 13 and 14."

"I'm glad you've got these tabs on your Bible," Kris grumbled, "Or else, it would take me forever to find anything. Even with the tabs, it took her a few moments to find the book of Ecclesiastes. "I don't think I've read anything in this book yet," she mumbled. She found the chapter and verses Amanda had quoted and read them aloud. "Let us hear the conclusion of the whole matter: fear God and keep His commandments, for this is man's all. For God will bring every work into judgment, including every secret thing, whether good or evil." Kris looked up from her reading. "How in the Hell have you memorized all these? I can't remember most of what I read an hour ago."

Amanda smiled and sipped at her coffee. "The more you get into it, Kris, the more sense it will make. You'll discover favorite verses, favorite stories, and, you will want to go back to those again and again."

"Hmm..." Kris mumbled. "That last one there – is it telling me that it's not up to me to judge these people who took Charlotte? Does that mean that it's okay I'll never be able to forgive them for what they've done?"

"That's right, Kris. It's not our place to judge," Amanda nodded, "These people, if they go to Heaven, will have to stand before God one day and be judged by Him for the things they have done. It's not our place to know their hearts, or to understand why they've done the things they've done."

"And will God forgive them for what they've done?"

Amanda nodded. "If they are truly repentant for what they've done and ask His forgiveness, then... yes, He will forgive them."

"Just like that, huh?" Kris sounded bitter. "Well, I guess He's gonna be pretty pissed with me because I'll never forgive the bastards..."

Amanda kept quiet for several minutes. She watched as Kris first closed the Bible and then her eyes. Her best friend looked so very tired. "The forgiveness is for your benefit, Kris, not for the kidnappers. You won't have a choice. If you're going to be able to move forward with your life, then you have no choice... you will have to forgive them. If you don't, then it will be like a poison slowly eating away at your insides. For your sake, and for Charlotte Grace's sake, you will eventually have to come to a place in your heart where you truly do forgive them."

"Well," Kris said as she shoved her chair away from the table. "I can tell you one thing for certain. That day won't be today." She rubbed the bridge of her nose and yawned softly. "I'm going to bed now. Why don't you stop by the coffee shop tonight and I'll treat you to one of those giant cinnamon rolls you love so much?"

"I just may do that," Amanda grinned. "Get some rest."

An hour later Amanda bounded through the café's front door, grinning as the angelic chimes announced her entrance. "Good morning, everyone!"

"It's just me this morning," Max yelled back from the kitchen. "Get yourself in here and sample this omelet casserole. If you like it, I'm going to add it to the menu tomorrow morning."

"Where is everyone?" Amanda asked. "I mean, I know

they don't have to be here first thing in the morning, but I don't think Bertie and Doug have missed a morning yet since I started working here."

"Oh, they'll be back any minute now. They were listening to the CB radio in the back and heard there was a crash on the interstate involving one of our regular truckers."

"Oh, no!" Amanda cried.

Max waved his hand and shook his head. "No, no, he's okay. It's just a small fender bender, or at least as small a fender bender can be on an eighteen-wheeler." Max grinned. "They rode out to take him some coffee and biscuits while he's waiting to settle things."

"Aw, that is so nice of them," Amanda shook her head. "You know... both of them... Doug and Bertie... they're always there to help when someone needs it."

"Well, now, isn't that the way it should be?" Max asked. "Folks helping one another and not expecting anything in return?"

Amanda's eyebrows rose in mock disbelief. "I wish!"

Max handed her a plate filled with the steaming casserole. "It has to start somewhere, Amanda. One good turn deserves another."

Amanda was quiet while she shoveled the omelet casserole into her mouth. She closed her eyes and savored the rich, buttery flavor mingled with cheeses, country ham bits, and scallions. "Oh, Max..." she sighed, her eyes rolling back into her head.

"I take it that you approve of the casserole?" Max grinned. "I'll make sure it gets put on tomorrow's menu. There's some chocolate milk in the fridge if you want something to wash it down."

"Just coffee, please. Chocolate milk might interfere with all these scrumptious flavors."

Max began wiping down the counters and looked at the clock. "The parking lot should start filling up any time now. By the way, I've been meaning to ask you... I heard that Kris has started going to church. Is that true?" Of course, Max already knew the answer to his question.

Amanda stopped chewing and perked up. "You heard right! That is most definitely true! I've been meaning to tell y'all about that, but I always seem to get side-tracked. Oh, and get this, Max... I found her reading my Bible this morning."

"You don't say?" Max grinned. "Now that really brings a smile to my soul."

Amanda nodded. "She's changing, Max. I can see it a little more every day. She still has a long way to go, but I think she is learning to depend on the power of prayer."

"Well, that is a blessing, indeed," Max smiled.

Amanda nodded. "Yes, it is, but... like I said... she has a long way to go."

"It will take time, Amanda," Max interjected.

"I know, and, well... I know she has reason to be angry with the people who took Charlotte Grace, but, I think... well, I think she's going to have a hard time letting go of the hate she has for them. I'm not sure she will ever be able to forgive them, Max. Nope, forgiveness may never come for them... not from Kris, anyway."

"It may seem that way now, but... forgiveness will come in time," Max reassured her. "Once she gets a firm grip on her faith, forgiveness will soon follow. It's inevitable."

"You sound pretty sure about that..." Amanda began, "But how can you be so sure it will happen for Kris?"

Max had his back to Amanda but he had heard her last question. He was about to do something that went against the rules, especially his own rules. He had only done it a few times in the past hundred years, but he felt the timing was right; and, he felt that Amanda was the right person to see it.

"Oh... my... God!" Amanda's hands flew to her mouth and she gasped loudly when Max turned back around to face her. She almost choked on her last bite of omelet. She watched in awe and amazement as the most brilliant hue of gold she had ever seen emanated from Max's entire body.

"Oh... my... God..." Amanda repeated as she gulped in

more air before falling to her knees.

    Max chuckled. "Well, no... I'm not God, but..."

CHAPTER 32

Contact with the Kidnappers

Amanda remained in a kneeling position, utterly transfixed at the transformation taking place before her very own eyes. She was so mesmerized at what was happening that she didn't hear the door chimes sound; so, she wasn't immediately aware of Amos Brown's presence behind her, filling the doorway to the kitchen. She never once took her eyes off Max; she couldn't have even if she had wanted to – which she didn't. She knew her mouth was hanging open in awe but she was powerless to close it. She didn't dare blink and she wasn't sure when she had taken her last breath.

Amanda decided that breathing might be a good thing, so she slowly closed her mouth and inhaled deeply through her nose. She felt someone kneeling down beside her and finally glanced over when a large, black hand rested upon her own.

Amos had quickly joined her on the floor. His eyes were also glued upon the glorious transformation taking place less than ten feet from him. He shook his head gently from side to side and mumbled, "Oh, sweet, Jesus…" He closed his eyes, silently wishing that his father and brother were here to witness and share this blissful scene with him.

While Amos' eyes remained closed in silent prayer, Amanda continued to stare at the man before them whose feet now floated a good foot off the ground. She marveled at the shards of gold and white beams that seemed to burst all around him, serving to illuminate his presence. Even though Amanda saw neither wings nor a halo, there was no doubt in her own mind that an angelic presence now stood before her and Amos.

"Max?" she whispered, pulling her hand from beneath Amos' touch, and holding it up toward Max.

Amos's head was still bent in prayer, his eyes squeezed shut, and both hands now folded tightly against his chest.

Max floated slowly downward until his feet were firmly planted on the kitchen floor. He held both hands out toward them and smiled, "Please... both of you... come on, get up off that floor. Trust me, there's only one person deserving of your worship, and... that person is, most definitely, not me!" Max directed his next smile to Amanda. "Amanda, why don't you help Amos stand up?"

Amanda reached over blindly, feeling for Amos' hand, still not daring to take her eyes off Max. Somehow, she managed to assist Amos to a standing position; or was Amos the one helping her to a standing position? She blinked hard as it suddenly dawned on her that Amos did not appear to be as shocked as she was at Max's angelic transformation. True, he had not said a word since mumbling "*Oh, sweet, Jesus*", but there was a soothing calmness about him that she was lacking entirely. Amanda looked deep into Amos's soulful brown eyes, glanced back at Max, and returned her attention back to Amos. "Oh, my God! You knew?" she choked. "How... why didn't..."

She looked back at Max, an angel, whose feet now touched the same floor she and Amos stood upon. She followed Amos's suit and squeezed her eyes tightly closed. "Good Lord... I think I need another cup of coffee..."

Amos nodded his head and grinned his toothless grin. "That's a mighty good idea, Miss Amanda... yes ma'am...maybe coffee is what we's all need right about now..."

The golden glow was gone.

Max was just Max again.

He walked over, stood between Amos and Amanda, and placed a hand upon each of their shoulders. "You deserve an explanation, Amanda, and I promise we will sit down and discuss this at length later, but, I'm afraid we just do not have time for that right now. I do realize that I probably didn't pick the best time to reveal myself to you, but I also know it was the right thing to do."

"Uh-huh..." Amanda nodded.

Max grinned and hugged her tight. "I also know that I can trust you... and Amos... to keep this little revelation to yourselves."

While Amos and Amanda remained in a subdued, dumbfounded state of mind, Max rubbed his hands together and grinned. "Well, alright then, we have work to do. The café will be filling up any moment now and we've got a lot of hungry mouths to feed this morning. Oh, and by the way, Princess... yes, it is true... Amos did know the truth about me." He smiled again and watched as Amanda opened her eyes, only to immediately close them again, shaking her head in obvious disbelief. "Open your eyes, Amanda. It's true. I am a messenger of God, not a Heavenly angel, per se, but an angel nonetheless. I have been around for a very, very long time."

Amanda opened her eyes at the same time Amos squeezed her hand tightly in support. "I honestly don't know what to say. I mean... I keep waiting for someone to pop out with a camera and say that I've been punked or something... that maybe I've been part of a reality show all these months and didn't know it, but..." She looked over at Amos who was beaming from ear to ear. "And, you! You knew..."

"Well, let's just say, it be something I kinda suspected for a while now. It's a long story, Miss Amanda," Amos nodded. "And, I's be proud and glad to tells you all about it sometime soon."

"Oh you can bet you will!" Amanda grinned as her mind finally began to accept the reality of what was happening. She looked up at Max and took a deep breath. "Okay, so...you're an angel... okay... yep, you're an angel. So... now that I've seen you transform yourself from a greasy spoon cook to an angelic being, I'm guessing that you just expect me to go out there, work all day, and pretend like this is just another normal day at work, right?"

Max laughed a deep, bellowing laugh. "I know it is a lot to ask, Princess, but, for now... well, yes, that is what I need you to do. Besides, that is what we hired you for, right?"

Amanda threw up her hands and nodded her head. She wanted to give Max a hug but now that she knew he wasn't just her boss, and not just a cook at an out-of-the-way diner, she wasn't sure how appropriate that might be. "Okay, okay... I think I can do that, but... I do have one question that has to be answered right NOW..."

Max watched her pretty face pucker into one of stubborn determination. "Why does that not surprise me? I already know what you're going to ask, Amanda; and, yes... Bertie and Doug are angels, too."

"I knew it!" Amanda shouted. "I knew Doug was too handsome and good to be just one of the guys. Bertie, though? Now, that's definitely a surprise!" She turned to leave, arm in arm, with Amos.

"Oh... and, Amanda?" Max's voice had a teasing quality to it.

Amanda turned back and saw his beaming smile. "Yes?"

"It's okay, you know...you can hug me if you'd like."

"Oh, no..." Amanda sighed with slumped shoulders. "You can read minds, too!"

* * * *

Kris had slept soundly until one o'clock that afternoon when she heard the mailman dropping her mail into the metal box outside the front door. She roused herself slowly, splashed some cold water on her face, put on another pot of coffee, and padded to the front door to collect the mail.

It felt strange, after so many weeks of not noticing whether the sun rose or set, but the first thing that grabbed Kris' attention when she opened the door was the sound of birds singing and dogs barking playfully in the distance. It suddenly dawned on her that her mind must have temporarily shut down to the daily sounds of routine life.

Something felt different for her now. Since she had been attending Dean's church and reading Amanda's Bible, she had begun to experience a slow, gradual loosening of the overwhelming tightness within her chest. That was the only way she could describe the feeling; that tight, constriction of her heart seemed to be dissipating slowly.

Kris smiled as she watched two neighboring pups chase each other along their adjoining fence line. The smiling sensation felt strange upon her lips, but she liked it. She sighed deeply, took one last look at the pups, and reached inside the mailbox to collect the day's mail.

She tossed the mail onto the kitchen table, pulled out a frying pan, and gathered the ingredients to make a grilled cheese and bacon sandwich to go along with her coffee. Her appetite was slowly returning along with a distant, but still dull, sense of hope. She wasn't quite sure from where that sense of hope generated, but she assumed that her daily prayers had a lot to do with her newly-found sense of optimism.

She cut her sandwich into quarters and sat down at the table. She took several sips of coffee while she sorted through the mail. "Bills, junk mail, more bills..." she muttered, until she picked up the last envelope in the stack.

She couldn't explain it, but something about the envelope caused the hairs to stand up on her arms. It did not appear to be junk mail. There was no return address, and her own name and address had been typed in large, bold, black lettering. She started to open it, and then decided it must be junk mail. She was about to toss it, unopened, with the other junk mail, but a sudden shiver coursed through her. She suddenly knew that this letter was not junk mail.

Kris turned the letter over and over, unable to explain her quickening heartbeat. Her hands began to tremble as she slid her finger under the sealed seam. Her heart rate increased and she could feel it pounding against her chest wall as she slowly opened the letter. She closed her eyes briefly before looking inside and removing a single, typewritten page; a Polaroid picture was wrapped inside that single, typewritten page. Kris turned the picture over; it was a picture of a smiling baby with curly red locks, her hands reaching upward.

It was a picture of her baby… a picture of Charlotte Grace.

Kris didn't know how long she sat at the table looking at the picture as tears rolled freely down her face. It felt like hours, but it was only a couple of minutes before Kris placed a call to Dean and read him the letter from the kidnappers.

Her next call was to Amanda at the Heavenly Grille.

"Who the Hell still uses a Polaroid camera?" she marveled out loud, while she waited for her reinforcement team to arrive.

Amanda hung up her cell phone and stared at Max, Bertie, and Doug.

"What?" Bertie asked. "You look like you've seen a ghost, Amanda! What's wrong, Princess?"

Amanda quickly relayed the news about the letter and picture Kris had received.

"Well, what the Hell are you two waiting for?" Bertie demanded.

Max and Bertie shooed Doug and Amanda out the café door. "Don't y'all worry about the café; we've got it covered.

You just be sure to keep us posted on what's going on!" Bertie yelled after them.

Bertie looked over at Max and sighed. "Well, I wonder what possessed the kidnappers to send a letter like that?" She shook her head and looked up at the gentle giant standing beside her. "From what I hear, it's been quite a day, big fella, hasn't it?"

Max knew that Bertie was referring to more than just the letter and picture Kris had received from the kidnappers. He nodded and tried to ignore Bertie's implication of his transformation before Amanda. "There's a reason that letter was mailed, Bertie, and it just might be the break that everyone has been praying for…one way or another, I have a feeling that things are coming to a head pretty soon. Yes, indeed, it has been quite a day." He turned to go back into the kitchen area. "But, it's not over yet, and we still have a room full of customers to take care of, so just keep all those opinions to yourself…at least until we get a break."

Bertie grinned and punched him on the shoulder when he turned away from her. "Humph! Don't you go thinking that you're getting off that easy, either. You have a lot of explaining to do, Maximus – maybe not to me, necessarily, although I'll be glad to lend an ear if you feel like talking about it. You know how much I love a good story. Yessirree, you can be sure I've got one or two opinions to discuss with you, alright!"

Amanda pushed open the front door and rushed inside the duplex.

Doug was right behind her, trying to keep up.

Dean had already arrived and was sitting beside Kris, looking very professional in his crisp, dark uniform.

Two other officers, one male and one female, were also in the room. They appeared to be discussing the contents of the evidence which was now secured in separate, plastic bags.

Dean had used Amanda's printer to make copy of the letter, and the other officers were going to rush it, and the picture, to the Tallahassee crime lab for further testing.

The two officers nodded to Amanda and Doug as they passed them on their way out the door.

Amanda waited for the officers to close the door. "I can't believe it!" she gushed as she ran over and put her arms around Kris. "They actually sent you a letter? Can I see it, or did those other cops take it with them?"

Dean motioned to the single piece of paper lying on the coffee table. "They took the original for testing, but we made a copy of it." He looked over at Kris. "Is it okay for them to read it?"

"Of course it is..." Kris said, blowing out a giant breath she hadn't been aware she'd been holding inside. She squeezed her fingers tightly around Amanda's hand.

"Just checking," Dean grinned awkwardly as he handed the paper to Amanda.

Doug moved to stand behind Amanda and Kris, who sat close together on the sofa.

Amanda turned the paper over and began to read the kidnappers' letter. She positioned it to where Doug could also read it from his position behind her. They both read the letter, in stunned silence, to themselves.

Kris Devone,

We have watched and listened to your constant pleas on television for the safe return of your baby girl, and our hearts go out to you for the suffering you must be going through. However, we believe with all our hearts that we can offer your baby a much better life than she would have with you. We know your story. We know your baby is illegitimate, and we think she deserves so much more. She deserves a mother AND a father who will love her and raise her in the eyes and glory of our Lord. As you can see from her picture, she is very happy in her new home. We are taking extremely good care of her and will continue to love her as our own. We do not desire to cause you any more pain by sending this letter; rather, it is simply our way of reassuring you that your daughter is happy, healthy, and safe. We know we may have taken a stupid risk in mailing this letter, but we are good Christians, and felt that we needed to give your heart some peace in knowing that your baby is in good hands. We hope that you will be able to move on with your life, maybe even have other children one day. For your sake, and the baby's, we pray that you will be able to do this.

Amanda turned the letter over and looked at the coffee table. "They sent a picture? Where? Where is it?"

Kris shrugged and pushed her face together between her open palms. "The other officers took it with them to the crime lab."

"Oh, Kris," Amanda almost cried. "How did she look? It was really Charlotte Grace, right? I mean, of course it must have been Charlotte Grace…"

The tears began flowing down Kris' cheeks. "Oh, Amanda… she was so, so beautiful. She looked a little bigger, and her hair is starting to curl some…" Kris gulped in air and tried to catch her breath.

Amanda moved even closer and rocked back and forth with Kris in her arms. "This is a good sign. They're going to find her, Kris," she smiled as tears rolled down her own face. "I have such a good feeling about this." Amanda looked over at Dean and asked, "Right, Dean?"

Dean didn't hesitate. "Absolutely," he nodded, trying hard to retain a professional composure. "Absolutely… as a matter of fact, we're now fairly certain that Charlotte Grace might still be in Florida."

"Really? What makes you think that?" Doug asked calmly.

Dean looked at Kris who smiled back at him. "Well… because of the post mark on the letter. The idiots mailed it from Tampa. We'll be focusing all our resources in that area now."

Doug shook his head in disbelief. "That's wonderful

news."

"Tampa?" Amanda asked, a hoarseness creeping into her voice. She looked over at Kris, wondering if she was thinking the same thing that had just crossed her mind. "We were just there a month or so ago…"

Kris nodded as fresh tears moved down her drenched cheeks. "We were in the same city as my baby girl, Amanda. We were so close…"

CHAPTER 33

–Heaven–
Doug Returns Home

I t was Sunday, February 5, 2012 and the souls in Heaven were rejoicing with gleeful gusto. Max and Bertie listened to the singing and laughter along with Martin and Doug. They smiled at each other, content in the weekly fellowship that renewed their Heavenly spirits.

It was Doug's first trip back Home since he had taken the assignment at the Heavenly Grille. As much as he had wanted to make the trip Home today, his first thought was that he should remain behind to keep a close eye on Amanda and Kris. He still had no clue how things would unfold, but something in his gut told him that things were coming to a head soon and he wanted to be there to support them whenever that happened.

Bertie and Max had been quick to reassure him that the trip Home would do him good and give him the strength he would need to help the two young women who had become like sisters to him.

Martin placed an arm around Doug's shoulder. "I'm really glad you decided to come Home today, Doug. It's been a while…"

Doug nodded and looked around him, listening again to the

wonderful, happy sounds of all the reunited souls. "Too long, I think... with everything going on down on earth, it's easy to forget sometimes how good it feels to be here."

Martin raised his eyebrows in disbelief. "Only six months and you've forgotten us!"

"I suppose that was a bad choice of words," Doug grinned. "No, I could never forget all this," he added as his eyes took in the white serenity that enveloped them. "I think I understand now why Bertie and Max come Home every Sunday. The feeling is amazing. I'm already feeling... how do I describe it... recharged!"

Max made his way over to the two men and joined in the group hug. "Oh, it definitely does that, my boy. Bertie and I feel like we can conquer anything back on earth after spending just a few hours back Home."

Bertie's eyes had been closed as she listened to the joyous reunions taking place throughout Heaven. There were fathers and sons, mothers and daughters, sisters and brothers...all being reunited once again. She knew that before she left here today that she would spend some time with her own family; they were all there now - her mother, father, siblings, husband, her two precious children and even a couple of her grandchildren. Oh how she loved these reunions! She opened her eyes and smiled, took a deep breath, and slowly made her way across the space to join her friends. She punched each of them on the shoulder. "So, Martin, you old geezer...have you told our Dougie why it was so important that he come Home with us today?"

Martin rubbed his shoulder. Oh, how he wished he could cure Bertie of that nasty habit. If pain was possible in Heaven, he was sure he would be black and blue by now from Bertie's constant punching. "Not yet, but since you've gone and spoiled the surprise, why don't you tell him?"

"Don't mind if I do!" Bertie laughed loudly. She took Doug by the elbow and guided him to the far right edge of the area they were occupied. Gold trails extended in all directions as far as the eye could see. "Do you hear them, Dougie? Listen to how happy everyone is."

Doug nodded. "It's good to hear it again, Bertie. Something about their laughter just calms the soul, doesn't it? I really hadn't realized how much I missed it all... until now. I promise I won't stay away so long from now on; I will definitely have to make more trips Home with you and Max. That's a promise."

Bertie punched him as Max and Martin moved in behind them. "Yeah, yeah, everyone's happy, that's a given," Bertie moved her head in exaggerated nods from side to side. "But listen more closely... what do you hear?"

Doug shrugged. "I'm not sure what you're getting at, Bertie. I hear... pure joy and happiness from every direction."

"No, no, no! Oh, for goodness sake... close your eyes for just a minute," Bertie instructed impatiently, "And don't open them until I tell you to."

Doug knew better than to argue with Bertie, or to question her intentions, so he did as he was instructed.

Max and Martin shook their heads but remained silent. Leave it to Bertie to insist on theatrics, even in Heaven.

Bertie moved in closer, squinted her eyes and wrinkled her nose, to ensure Doug's eyes were really closed. She then looked behind her and motioned for the two figures in the distance to come forward.

The two women – sisters - had died together several weeks ago from carbon monoxide poisoning, at the ages of eighty-nine and ninety-one. However, their Heavenly bodies projected the healthy bodies of two women in the prime of their life, certainly no more than forty-five.

The sisters held hands as they glided toward Bertie and the young man.

When the women got within a few feet of her, Bertie whispered to Doug. "Okay, open your eyes, handsome..."

Doug's half-smile froze upon his face as he stared at the two women before him.

No! It couldn't be! Even though they were older than the last time he had seen them, he would have recognized them anywhere. He rushed forward and grabbed both his sisters in a fierce hug. His broad, masculine shoulders shook as tears of joy flowed freely down his cheeks. His chest heaved as giant sobs escaped from somewhere deep inside him. It had been so long... sixty years since he last saw his sisters waving good-bye to him in 1952 as his train pulled out to take him to basic training.

Doug had only been nineteen at the time. His older sisters, Sarah and Hannah, had been thirty-one and twenty-nine then, respectively.

Martin glanced at Max and nodded toward Bertie, who was wiping away her own tears.

Bertie reached over and punched them both. "Oh, shoosh! Both of you, don't even say it!"

Doug finally composed himself and, still hugging both his sisters against him, said, "How long have you been here?"

Sarah, the oldest of the three siblings, smiled and said, "Oh, not very long, just a couple of months now." She reached up and cupped Doug's face. She couldn't take her eyes off the handsome brother that she had said good-bye to so many years ago.

Doug wiped away tears and looked back at Max and Bertie, "Why didn't you tell me? I would've come Home sooner."

Hannah laughed and moved in closer to hug her brother tightly. "Well, it seems like we've only been here a few hours, but we know that you're doing important work back on earth. We didn't want to interfere with that in any way."

"Not to mention the fact that we've been just a little bit pre-occupied ourselves," Sarah added. "From what I understand, this whole transitioning phase can be...how I should say...a bit overwhelming, at best!"

Doug couldn't stop staring at the two women on each side of him. He hugged them tight again. "We have so much to catch up on. Have you seen mama and papa yet?"

Sarah and Hannah shook their heads.

"No, Dougie... just you. You're the first family member that we've seen," Hannah answered back. "I was afraid to ask about anyone, afraid that maybe... well... that they might not be here...if you know what I mean. You remember how papa used to love his drinking and cursing."

"As if cursing is enough to keep anyone out of Heaven," Martin mumbled beneath his breath so that only Max and Bertie could hear.

Bertie glared at him and gave him a good punch.

"Oh, they're here!" Doug laughed. "Truth be told, papa would probably still love to have a cold beer, but mama keeps him pretty

busy." Doug wiped the tears from his eyes and grinned widely. "Oh, I've been waiting a long time for this reunion! I can't wait to see their faces when they see the two of you."

Martin stepped forward and addressed the trio. "Well, there's no time like the present, I say. Go on now! What are you waiting for? Don't keep your parents waiting one minute more."

Sarah and Hannah looked at each other.

"Go where?" Sarah mumbled.

Doug laughed out loud and hugged his sisters to him once again. "Oh, this is the easy part. One of the best things about Heaven is that all you have to do is close your eyes, think about the person you want to see, and… in an instant… you will be reunited with that person."

"You've got to be kidding?" Hannah asked.

"It's pretty fun once you get the hang of it," Doug replied.

"You can explain all that to them along the way, handsome. Get going, scram!" Bertie shouted. "Your parents have been patient a long time now. They're waiting for you all!"

"Here goes nothing…" the sisters said in unison as they each grabbed a hold of Doug's hands.

Doug held on tight and said, "Now, just close your eyes and picture their faces…"

The siblings all closed their eyes and, within a split second, vanished.

Max, Bertie, and Martin looked at each other and burst out laughing.

"I love my job!" Martin grinned.

"Yeah, me, too," Bertie sighed, "Ours may not be quite as exciting as yours, but we have our moments, too. Don't we, Maximus?"

Max nodded, his thoughts quickly returning to their earthly charges. "Oh, yes… we certainly do."

"Speaking of some of those moments," Martin cleared his throat and turned to Max. "That reminds me… would you care to explain why you felt the need to expose yourself to young Miss Turner and Amos Brown?"

"You do know that expression kinda means something else these days, Martin," Bertie laughed, "But we both know what you mean." She also turned to face Max. "Yes, Maximus... I've been wondering the same thing myself... why did you **expose** yourself?"

"What?" Martin queried, a puzzled expression upon his face. "What does the expression mean these days?"

"I don't think we need to get into that explanation just now," Bertie grinned. "But... hey, Martin... maybe you can Google it later and find out for yourself!"

Max lifted his head high and straightened his massive shoulders. It was easy to envision him in his gladiator attire, so proud and strong, conquering anything and anyone who challenged him. "Neither of you needs to remind me; I know it is generally prohibited and greatly frowned upon," Max replied. "I also know that I've slipped up a few times and exposed myself in the past. Trust me... I've heard about those times from our Lord, but He has also told me that He understands when I feel the need to do it. As far as Amos and Amanda... well... the time just presented itself, and I acted upon it. There's no doubt I will have to make atonement for my actions."

Bertie shook her head, trying hard not to grin at Max's discomfort. "Well, I've managed to avoid any long conversations with Amanda or Amos, but I suppose we'll need to sit down and discuss things with them soon. Amanda has been looking at me all week like I've suddenly grown two heads. You can tell she wants to say something, but I think she's waiting for us to start the conversation."

"And we will..." Max agreed. "When the time is right, but, in the meantime, I have no doubt that our secret is safe. I never would have shown my true self to them, if I ever thought otherwise. Amos has suspected for some time now, but poor Amanda is still in a state of shock and disbelief, I think."

Martin smiled. "One of the few times the young lady has been speechless, no doubt."

Max nodded his agreement. "Anyway, we will sit down with Amanda and Amos next week and make sure they understand exactly what they saw."

"I can't wait," Bertie grinned.

"I'm sure you can't," Martin remarked, "But, wasn't there something you needed to do while you were here today, Max?"

"Yes, my friend," Max answered back. "I do have several things to check on while we're here today. I have a strong feeling that things with Kris and the baby will be coming to a climax very soon, and… well, not knowing exactly how the situation will unfold… we need to be prepared to help Kris through this."

"I can't believe those idiots sent that letter to her," Bertie said.

"Well, actually…" Martin began, "As it turns out, it was only one of those idiots that decided to send the letter."

"What do you mean?" Bertie and Max asked in unison, surprised at Martin's revelation.

Martin led them to the large video screen at the end of the room. "Watch this."

The images of Jack and Susan Peterson appeared instantly on the screen. Bertie and Max watched and listened intently to the end of the couple's conversation taking place in their Tampa home.

Jack Peterson collapsed onto the sofa and looked up at his wife. "Oh, dear, God… Susan, I can't believe what you have done…"

Susan Peterson sat down next to her husband, wringing both hands nervously in her lap. "Please don't be angry, dear. I'm so sorry, Jack. I guess I wasn't thinking straight; all those medications… sometimes, they make my head so foggy, I just…"

Jack placed both hands against each side of his head. His shoulders collapsed in defeat. "You mailed the mother a letter, Susan… why on earth would you do that? Why…"

Susan put an arm around her husband and laid her head upon his shoulder. "She was just so sad, Jack. It broke my heart every time I saw her on television. But I was very careful, dear. I didn't hand-write the note, so they can't trace that back to us. It was typed and… oh, yes… I made sure not to put our address on it… I didn't sign it. You read the copy I kept. I didn't say anything that would let them know who we are, or where we are. I even washed the color from the baby's hair before I took the picture, so they wouldn't know we had changed the hair color. Oh, Jack... I just needed to do something... something to help that poor mother to be able to move on with her life."

Kelly was crying softly in the back ground. It was time for a feeding.

Susan was torn between attending to the baby and attending to her husband. She pushed Jack's thinning hair off his forehead and kissed him there. "Please don't be angry with me, Jack... please. I told you, I didn't put our address on anything. It's okay; you'll see... everything will be okay."

Kelly continued to cry.

Jack looked at his wife, who was still so beautiful in his eyes, in spite of the obvious effects of the cancer eating away inside her. He took her into his arms and held her until she stopped shaking. "Go see to the baby, love..." he whispered.

Susan smiled as she rose to leave, content in her belief that she had not done anything to jeopardize their situation.

Jack watched her leave the room and his heart sank. He didn't have the courage or heart to say it out loud, but he thought it to himself, *"But the letter had a Tampa postmark..."*

Martin's screen moved to the room where the baby pulled herself to a standing position in her play pen.

The crying baby, with a head full of beautiful red curls, sat down in the play pen and rocked back and forth on her knees, demanding to be fed.

Susan had sat down in the rocking chair beside the play pen.

Jack entered the baby's room and stroked his wife's head. "We need to touch up her hair again today..." Jack whispered, unaware that Susan's eyes had already closed in drugged sleep.

Our soul waits for the Lord; He is our help and our shield."

-Psalm 33:20 (NKJV)

CHAPTER 34

The Petersons Face Reality

The trip Home had definitely recharged the angels of the Heavenly Grille Café. They went about their daily routine with, not only extra energy, but also, renewed purpose. Although they were not privy to God's overall intents and purposes, they all felt that this particular chapter in Kris' and Amanda's life was coming to fruition soon.

During the past several weeks, the angels had taken every available opportunity to talk with the two women about what was going on in their lives, from what they had for breakfast to what they wanted to do with the rest of their lives. It was easier for them to talk openly and candidly with Amanda since she now knew the truth about them; however, all three of them took immense satisfaction and gratitude in knowing they were having a part in bringing Kris closer to a true relationship with God. They had prayed with her and answered all her questions about God and the Bible, to the best of their abilities. Amanda had teased them, in private, telling them that Kris confided to her that she thought Max would make an even better preacher than he was a cook.

Max knew that he couldn't put off the conversation he needed to have with Amos and Amanda, regarding his transformation before their very eyes, so he and Bertie had left Doug behind and returned earlier than usual from their weekly visit Home. Max had been duly reprimanded by his Father and reminded of the necessity to convey the importance for the two mortals to keep their secret and not tell anyone the truth about the three angels. He and Bertie had arranged for Amos and Amanda to join them at the café when the angels returned from Home on Sunday night.

The meeting lasted three hours, and in the end, the angels agreed that it had been a good meeting. Amos had been quiet and accepting of their explanations; however, their precious Amanda had been full of questions and awe – thus, the need for a three-hour meeting. It took the entire three hours, but in the end, Amanda had eventually come to terms with the fact that she had been employed by angels for the past six months of her life. She had asked numerous questions about her parents and the dreams she had been having. Max had reassured her that she was not losing her mind and that, most likely, she would continue to be able to communicate with her parents via the dreams. Amanda had seemed truly disappointed when she learned that she would not be able to share her new-found angelic knowledge with Kris, but she promised to keep the angels' secret.

The Florida police had been busy since Kris received the letter from the kidnappers. They had been able to pull fingerprints from both the letter and the picture; unfortunately, the prints did not match any that were in their current database. They were able to conclude that the prints, most likely, belonged to a female. There had been a lot of discussion among the primary investigators as to whether or not they should advertise the fact that they knew the letter came from the Tampa area. They were concerned that the suspects would flee the state, and possibly the country, if that bit of evidence was advertised; they knew this would require law enforcement staff to start the investigation over from scratch. However, on the flip side, they felt that broadcasting the new information might alert more people to be on the lookout for the baby.

In the end, they had decided to go public with the information, but they waited until the morning of Monday, February thirteenth to do so. The police released a statement to all major newspapers and television networks that they suspected the kidnappers were in the Tampa area.

Ida Brooks, the elderly neighbor of Jack and Susan Peterson, was sitting at her kitchen table reading the newspaper when she saw the article about the missing baby. "Well, I'll be..." she clucked. "That precious little baby is somewhere here in Tampa..." She looked at the color picture, included in the article, of Charlotte Grace; it was the Polaroid picture the kidnappers had sent to the baby's mother. She traced her finger around the picture of the baby's face. "What a beautiful little girl... such pretty red hair," she sighed. She put the paper down, clasped her hands before her, closed her eyes, and prayed. "Oh, Lord... I pray that it is your will for this precious child to be found soon and reunited with her mother. Please keep her safe, Lord, and... forgive the people who took her away from her mother... Amen."

A very different scene was unfolding inside the tidy house, next door, with the paradise-back yard.

Jack's morning paper fell from his hands. He quickly picked up his cup of coffee to calm himself, but his hands began to shake so badly that the hot coffee dripped onto the newspaper, smearing the article he had been reading.

It was Monday morning, February thirteenth, and Jack was having a quick breakfast before heading off to work. As his hand continued to shake, he turned to check on Susan and the baby; they were both sitting on the lanai, enjoying the early-morning sunshine. Jack squeezed his eyes and bit his upper lip while he listened to his wife singing a weak lullaby to their baby girl. He sat at the table for another ten minutes, unable to move after reading the article outlining the police's certainty that the kidnapped child was in the Tampa area. He knew he should get up and tell Susan about the article, but his legs felt like they had been immersed in concrete beneath him.

He could not move.

Susan found him sitting at the table with his forehead lowered into both hands. "Jack? Are you all right, dear?"

Jack sighed deeply before looking up into his wife's worried eyes. He couldn't say anything; all he could do was to return her concerned look.

Susan clutched the baby tightly against her and pleaded with her husband. "Jack... you're scaring me... what's wrong?"

The baby squirmed in Susan's arms and began to slip. The feeling returned to Jack's legs just in time. He jumped up instantly and caught Kelly beneath her arms. He hugged the baby tightly against him and inhaled her sweet-baby fragrance. The baby grabbed his nose and cooed.

Susan's face had paled when she realized she was about to drop the baby. She grabbed onto the edge of the kitchen chair, pulled it out and collapsed onto it. She continued to stare into her husband's worried face. "Oh, God... what's wrong, Jack? I know something is wrong..."

Jack glanced quickly at the wet newspaper.

Susan followed his gaze and saw the newspaper covered with the stain from the spilled coffee. She looked at Jack, and then back at the newspaper. She pulled the paper closer to her and looked at the blown-up picture of a smiling, Charlotte Grace Devone. "Oh, God..." she whimpered, immediately releasing the paper as if it had burned her fingers. She looked back at her husband. "Jack? That's the picture I sent the mother..."

"Go ahead," Jack motioned at the paper, "Read it..."

Susan retrieved the dropped paper and read the article.

Jack watched his wife closely as her worried expression

quickly turned to one of pure panic.

Susan put the paper back on the table and slowly lifted her head to look at her husband. She reacted instantly to the fear evident in his tired face. "Oh, no...Jack? What are we going to do? We've got to leave, but... oh, God... where do we go?" She attempted to push herself up and away from the table, but her knees shook so badly they gave way and she collapsed onto the tile flooring.

It all happened so quickly. Susan's skeletal frame met the hard surface of the floor with a sick plop. Her eyes opened wide as she grabbed her throat with one hand and held the other one upward toward her husband.

The baby squirmed against Jack's hip and his ability to breathe temporarily escaped him.

Susan closed her eyes and whispered hoarsely, "Can't... breathe..."

Jack's own ability to breathe was quickly restored and he reacted instinctively as Susan's frail body lay crumbled before him. He bent down quickly, intent on assisting his wife, and forgot for a moment that he still held the baby in his arms. "Susan! Oh, God... hold on Susan!"

He rushed onto the lanai, dragged the playpen inside, and placed the cooing child inside it.

He raced back into the kitchen and the first thing he noticed was that Susan's lips were already turning blue. He saw her eyes opened wide in apparent panic, staring at him; she was holding her throat and gasping frantically for air. Jack's eyes roamed the room until he spotted his cell phone on the foyer table. He grabbed it and immediately dialed 911.

The 911 operator was still asking him questions when he dropped the cell phone and cradled Susan in his lap, careful to keep her head elevated. He kissed the top of her head just as she lost consciousness.

Charlotte/Kelly cooed in the background.

Jack was on his knees, rocking back and forth, with his wife's head on his lap. "Hang on, love, please hang on..."

Ida Brooks heard the siren. It sounded like it was outside

her front door. She rushed as quickly as any seventy-seven year old could to the front window to see what was going on outside. She opened her blinds just as her neighbor, Susan Peterson, was being loaded into an ambulance. "Oh, sweet, Jesus!" Ida exclaimed. She grabbed her cardigan and ran as quickly as she could to the Peterson's driveway. She stopped and tried to catch her breath when she saw Jack Peterson standing helplessly in the driveway, holding their baby against his chest. She reached out and touched his arm. "Oh, Mr. Peterson, what's wrong? Is there anything I can do to help?"

In spite of the trauma unfolding before him, Jack was coherent enough to realize he had a true dilemma on his hands. He couldn't deny it any longer, and he hated to finally admit it to himself, but he knew that Susan was dying. His wife was literally dying right before his eyes; and, he found himself torn between riding with her in the ambulance, and following in his car, with the baby. He bounced the baby, who was bundled in a light blanket, against his shoulder.

Ida's first thought was that he looked like a small child who had just lost his best friend. She touched his shoulder once again. "Please, Mr. Peterson... let me help. What has happened?"

The concern in the old lady's face was his downfall. Jack looked back and forth between Mrs. Brooks and the ambulance.

The ambulance driver was still holding open the vehicle's doors. "Sir? We need to go! Will you be riding with your wife?"

Tears slowly began to run down Jack's face and dropped onto the baby's blanket. He made an instant decision that he hoped he would not live to regret. "Mrs. Brooks... I have to go with Susan. She's very sick. She has cancer and..." He choked up and held the baby out to his neighbor. "Can you please stay at the house with Kelly until I get back? Her bottles are in the fridge and her diapers are in the nursery."

Ida immediately took the smiling baby from his arms. "Of

course, I can, dear. Don't you worry one bit about her. I promise I will take good care of her. You go with your wife and don't you worry about this precious child."

Jack still doubted his decision but he knew he had to be with Susan now. He would never forgive himself if he wasn't with her when the end came. "Thank you so much, Mrs. Brooks. I'll call you as soon as I can," he called out to her as he climbed hurriedly into the back of the ambulance.

Ida watched the ambulance speed away before turning to go back to her own house to get her keys. She shifted the baby to her other hip and locked her front door. The baby pulled at Ida's gray curls and cooed. "Oh, yes," Ida smiled and kissed the baby's nose. "We're going to be just fine, aren't we, precious?"

Ida began the short walk toward the Peterson's yard. She watched as several neighbors slowly made their way back to their own homes. One of them waved to Ida and yelled out, "Do you need any help?"

Ida shook her head and waved back, "We're fine..." She felt another tug on her gray curls. She looked down at the beautiful baby she held against her. "Are you trying to tell me something, little one? Are you hungry? I bet you are, yes I do... let's go get you a bottle."

The baby looked back at Ida with the bluest eyes she had ever seen. She smiled and cooed in response to Ida's gentle voice.

Ida took that as an affirmation to her question. She patted the baby's bottom and laughed when the baby reached and tweaked Ida's nose. "Oh, and I dare say we need to check that diaper, too, little one!" she laughed as she slowly made her way between the two yards to her neighbor's front door.

Max stood in front of his grill, turning the bacon and sausages with one hand, and stirring the huge pot of cheese grits with his other hand. Suddenly, he stopped. A slow smile began to spread across his face. He leaned his head back and looked upward at the same moment that Ida Brooks sat down on the couch to feed Kelly Peterson her morning bottle. "Well… finally… the time has come," he sighed. His smile broadened and he began whistling - out of tune, as usual - one of his favorite hymns, "Just a Closer Walk With Thee."

Amanda poked her head into the kitchen and grinned. "Hey, I know that one!" She began singing the words along with Max's whistling tune.

It only took a few verses before the customers in the dining area joined in. "Just a closer walk with Thee, grant it, Jesus, is my plea. Daily walking close to Thee, let it be, dear Lord, let it be…"

CHAPTER 35

Death Rush to Hospital

Jack hated hospitals. He appreciated the often thankless job the doctors and nurses performed on a daily basis, and he had the utmost respect for the work they did; however, he often wished that they could have performed their duties in his home instead of the sterile surrounding of the private room his wife now occupied.

Dr. Matheson was Susan's oncologist and primary physician. He had discussed Susan's disease, prognosis, and her eventual need for Hospice care with them both. He noted in his chart that the husband had been receptive to the idea, but that Susan had been adamant that she was not ready for that kind of care. The husband had told him, repeatedly, that Susan was not ready to give up.

Yes, Jack hated hospitals. He hated everything about hospitals. He hated the antiseptic smells that valiantly attempted to cover up the even more unpleasant smells of sickness and death. He hated listening to the wailing of people in pain and agony. He hated the matter-of-fact way some of the nurses attended to their patients. However, more than anything, he hated knowing in his heart that today might be the last time he would bring Susan here.

Jack sat beside his wife's hospital bed, holding her cold and lifeless hand between his own. He listened, reluctantly, to the awful gurgling sound, commonly referred to as the death rattle, coming from deep within her lungs. He watched and listened to all the machines that were keeping Susan alive; the constant beeping of the machines was enough to shatter his last illusion of reality. He wished he could turn an OFF knob and vanquish the intrusive sounds. Instead, Jack continued to sit beside his wife, and tried to rub warmth back into her cold, mottled, and clammy hands.

"Mr. Peterson?" Dr. Matheson spoke from the doorway. He motioned for Jack to follow him outside the room.

Jack released Susan's hand and kissed her forehead. "I'll be right back, love..." he whispered in her ear.

Dr. Matheson waited patiently outside Susan's room. It was his own personal belief that, even while asleep or in a coma, the patient might still be able to hear sounds and voices around them. Therefore, he made it a practice to never discuss a comatose patient's condition in front of the patient.

Jack took one look at the doctor's face and buried his own face in his hands. He rubbed at his eyes and looked at the doctor again. In his heart, he knew it, but he still didn't want to admit that it might be true. "Is this it? Is this the end?"

Dr. Matheson touched his shoulder. "I can't confirm that with any certainty, Mr. Peterson; every patient is different. Some may experience pain and shortness of breath, while others will feel no pain at all and are able to breathe comfortably on their own. Some people will decline rapidly while others will fight it to the bitter end, despite all odds."

Jack took a deep breath and asked, "But you do think it's the end for Susan, don't you?" He needed to hear the actual words before he would allow himself to finally believe the truth of what was happening.

Dr. Matheson paused for just a moment before replying. "Yes, I do."

Jack nodded his head and rubbed the bridge of his nose. "Will she wake up?" He quickly released another deep breath he hadn't realized he had been holding in.

Dr. Matheson rubbed the back of his neck. "That's hard to say. She might, but if she does, she may not be able to talk, even if we removed the breathing tube. There is the possibility that she may not even realize who you are or where she's at. We have her on a very high dose of morphine to help with the pain. I'm afraid the cancer has spread even quicker than we anticipated. It has moved to the bones in her chest and spine. Quite frankly, Mr. Peterson, it's a testimony to her strength and determination that she's lasted as long as she has."

Jack leaned back against the wall for support. "She's always been very determined about everything she does. You don't know this, but, we, uh… we adopted my brother and sister-in-law's baby girl a few months ago. They were killed in a car accident, and the baby… the baby has been a Godsend for Susan. I think she really believed that she could beat this disease long enough to…" Jack couldn't finish his sentence. He bent his head and his shoulders shook with unreleased sorrow.

Dr. Matheson touched Jack's shoulder again. "I wish I had better news, Mr. Peterson. I'm sure you and Susan have both been under tremendous stress and pressure, and, I'm sure the baby has been very… therapeutic for your wife. I have to admit, though, that I am very surprised that Susan has had the strength and energy to care for an infant."

"She's done what she could, but I suppose most of the care has fallen on me," Jack answered back. "It's been a huge help that I've been able to work from home, so I'm there with them most of the time."

Dr. Matheson nodded. "We'll do what we can to keep her comfortable, but… if you have family, well… you may want to notify them."

Jack stared vacantly into the doctor's eyes and shrugged. "No… there's no one else. It's just the three of us." He took another deep breath. "That reminds me… I need to call our neighbor. She's looking after the baby for me."

Dr. Matheson touched Jack's shoulder a last time and said, "I'll be checking back in a couple of hours. Have the nurse notify me if you need me before then."

Jack shook the doctor's hand. "Thank you, Dr. Matheson… for making her comfortable. I don't want her to suffer any more than she already has."

Back at the Peterson home, Ida Brooks bustled about the kitchen, wiping counters, and rinsing the breakfast dishes that had been left on the table and in the sink. It felt good to be needed again. She saw the morning paper on the table and, once again, looked at the image of the missing baby from Monticello. She was about to sit down and re-read the article when she heard cooing coming from the nursery. "Oh, the little one is awake from her nap…"

The house phone rang as Ida turned to go to the nursery. She debated whether or not she should answer it, until she remembered that it might be Mr. Peterson calling. She had left her home number with Susan a few weeks ago, but she wasn't at home to answer her phone, now was she?

"Hello? Peterson residence…" Ida answered hesitantly.

"Mrs. Brooks? How is the baby?" Jack croaked out the questions.

Ida picked up on the hoarseness in his voice. "Oh, it's you! Hello, Mr. Peterson. Don't you worry about the little one; she is just fine. She's such a good baby. How is Mrs. Peterson? Is she going to be all right?"

Jack couldn't answer right away. He wasn't sure if he could say the actual words and he surprised himself when he blurted out, "No… she's not all right… she's dying, Mrs. Brooks… my wife is dying."

"Oh, dear, Lord…" Ida gasped. "I am so very sorry. I… what can I do to help?"

Jack waited a moment before continuing, trying to compose himself. "You're already doing it, Mrs. Brooks, by taking care of Kelly for us. If it's not too much of an imposition, would it be possible... would you mind staying for a couple of more hours? I want to talk to the doctor when he makes his rounds, and then I'll come home to relieve you."

"Don't you worry about us, Mr. Peterson. The baby and I are just fine. Now, you just take all the time you need and don't you worry about us now, you hear? There's no need for you to rush back. Take all the time you need, really..."

"Thank you, Mrs. Brooks. You have no idea how much you are helping us right now."

Ida hung up the phone. "Oh, you poor man..." Her thoughts stopped as the sound of Kelly's cooing changed from happy to demanding. "I'm coming, little one, I'm coming."

Ida played with Kelley for the next hour before looking at the time. "Well, your Daddy should be coming home soon." She gave the baby a playful tickle and said, "What do you say we get you fed and give you a nice warm bath before he comes home? That way, all he'll have to do is hug you and hold you tight. What do you say?"

The baby appeared to look deeply into the old woman's eyes before a wide grin spread across her tiny face.

"I thought you'd like that idea," Ida cooed back at her. "Yes, indeedy, a nice warm bath is just what the doctor ordered. Maybe we'll do that before we feed you." Ida looked around the nursery and spotted the portable baby bath in a corner. "Oh, poo, we don't need that clumsy thing, now do we. I'll just fill some water in the kitchen sink and we'll get you all nice and clean. We'll even wash those pretty curls of yours... yes we will!"

The baby cooed and seemed to follow Ida's every move.

Ida filled the deep kitchen sink with warm water and lined up the baby shampoo, soap, and towels within easy reach. She removed the baby's clothes and tested the water's temperature before easing Kelly slowly into the water. She received a mini splash and laughter as thanks.

While the baby splashed happily in the sink, Ida used a baby wash cloth to drizzle warm water over Kelly and used baby talk to entertain her. "Now, what do you say, little one... let's wash that pretty hair..." Ida used the wash cloth again to drizzle water over the baby's head, being careful not to get any into the infant's eyes. She flipped open the shampoo bottle and squirted a small amount onto Kelly's small head. She rubbed the shampoo in and gently massaged the baby's head, working up a rich lather of suds. In a matter of seconds, the foamy suds on Ida's hands turned from white to grey. "Oh, my..." Ida laughed, "You really did need a bath, didn't you, little one?"

She reached for a small cup she had sat on the counter and used it to rinse the suds off the baby's head. Ida Brooks gasped in shock and disbelief when the color of the baby's beautiful black hair began a slow but steady transformation to a coppery shade of red. "Oh, my goodness..."

Mrs. Brooks was stunned and dumbfounded. She stared at the baby with the red curls and, at first, didn't know what to make of the situation. "Who would want to dye a little baby's hair?" she mumbled, half-way hoping the baby would magically offer up a logical explanation of her own.

Ida Brooks may have been seventy-seven years old, but her mind was as sharp as it was when she was twenty-seven. She may have been trusting and naïve, but it only took her a few moments to make the connection between the squirming baby in the sink to the one whose picture filled the morning's paper. "Oh, my goodness..."

CHAPTER 36

Charlotte Grace is Found

Kris had been at work for about an hour and was behind the counter, putting on more coffee and chatting with a customer when the front door opened. "Just have a seat anywhere..." she yelled out, stopping in mid-sentence when she recognized the two police officers standing at the door, apparently searching the coffee shop. They were the same officers who had met Dean at her house the day she received the letter and picture from the kidnappers.

Kris put the coffee pot back on the warmer and wiped her hands on the short apron tied around her waist. The customer was saying something to her, but his voice sounded like it was coming from far away. Her attention zeroed in on the officers as she watched them remove their hats. It was obvious they had spotted her when they made their way through the crowd to the counter. She had not realized she had been holding her breath, while trying to read their faces, until one large gasp escaped from her throat.

The customer was still babbling about God knows what when the front door opened again.

Her knees buckled slightly when she spotted Dean, looking handsome and professional in his crisp uniform. She watched as he, too, removed his hat. His face was easier to read.

The minute he spotted her behind the counter, Dean began grinning from ear to ear. As much as he tried to control his emotions, he felt the tears begin to well up in his eyes. He just looked at Kris, continued grinning, and nodded his head.

Kris grabbed the counter and held on tightly with both hands. She bent her head forwards and her shoulders shook with barely suppressed sobbing.

The customer had finally quit talking when Dean and the two officers approached the counter.

Kris lifted her head and stared into Dean's smiling face. He was still nodding. The two officers were also smiling now. Kris slapped one hand against her mouth and dropped to her knees. "Thank you, God... thank you so very much..." Her own tears came flowing in a torrential downpour as she repeated, "Thank you..."

The customer threw some money on the counter and left.

Mumbling began among the other customers in the coffee shop.

Kris' boss had been in the kitchen when he, too, saw the officers enter the shop. He and Dean reached Kris at the same moment, and they both helped her to a nearby booth.

The customers' mumbling had turned to light chatter as they continued to watch the scene unfolding before them. It had not taken them long to figure out what was happening. The majority of them had been strong supporters of Kris' since the kidnapping.

Dean knelt before the booth she sat in and wrapped her hands inside his own.

Kris searched his face again to make sure he was still smiling; a smile usually meant good news, but she desperately needed to hear the actual words.

Dean dropped her hands and slipped into the booth beside her. He held her face between his hands and stared deeply into her eyes. He did not make any attempt to control his own flow of tears. He was still grinning when he touched his forehead to hers. "We found her, Kris... we found her, and she's fine."

Kris stared back at him and begged, "Say it again... I need you to say it again..."

Dean kissed her lightly upon her trembling lips. "She's just fine," he smiled, "She really is."

Kris' boss slapped the top of the table and shouted, "Hot damn!" He turned to the crowd of customers and grinned, "They found Kris' baby!"

Kris wrapped her arms around Dean and buried her face into the crook of his neck. Sobs of extreme joy shook every fiber of her body. She looked up at him and returned his gentle kiss with a more fervent one of her own. "It's true what you said, Dean... it works. Prayer really, really works... I never really believed it was possible, but it works..."

Dean nodded and hugged her against him. He kissed the top of her head and whispered, "Yes, baby... it most certainly does..."

Loud cheering, clapping, and whistling erupted behind them from customers, employees, and Dean's fellow officers.

There was not a dry eye in the building.

Amanda was finishing up her shift at work, wiping down tables, when Bertie breezed through the front door. Amanda waved and grinned, "Hi, Bertie!"

"Well, hey there yourself, Princess," Bertie waved back to her. "Are you about ready to call it a day?"

Amanda walked over to help Bertie with the box of supplies and groceries she carried. "Here, let me help you with that. Where's Doug? He should be carrying this for you!"

Bertie grinned. "Oh, he's right behind me with his own boxes. We had to make a quick run to Sam's before the night shift got going. Max said he was expecting to do a lot more cooking than usual tonight and tomorrow."

"Really?" Amanda asked. "He didn't mention anything to me about it. Is there a special party or something?"

"Well..." Bertie whispered as she moved into the kitchen where Max was grilling hamburgers and hot dogs. She nodded and smiled at Max. "I think he wanted it to be a surprise."

Amanda was right behind her but she turned when she heard the angelic chimes and saw Doug entering with three more huge boxes of supplies. She watched as he used his foot to close the door behind him and joined them in the kitchen. "Okay, you three... what's going on? And don't say it's nothing because you're all grinning like Cheshire cats who found a bounty of wild mice to eat."

"Oh, you'll see," Max smiled as he turned away and began his usual out-of-tune whistling.

Amanda watched while Bertie and Doug put away the supplies and groceries. "That's not fair! Y'all need to tell me what's going on..." Her cell phone began ringing, interrupting her conversation with the angels. She saw Kris' name pop up on the phone. "Don't y'all dare move!" she ordered them. "I want to know what the surprise is..." She walked out the back door and sat down at the picnic table. "Hey, Kris... what's up?" She knew that Kris was at work, working a double shift, and hoped that everything was okay.

Amanda sat at the picnic table, in silent shock, while she listened to Kris repeat Dean's news about Charlotte Grace. Her free hand flew to her mouth. "Oh... my... God..." she said when she was able to take in a full breath. "Oh, Kris... thank, God! We've all been praying so, so hard for this..."

Amanda talked with Kris for a few more minutes and learned that a police helicopter was flying Kris and Dean to Tampa to pick up Charlotte Grace. When she finally ended the call, she closed her eyes and offered her own silent prayer of thanks to God. She opened her eyes and saw her three guardian angels grinning at her from the doorway.

"Get in here, Princess!" Max laughed. "Looks like you may be working a little overtime tonight."

Bertie walked out to where Amanda still sat at the picnic table. She gave her a playful punch on the shoulder, grinned, and wiped a tear from her eye. "That's right... come on now... we've got a real celebration to get ready for!"

CHAPTER 37

The Death of Susan Peterson

Jack sat alone at Susan's bedside and held her hand. He cringed inside at each rattled breath she took, wondering if that one would be her last. His last conversation with the doctor had not offered any hope or encouragement that Susan would improve. Her condition was deteriorating rapidly and her doctor thought it was doubtful, though not impossible, that she would even awaken again. They were keeping her as comfortable as possible.

Jack knew this was the end of the road for the woman he had shared his life with for the past sixteen years. They had been sixteen wonderful years and tomorrow would be their seventeenth wedding anniversary. He watched as Susan seemed to fight for each and every breath she took, and he wondered if she would even live long enough to see their seventeenth anniversary.

As hard as it was for Jack to let her go, he closed his eyes in prayer. "Please… God… I beg of you… please be gentle with her… don't let her suffer unnecessarily." He had known too many friends who had to watch their loved ones linger, against their will, while they waited for the Angel of Death to release them from their pain and suffering. Tears trickled from the corner of his eyes as he continued to pray. When he finally opened his eyes, he saw Susan's fluttering eyelids. "Susan?" he whispered as he lowered his face closer to her own. He kissed her cheek.

Susan's eyes opened. It took her a moment to focus on the man shimmering before her face. She tried to speak; instead, she gagged. The inserted breathing tube prevented that from happening.

Jack's heart was breaking as he watched the woman he loved try to convey her message. She looked so weak... so very tired.

Susan blinked repeatedly as her own tears began to trickle down her face. It took all the energy she had, but she managed to pull her hand from Jacks' grasp. She joined her thumb and index finger together and made a writing motion in the air. Her eyes searched his, hoping desperately that he understood her request.

He did.

Jack moved around the room quickly, searching for a pad and pencil. He found both, next to a small Bible, inside the table drawer next to the bed. He placed the pencil in Susan's trembling hand, and held the pad steady atop the bed sheet.

Susan used the entire page to scribble the two words – SEE BABY.

Jack smiled down at her and said, "Kelly is fine, love. Mrs. Brooks is watching her for us until we get you back home." He recognized the look of panic that immediately filled her eyes and tried his best to calm her. "It's going to be okay, really... it is. Mrs. Brooks is taking good care of her. Nothing is going to happen. You'll see. You just have to focus on getting stronger so that I can take you home."

Susan's panicked expression was steadfast as she moved her head slowly from side to side.

Jack took the pencil from her hand and lowered his head upon his wife's belly. He felt utterly helpless as he listened to her forced breathing. He felt her frail body trembling. However, with his own face pressed into her sheets, he failed to see the real cause of her trembling; he failed to see the sudden look of fear and defeat that filled her tear-soaked eyes. Jack's head rose slightly with each labored breath Susan attempted. He knew he needed to get his emotions under control before raising his head. When he finally looked up at her again he noticed that she was not looking at him, but rather beyond him. "Susan?"

She wasn't blinking and Jack's first thought was that she was dead. A cold shiver coursed involuntarily through his body just before he turned his own gaze in the direction to which Susan's eyes appeared to be glued. "Oh, dear, God... not now...not here, please... God, please..." he whispered so low he barely heard himself.

Susan had not died. Her gaze was frozen on the two police officers who towered in the doorway. However, it wasn't the police that captured Susan's attention; it was the woman who stood directly behind them that did that; that woman was holding Kelly in her arms. The fourth member completing the unexpected entourage of rescuers was Ida Brooks.

They all entered the room slowly, one by one.

The room began swaying before Jack. His attention was torn between the precious baby being held by the strange woman, and the woman dying on the bed bedside him.

"Jack Peterson?" one of the officers asked.

Jack didn't acknowledge the officer at first; instead, he looked back at Susan.

Susan's rapid breathing became even more labored, but she, too, only had eyes for the woman who was holding the baby... her baby.

Mrs. Brooks remained in the background, trembling, and whimpered, "Oh, my goodness..." She momentarily doubted her decision to contact the authorities.

Jack finally stood up and faced the officers. "Yes, I am Jack Peterson."

"And is this Susan Peterson?" the same officer asked,

nodding in Susan's direction.

Jack took a deep breath, squared his shoulders, and nodded. "Yes… this is my wife."

The two officers looked at each other and the one who had spoken began reading Jack and Susan their Miranda Rights. "Jack and Susan Peterson… you are both under arrest for the kidnapping of the infant, Charlotte Grace Devone. You have the right to remain silent. Anything you say may be used against you in a court of law. You have the right to consult with an attorney and to have an attorney present during questioning. If you cannot afford an attorney, one will be appointed for you. Do you understand these rights as I have read them?"

"Please…" Jack began as he looked back at Susan.

Susan gagged and lifted her right arm toward her husband.

"Do you understand these rights as I have read them?" the officer repeated.

Jack took Susan's upheld arm and kissed her hand. Tears were pouring down both their cheeks.

"Sir…" the other officer began.

"Yes," Jack nodded, affirming a weak response. "Yes… we do…"

Ida offered a small gasp as someone shuffled behind her.

Dr. Matheson moved into the room and demanded, "What's going on in here?"

The officer who had read Jack and Susan their rights pulled out a pair of handcuffs and motioned for Jack to turn around. He hadn't known what to expect from the kidnappers, but he was mildly surprised when Jack Peterson dutifully turned around so that the cuffs could be secured around his wrists.

"What is the woman's condition?" the other officer directed his question to Dr. Matheson.

Dr. Matheson looked at Jack.

Jack nodded and closed his eyes.

Susan's expression had not changed; it remained one of

pure panic.

Dr. Matheson looked at Susan for a few moments before answering. "The patient is dying."

Susan looked away from Jack and back to the woman holding her baby. Using what little energy she had left, she slowly lifted both hands toward Charlotte Grace.

The woman looked at the officer, lifting her eyebrows in query.

The officer looked at Susan, and back at the doctor. "How long does she have?"

Dr. Matheson looked at Susan and Jack again before answering. "Not long, I'm afraid." He detested talking about his patient as though she weren't even in the room. He didn't know exactly what was going on, but the defeated look on Jack Peterson's face spoke volumes to him. "She could go at any time now."

The woman holding the baby decided not to wait for the officer's confirmation or approval. She moved closer to the bed. "It can't do any harm," she said as she looked over at the officer. She placed the smiling and cooing baby into the dying woman's outstretched arms.

Jack looked back at the officer who had cuffed him. "May I?" he asked, nodding toward his wife.

The officer hesitated briefly before offering a silent affirmation to Jack's request.

Jack moved closer to the bed and bent his face closer to his wife and baby. He shuddered at the fresh baby smell that eerily intermingled with the smell of death. He kissed each of his girls on their cheeks, and the baby reached over to grab his nose.

The officer's move was silent and subtle.

Jack lowered his head and sighed in relief when he felt the cuffs being unlocked behind his back. He looked back at the officer and mouthed, "Thank you…" He rubbed his wrists before leaning over the bed. He cried openly as he took them both into a final embrace. He choked on tears that had become mixed with those of his wife's.

Susan gagged and moved her head slightly so that she could look into the eyes of the man who had sacrificed everything for her... for them. The baby cooed and wriggled in the nook of her left arm. Susan tried to smile, but the inserted breathing tube made it difficult to do. Instead, she stared intently into Jack's eyes, trying to convey all the love and happiness she had been blessed with for the past sixteen years. She could only hope and pray that he knew how much she appreciated what he had done for her. She blinked slowly three times... her private message of love to her husband... I LOVE YOU. Tears flowed freely down her mottled cheeks.

Charlotte Grace cooed and reached out for Jack's offered finger.

Jack touched the baby's coppery curls, quickly realizing how the truth had come about. He kissed his wife on the forehead. He kissed Charlotte Grace on her cheek and, ever so slowly, removed his finger from her tiny, yet firm, grip. He looked back at Susan and stroked her thinning hair. "I love you, too... happy anniversary, my love..."

Susan blinked three more times, very slowly, took a final look at the baby she had always wanted, and slowly closed her eyes for the last time. She was finally at peace.

Jack held his wife's face between his palms and kissed her cheeks until the heart monitor indicated a straight-line reading. Tears streamed down his cheeks and he kissed Susan's forehead one final time.

Charlotte Grace wiggled and reached toward him.

Jack allowed her to grasp his finger. More tears flowed down his face when the baby smiled and cooed at him. He ran his fingers through her coppery curls and kissed the top of her head. "God bless you, always, little one..."

The Department of Children's Services representative stepped to the bedside. "I'll take her now, Mr. Peterson."

Jack slowly pulled his finger from the baby's tiny grasp and nodded.

The woman removed the baby from Susan's lifeless arms.

Mrs. Brooks shook her head and cried, "Oh, my goodness…"

CHAPTER 38

Kris Makes Peace

It was Sunday, October 14, 2012.

Kris sat at the long table in the prison's visitation room. It hadn't been too many years ago when she had envisioned herself being in a place like this... but not as a visitor. She had initially thought she would never be able to do what she was about to do. However, her spiritual faith had grown at such a rapid pace over the past few months that she knew, without a doubt, that she needed – and wanted - to confront Jack Peterson.

The day of today's confrontation was also extremely important to Kris. She knew, in her heart, that it needed to be done today because as she sat there waiting for the man who had kidnapped her daughter to walk through the door, something more important was occurring in a small café in Monticello, Florida. A small, collective group of friends were gathering later at the Heavenly Grille Café, which was normally closed on Sundays, to celebrate the baptism of Kris and Charlotte Grace Hall. Kris knew that her own baptism would be meaningless to her unless this long-delayed confrontation occurred.

She clasped her hands securely in her lap and watched as surrounding family members were reunited with their loved ones. She couldn't help but wonder about the prisoners' stories and what had transpired in their lives to have them end up in a place like this. She knew she was so lucky that her own life had turned around because she had no doubt that she could have been one of those unfortunate souls locked away for years on end.

It had taken Kris a long time to get to this visitation, but once she had committed to, and scheduled her and her baby's baptisms, she knew it had to be done. She had contacted her attorney and requested the visit with Jack Peterson today.

She had never spoken directly to him, not even at his sentencing hearing. She had thought that she would because she wanted the judge, and the world, to know how much agony and torment Jack's actions had brought upon her and her child. However, when the time came for her to make a statement, she had quietly declined to do so. Instead, she had watched and listened as Jack Peterson turned toward her and directed his sincere apology for what he and his wife had done. His apology had fallen upon empty ears.

The unlocking of the steel door brought Kris' attention back to the present. She saw Jack Peterson shuffle in, chained at the feet and his hands secured behind him. She watched as the correction officer unlocked the handcuffs and motioned him forward, and wondered if it was too late to change her mind. No… she needed to do this… for herself and for her child, who was too young to speak for herself.

Kris stood up as Jack approached the table. She looked him squarely in the eye, unsure of what exactly she expected to see. It wasn't the look of peace and serenity she saw reflected in his thin, drawn face.

Jack smiled at her. "I've been praying for this day for such a long time, Miss DeVone."

Kris scrambled to sort through her own feelings and responded, "It's Mrs. Hall, now…"

"May I?" Jack motioned to the bench seat across from her.

Kris nodded. The lump in her throat prevented her from saying anything further.

Jack positioned himself across from her and placed his folded hands upon the table. "Congratulations, Mrs. Hall. Marriage is a wonderful gift from God. I hope yours will be as blessed as my own was."

Kris had created a list of questions she had intended to ask Jack Peterson, but they all vanished from her mind as she stared at the lonely man sitting across from her. "You must have loved your wife very much, Mr. Peterson... to have done what you did."

Jack nodded and looked down at the table. "My wife was everything to me. I don't expect you, or anyone else, to understand why we did what we did. The decision we made came about as one focus point in our lives. You see, I knew that Susan was dying and I also knew I had to do everything in my power to give her the one thing she had always wanted."

"A baby..." Kris mumbled.

"Yes," Jack replied, never taking his eyes off the woman who sat trembling across from him.

Kris's own gaze was as direct as Jack's. "But... why my baby, Mr. Peterson? Why did you have to take Charlotte Grace from me?"

Jack sighed and offered a weak smile. "Susan and I saw you for the first time at the Heavenly Grille Café, late last summer. You were very pregnant at the time. We were sitting close to you and your friend, the young lady who worked there. We overheard you talking about your upbringing... about your alcohol and drug problems."

"You were eavesdropping?"

"Not intentionally, no... but... well, we had just come from another doctor appointment and received confirmation that Susan's condition was deteriorating. Susan was in denial but we both knew that she didn't have much time. Anyway, once we got home that night, we rehashed what we overheard you saying to your friend. I think that's when the idea first came to fruition for us."

Kris nodded, more to herself than to acknowledge Jack Peterson's comment. "Amanda and I had a lot of conversations in that booth, but I never realized that anyone was listening to us." She looked back at Jack, distracted momentarily by distant memories. "You know, I never realized it until now, but I think I actually remember the two of you. You were at the restaurant more than once, weren't you?'

"Yes, we were. We tried not to be too conspicuous because we didn't want anyone to remember us. More often than not, we simply watched you. We watched your house, we parked outside the coffee house where you worked and watched you through the windows, and we even parked near the café several times. We were parked outside the day those three café workers closed the café and rushed to the hospital; we followed them because we knew your delivery time could happen at any time. We tried to convince ourselves that you didn't deserve that baby... that we would make better parents and be able to give her a better life than the one she would have with you."

Kris couldn't help blurting out, "What an incredibly selfish thing you did..."

It was an emotional reflex when Jack reached out to touch her hand; the correctional officer's slight movement and grunt quickly reminded him of the prison's "no touching during visitation" rule.

Jack withdrew his hand, which trembled now against his will. "Yes... it was... it was a very selfish act on our part, but you have to realize that we were desperate... so very desperate to be a family before Susan died. We both knew she didn't have long. She actually lasted longer than I thought she would; her cancer was so far advanced by the time they discovered it. Anyway... I really thought that we could take the baby, pretend to be a family for a couple of months, and then... I don't know... return her to you... or to a church, or a hospital. We really did not plan it out all that carefully, other than to move to Tampa right away. I see now, in hindsight, that we probably should have left Florida altogether, but..."

Kris interrupted him. "That day in December... when Amanda and I came to your house... to Amanda's house... I still can't believe that I was within arm's distance of my baby."

Jack nodded. "I actually thought we had been found out when I saw the two of you standing at the door. I had already made my peace with God about it and hoped for mercy on the court's part. I was in total disbelief when I didn't see any police cars with you that day. I think we convinced ourselves that day that it must be God's will for us to keep the baby rather than return her to you."

"The baby was sleeping that day," Kris remembered. "I couldn't see her face, but I remember the head full of black hair. Amanda and I talked later about the baby being small for her age. I think I was still in a state of denial back then, and all I wanted was to get as far away from your baby as possible. It was too painful a reminder of what I had lost, or rather, what had been taken from me."

There was a moment of silence between them before Jack spoke again. "I'm very sorry for that..." his voice cracked as tears formed in his eyes. "What we did to you was a horrible, horrible thing. No parent should ever have to go through something like that. If I could turn back time, I would never have allowed it to happen. You know... it wasn't even Susan's idea. In fact, she fought me on it at first, but I managed to persuade her that we would be doing what was right for the baby... that the baby needed her more than it needed you, and quite frankly, in her condition... well, it wasn't hard to convince her that it was the right decision." A lone tear rolled down Jack's face. "Please, Miss DeVone... I'm sorry... Mrs. Hall. Please don't think badly of Susan. All she ever wanted was to be a mother. She was a good person, truly she was..."

Kris remained silent and watched as the tears flowed

down Jack Peterson's thinning face. He had aged considerably since she had last seen him in the courtroom. She could only imagine what prison life must be like for someone like him. She continued to watch him and tried to rebirth the revengeful feelings she had when Charlotte Grace had first been abducted; but, those feelings of hate, anger, and revenge were gone. She knew in her heart that God had taken them away. She had prayed time and time again for that to happen.

Jack's folded hands trembled upon the prison table.

Kris slowly reached out and placed her hand upon his. She saw, out of the corner of her eye, the guard move in their direction. She looked over at the guard with a silent plea evident in her eyes. They stared at each other for a moment before the guard nodded and moved back to his position at the door.

Kris enveloped Jack Peterson's hands, within her own, and felt them tremble. She had no way of knowing that this was the first kind touch he had received since Charlotte Grace had released her grip on his finger eight months ago. "I believe you, Mr. Peterson..."

Jack opened his eyes and stared into the forgiving eyes he never expected to see. He was overwhelmed with emotion at the genuine kindness in her voice. "You do?"

Kris nodded. "Yes, I do. Your wife was a very sick woman. You loved her more than you cherished your own life. For the first time in my life, I understand that kind of love... I would do anything to protect my child and my husband."

"You have every reason to hate me," Jack cried openly. "I have prayed for your forgiveness from the moment I knocked you down in the parking lot that day... I don't deserve it."

"Maybe you don't," Kris answered back. "But I've been praying for the strength to forgive you. I honestly didn't think I had it in me to forgive you for what you did. I wanted you to rot in jail for what you put me through, but..."

Jack shook his head, "Oh, no... you're right to think that.

I should rot in jail for what I did. I deserve this punishment. I only hope that God forgives me and that I am not condemned to Hell for what I did."

"Well..." Kris sighed. "I'm pretty new to all this God and religion stuff, but the God I'm learning about is not a vengeful God. If you have truly prayed for His forgiveness, I don't think you have to worry about going to Hell."

"God's forgiveness is what's most important to me..." Jack agreed. "But, I had also hoped that one day you might be able to forgive me... and Susan, for what we did."

Kris stared at Jack Peterson for several moments before, finally, releasing the tears that she been holding in. "That's why I'm here today, Mr. Peterson. I needed to let you know that I do forgive you, and I forgive your wife. I... uh... also want you to know that I intend to speak to your attorney before I leave town. I want him to know that when the time comes... when you come up for parole... that I will be willing to stand on your behalf in front of the Parole Board."

Jack was dumbfounded. "You would do that?"

"Yes... I will do that," Kris smiled back at him. "I... I also have something for you."

Jack used the back of his hand to wipe away his tears. He sighed deeply as a sense of peace and hope came over him... the first feeling of hope he had experienced in months. "For me?"

Kris stood up and retrieved an envelope from her jacket pocket. She looked over at the guard and waited for his nod of approval. "I thought this might help you get through the next few months. I'll send you some more later on... until you get released."

Jack looked at the offered envelope. He reached across the table and took it from Kris. He didn't think he had any tears left but he was wrong. He cried openly when he pulled the picture of Charlotte Grace from the envelope.

"It was taken this morning," Kris said. "My daughter and I were baptized this morning."

"Oh, that is wonderful news..." Jack cried. "Look at her,

how big she's gotten. She is so beautiful…" He stared at Kris and smiled, "Just like her mother…"

Kris wiped away her own tears. "I thought it might help. I want to thank you for taking such good care of her while you had her."

"She's going to grow up to be a very special person…" Jack whispered.

"She already is," Kris smiled.

A brief, but comfortable, silence followed before Kris continued. "There is one more thing, Mr. Peterson… something else I have prayed about. If you want to, I'd like for you to be a part of Charlotte's life, to watch her grow up. I know a lot of people would think I've lost my mind to offer you an olive branch like this one, but I think it's what God wants me to do."

Jack put his head on the table and did not try to repress the giant sobs that shook his entire body. "I don't deserve this…" he choked.

"Maybe not," Kris answered back, suppressing her own sobs, "Maybe not… but I think Charlotte and Susan deserve it…"

There was another comfortable moment of silence between them before Kris cleared her throat.

"You know, an old man… his name is Amos… told me a few weeks ago that people come into our lives for a reason… some for a reason… and others for only a season, I believe he said. He told me that you and your wife came into my life for a reason. I believe, now, that had you not taken my baby from me that day, I never would have found my way to God. I truly believe that's the reason it all happened the way it did."

Jack reached across the table for her hand and smiled. "Would you pray with me, Mrs. Hall?"

Kris returned the smile. "It's Kris… you can call me, Kris." She stood up and walked around to his side of the table. She watched the correctional officer watching them and nodded silent thanks to him while the unlikely duo knelt side by side, holding hands inside a prison visitation room, and prayed to their God.

When Kris stood to leave, she reached over and hugged Jack Peterson. "Take care of yourself, Mr. Peterson."

Jack released her hands and held Charlotte's picture close to his heart. "I will, Kris. God bless you…"

Kris looked back at him as she turned to leave. "He already has."

CHAPTER 39

Farewell Celebration

Dean and Kris rode in companionable silence after they left the prison.

He knew that she needed some time to herself, to digest everything that had happened in her meeting with Jack Peterson. He turned on the radio and rolled down the window. The warm October air felt good blowing against his face. He glanced upward at the clear sky and offered God a silent prayer of thanks for this particular day. His wife and daughter had been baptized and officially welcomed into the family of God; that event had been heartfelt enough, but he knew that an even more emotional time was awaiting them. They would be gathering at the Heavenly Grille to, not only celebrate the baptisms, but to also say their good-byes to friends who had become like family to them over the past few months. That would be a very hard thing to do.

They were within a few miles of the café when Kris turned to look at her husband. "I forgave him, you know?"

Dean nodded. "I know. I thought you would. It was the right thing to do, Kris."

Kris smiled and looked down at her folded hands. "I did something else... something you might not be too thrilled about."

Dean raised his eyebrows and grinned. "I'm listening..."

Kris took a deep breath, still in a state of shell-shock herself, "I told him I wanted him to be a part of Charlotte's life when he gets out..." When he didn't reply and she couldn't read the expression on his face, Kris continued, "Dean? Say something... please..."

Dean rubbed the back of his neck with his right hand. "Well," he sighed, "I guess that depends on how much a part of Charlotte's life you intend him to be. I mean... should I be clearing out the room that's going to be my office and turning it into a spare bedroom for him..." He tried to convey a serious expression, but the upward curve of a smile gave him away.

Kris slapped him on the arm. "No, silly! I mean, I don't know what his plans are when he's released, but wherever he is, I want him to know that he will be welcomed in our home to visit her any time he wants. I intend to send him regular pictures of Charlotte so that he can watch her grow up."

"I think that's very... generous... of you, Kris. Have you given any thought to whether or not you'll ever tell Charlotte about what happened to her... tell her the truth about Jack and Susan Peterson?"

Kris nodded. "I probably will, when she's older. I'm not sure how she'll feel about the whole thing, but I'm hoping that by then, she will have come to know Jack Peterson better. I want to get to know him better, too. Does that make me some sort of sicko, or something? I mean what person in their right mind would want their kidnapper to be a part of their lives?"

"Well," Dean smiled. "It's definitely not the typical reaction you'd expect from the mother of a child who had been kidnapped, but... well, you've come a long way, spiritually, in the last few months, Kris. I'm very proud of you. I can honestly say, though, that I don't know if most women, put in your shoes, could be as forgiving."

"I can't worry about what other people will think; that will be their problem. It's just that, well... something about the man just screams out to me. I don't know how to explain it. I mean, he has no one in his life... no one. That was me a year or so ago. It was an awful, awful feeling, and I wouldn't wish that feeling on anyone."

Dean reached over and took her hand. "You will never walk alone again, Kris... never."

They pulled into the parking lot of the Heavenly Grille and Kris leaned over and kissed her husband. "What did I do to become so lucky... I'm going to hold you to that promise, you know!"

Dean laughed. "What makes you think luck had anything to do with it all? I knew from the first moment I saw you that I wanted you in my life."

Kris' shocked expression was genuine. "You're kidding! Now wait a minute; if I remember correctly, I was ragged-looking, crying, abandoned, and seven months pregnant at the time."

Dean nodded. "Yep... you were... and you were absolutely the most beautiful person I'd ever seen before in my life."

"Now, who's the sicko! Remind me to keep you away from pregnant women!" Kris laughed as she kissed him again. "Come on, let's get inside. Our little girl is waiting for us."

A festive, celebratory mood filled the Heavenly Grille café this particular Sunday afternoon.

Charlotte Grace was relatively new to walking and, at times, still preferred to crawl; she got to where she wanted to go, quicker, that way. She was crawling around the dining room, pulling herself up at each and every booth she came to. Every so often she would look back to make sure her Aunt

Amanda was within sight.

Amanda was on her own knees, following the baby's every move to make sure she didn't fall too hard. Charlotte Grace laughed out loud every time Amanda crawled toward her. She evidently thought it was a game.

Doug was behind the counter blowing up what, seemed to him, must be hundreds of blue and white balloons. Naturally, he never ran out of air, so the mountain of balloons grew quickly. He kept one eye on the balloons and another on Charlotte Grace, the little girl who had captured his heart from day one.

Ever since they had brought her home six months ago, Doug had not been far from her side. He felt the strangest connection to the baby and knew instinctively that God intended for him to be her guardian angel through life, and beyond. He wasn't sure how he would pull it off as the years went by, but he was equally confident that he would find a way to be a constant source of influence in her life. He may have to learn how to apply makeup in order to appear older as the years went by, but he knew he would find a way. Given permission to do so, he might even be able to tell her the truth about who he was.

Amos Brown was carrying paper plates and cups to the long table set up at the far end of the room. He was watching Doug watch the baby, and smiled his toothless grin. "She gonna be a hand full, that one is…"

Doug grinned back at him, wondering how long the old man had been watching his reactions to the baby. "She's already a hand full, Amos."

Amos stopped beside Doug on his way back from placing the plates and cups. "You thinks she'll ever guess the truth about you, Mr. Doug?"

Doug smiled. "What do you think, Amos?"

Amos looked over at the precocious one-year old. He raised his eyebrows in shock when the child suddenly turned and seemed to stare directly into his soul. When she giggled and moved on to the next booth, he looked back at Doug.

"Well, sir… somethin' tells me that child may already knows the truth… yessirree…"

Doug glanced back at Charlotte Grace and could have sworn the child winked at him. "Oh my, God… you may be right, Amos…"

The two men laughed in unison as Amanda caught up to Charlotte Grace and tickled her relentlessly.

Bertie sashayed from the kitchen carrying a large pan of Max's custard-bread pudding. She placed it on the table next to the plates and cups. On her way back to the kitchen, she made a quick detour, swooped up Charlotte Grace, and danced around the room with her.

Charlotte Grace laughed out loud as she was twirled around and around. Her chin-length red curls bounced around her head as she held tightly to Bertie's extended finger.

Kris and Dean sat shoulder to shoulder in their favorite booth by the front door. Kris looked down at the gold wedding band on her left hand and closed her eyes in quiet satisfaction. It seemed like everything had happened so fast.

Dean's proposal had come almost immediately upon Charlotte Grace's safe return. Kris never hesitated in accepting that proposal; and, their friends all gathered to celebrate their marriage two months later.

Dean subsequently began the process of formally adopting Charlotte Grace as his own child, with hopes that she would have at least two or three more siblings to boss around in the years to come. His request for a transfer to Tampa had been approved, and he considered himself to be the luckiest man alive.

Mrs. Brooks stood beside Max in the kitchen and admired his cooking skills. She was taking notes on how he prepared his country ribs and sauerkraut. She didn't even mind the out-of-tune whistling she had to endure while taking notes. "I hope you don't mind me watching you cook, Max," she smiled up at him. "It's just that I've never had ribs and sauerkraut cooked together like this, and it smells absolutely heavenly."

Max stopped whistling and grinned as he handed her a large spoon. "Here you go, Ida. Why don't you take a little sample and let me know what you think."

"Oh, my goodness," Ida laughed, "Well, I don't mind if I do."

Back in the dining area, Kris looked around at all the people who had come to mean so much to her and Charlotte Grace. Her life had changed so much in the past year. She felt like pinching herself to make sure that this was really her life she was experiencing. She didn't know what she had done to be so lucky in God's grace, but she never failed to count her blessings each and every day. She sighed and laid her head on Dean's shoulder. "I'm going to miss all of them, and this place, so very much."

"I know," Dean replied. "So am I..."

Kris glanced over at her husband. "Do you ever get the feeling that there is something, oh... I don't know... something kind of magical about this café? I mean, other than Charlotte Grace being kidnapped from the parking lot, I can't think of anything bad ever happening here. I've always felt so safe sitting inside this booth. I wish I could bottle that feeling up and take it with us to Tampa."

Dean hugged her against him. "It's not that long a drive. We can come back and visit as much as you want to. But... you're right, I know what you mean about the place having a magical feel to it. Hey! Maybe Max is really some sort of sorcerer and he's cast a major spell on all of us."

Kris pulled hard at his ear and grinned. "You may not be far off in that thinking," she thought. "No... not a sorcerer," she replied, "but... something..."

Doug allowed Bertie a few minutes with Charlotte Grace before he walked over to them and held out his arms. "Okay, my turn," he grinned as Charlotte Grace reached out eagerly to him. He grinned again as the baby pulled on his thick hair and laughed when he said, "Ouch!" Their bond had only strengthened in the past six months and Doug knew that he would be making frequent trips to Tampa as long as he could. Yes, if he could find a way to appear to age progressively, he planned to be around to see Charlotte Grace graduate from high school, maybe even college. *"Oh, why stop there..."* he thought, *"I may as well stick around until she becomes a grandmother!"*

Amanda walked over to the long table where Amos still stood and put her arm around his waist. "Bread pudding for dessert, huh? Shucks, I was kinda hoping for one last serving of Max's seven-layer coconut cake. That's my favorite, you know?"

Amos hugged her back and smiled his toothless grin. "Well now, you never knows what a little hope and prayer will bring, now do you, child?"

Mrs. Brooks walked out of the kitchen, as if on cue, carrying a seven-layer coconut cake. "I understand that we couldn't have a party without this," she smiled at Amanda. "The cook said he made it special just for you."

Amanda closed her eyes and inhaled the sweet, buttery aroma and richness of the cake. "Oh, I love all of Max's desserts, but this one is extra special. Just wait until you taste it, Mrs. Brooks."

Amanda took the cake from Ida and sat it carefully on the table, allowing it to take center stage, as it so well deserved. "I'm really, really glad you could be here with us today, Mrs. Brooks. The party wouldn't be complete without the woman who was responsible for bringing Charlotte Grace back to us."

"Oh, my goodness!" Ida laughed. "Enough of that! I didn't do anything special. Why, I almost had heart failure when that baby's hair turned from black to red. I'll never forget that moment as long as I live."

"Neither will we!" Dean laughed as he and Kris joined them at the long table.

"That's for sure," Kris smiled. "And just think...now we're going to be next door neighbors for a long, long time, and you can watch Charlotte Grace grow up."

"Not to mention, we'll have a built-in babysitter," Dean added.

It was Amanda's turn to laugh. "Yep, just imagine it. You three living in the house I grew up in, with the same babysitter I had growing up! What are the odds of that ever happening?"

Dean shook his head in minor amazement. "Well, when the house came back on the market last month, Kris and I took it as a sign, Amanda. We talked it over and decided it had to be fate that it became available when it did. Any sooner or later and we probably would've missed the opportunity to get it. After the department accepted my transfer request to Tampa, we started looking for something in your old neighborhood since it's so close to everything we need. When the real estate agent drove us to your old house to look at it, we both knew what we had to do. By the way, with the market like it is right now, and circumstances being what they were, we got it for a steal. Are you sure you're okay with us getting your father's house, Amanda?"

Bertie came up behind them and punched Dean on the shoulder. "What are you talking about? Of course our girl is okay with that. She's going to be much too busy at the Police Academy to worry about cutting grass and paying a mortgage. Besides, from what I hear, she's already claimed a spare bedroom in your new house."

Kris laughed. "I'm still having a hard time with that one! You, Amanda… on the police force! You'll probably have all the bad guys down on their knees, praying, after you catch them. They'll be repenting their sins before you even get the cuffs on them!"

Amanda laughed along with everyone else. "I never really thought much about being a cop… until everything that happened with Charlotte Grace. I don't know if they have any kind of special units that help find lost children, but if they do, you can bet I'm going to be one of the first to sign up for it. Oh, and by the way, Bertie, you are right… I want the spare bedroom closest to the backyard; the one that has its own door leading outside. Just wait until you see that back yard, Bertie. It's Heaven!"

"Is it now?" Bertie winked at her as she punched her on the shoulder. "Well, now, if it's anything like Heaven, then I know I have to see it!"

Amanda blushed, afraid that she had hinted too closely at the truth, but she relaxed when Bertie hugged her tight and winked again.

"Okay, everyone!" Max shouted from the kitchen. "Here comes the main course. Make way and grab a bowl!"

Kris held up her hand. "Not before we say grace!"

The friends gathered together and formed a circle around Charlotte Grace. They held hands while Max offered a prayer of thanks for the wonderful friends and food that filled the room.

"Amen!" they all shouted at the end of the prayer.

Charlotte Grace giggled and twirled around the adults. "A-M-E-N!" she echoed, speaking her first real word.

Several hours later, after the sun had set and everyone's bellies were full, Max motioned them all to the center of room.

The nine of them held hands again as Max led them in a final prayer. "Dear, Lord… life is all about getting through the changes… some of them good, and some of them not so good. We gather here today to thank you for all the blessings you have bestowed upon us all; we thank you for the friendships that have formed; and, most of all, we thank you for forgiving us our shortcomings and allowing us the strength to offer forgiveness to those who have hurt or deceived us. We pray for Jack Peterson as he begins the next journey of his heart. We thank you, Lord, for the time in which you have allowed us to build new friendships that will endure a life time… and beyond. As some of our friends leave us to begin their new lives in Tampa, we pray that you surround them daily with your angels to keep them safe, healthy, and happy. We ask these things in the name of Jesus Christ, our Lord and Savior... Amen."

"A-M-E-N!" Charlotte Grace shouted.

CHAPTER 40

–Heaven–
December 2012
The Angels' Next Adventure

*I*t was the Sunday before Christmas and Heaven was even more exhilarating than usual. Everyone was preparing for the celebration of their Lord's birthday. Fresh fruits and vegetables were everywhere. There was no meat eaten in Heaven but nobody seemed to mind the vegetarian requisite; after all, food was more or less an afterthought, totally non-essential.

Doug, Bertie, Max, and Martin watched and listened to all the happy commotion surrounding them.

"I'm glad all of you were able to come Home today," Martin smiled. "Your families will certainly be happy to have everyone together for this special celebration."

"I can't imagine being anywhere else today," Doug answered back. "Things have slowed down quite a bit at the café since Amanda moved to Tampa."

Martin watched Doug carefully. "You miss her, I know."

"We all do," Bertie sighed.

"Let me ask you all something," Martin began. "Are you

absolutely, totally sure that she can keep your secret for the rest of her life? Are you certain that she won't be tempted to tell anyone the truth about the employees of the Heavenly Grille Café?"

Max lifted his eyebrows and shrugged. "Without a doubt... that young lady will carry our secret to her grave."

"And, hopefully, that will be a long, long time away," Doug added. "I'm hoping and praying she has a long life ahead of her... a life time full of happiness. She deserves it."

"Well," Martin sighed, "That's not for us to know, but... if the three of you trust her to keep your secret, well then... that's good enough for me. I don't suppose you'll have to up and move the café for a few more years."

"Actually," Max smiled, "I've been doing some thinking along those lines. I was thinking of staying put for another year or two before moving to some place we've never been before. Well, that's not quite true. I've been there, a very long time ago, but I don't think any of you have."

Bertie punched him on the shoulder and laughed. "And where might that be, big fella?"

Max grinned mischievously and stood tall and proud before them. In an instant, his white and gold robe had been replaced with a gladiator's shiny shield of armor. His muscled arms and thighs glistened in Heaven's natural glow. Solid, but simple, sandals graced his large feet.

"Well... I'll... be... damned!" Bertie laughed, clapping her hands, and jumping up and down. "Hook up your chariots, my friends, it looks like I'm finally going to get to meet the Pope!"

"B-E-R-T-I-E!"

"Oops...my bad!" Bertie whispered before punching Max on his chiseled shoulder. She shook her hand in mock pain. "Ouch...damn! That hurt!"

"B-E-R-T-I-E!!!"

"For this is God, our God forever and ever; He will be our guide even to death."

-Psalm 48:1 (NJKV)

The End...for Now

www.ingramcontent.com/pod-product-compliance
Lightning Source LLC
Chambersburg PA
CBHW021230250626
47155CB00008B/2946